CHANGO PRESTO

"Let me see that," Brewster said, impressed by the large book. He read aloud the ornate script. "THE GRIMOIRE OF HONORIUS."

"THAT'S IT!" cried Brian the chamberpot. "Honorius! That's the wizard who enchanted me, curse his black, unlamented soul! The spell he used on me is in there! It has to be!"

"Then maybe the spell to reverse it is in there, too," said Mick.

Brewster opened the grimoire. "Let's see. . . . Spell to Transform People into Newts . . . Toadstools . . . Footstools—*footstools*?"

"He likes having his enemy under foot," said Brian.

"Spell to Transform People into Chamberpots," Brewster read.

Shannon grinned. "I suppose he also likes his enemies to catch—"

"We get the point," Brewster interrupted. "Here it is. To reverse the spell, repeat: "ABRACADABRA, change back."

"ABRACADABRA, CHANGE BACK? SIXTY MISERABLE YEARS OF BEING A LOUSY CHAMBERPOT AND *THAT* WAS ALL IT TOOK? AAAAARRRRRRGGGGGGHHH!"

ALSO BY SIMON HAWKE

The Nine Lives of Catseye Gomez
The Reluctant Sorcerer
The Samurai Wizard
The Whims of Creation
The Wizard of Camelot
The Wizard of 4th street
The Wizard of Lovecraft's Cafe
The Wizard of Sunset Strip
The Wizard of Whitechapel

Published by
WARNER BOOKS

THE
AMBIVALENT
MAGICIAN

SIMON HAWKE

ASPECT®

WARNER BOOKS

A Time Warner Company

WARNER BOOKS EDITION

Copyright © 1996 by Simon Hawke
All rights reserved.

Aspect® is a registered trademark of Warner Books, Inc.

Cover design by Don Puckey
Cover illustration by Jody A. Lee

Warner Books, Inc.
1271 Avenue of the Americas
New York, NY 10020

Visit our web site at
http://pathfinder.com/twep

 A Time Warner Company

Printed in the United States of America
First Printing: July, 1996

10 9 8 7 6 5 4 3 2 1

For the Sonora Writers Workshop,

with warm thanks to my students, Janis Gemetta, Carrie Cooper, Roger Hyland, Davis Palmer, Misha Burnett, Phil Fleishman, Barbara McCullough, Shiori Pluard, Dan Tuttle, Ron Wilcox and Toby Herschler, with all the best wishes in their own writing endeavors. Also, special thanks to Dave Foster, Margie and James Kosky, Bruce and Peggy Wiley, Bob Powers, Sandy West, all my friends in the ECS and the SCA, and Otis Bronson and my colleagues in the writing department at Pima Community College in Tuscon, Arizona. Thanks for the friendship and support.

THE
AMBIVALENT MAGICIAN

One

"*At last!* I've done it! After months of ceaseless scrying, spellcasting and divination, endless, patient searching through the vast, uncharted reaches of the ethereal planes, I've finally found him!"

"Found who, Master?" the wizard's hairy little troll familiar asked, pausing in his dusting of the ancient vellum tomes and scrolls that crammed the bookcases and were piled high on almost every available flat surface in the sorcerer's sanctorum.

"The voice in the ether!" Warrick Morgannan replied triumphantly. "That arrogant, omniscient spirit who calls himself . . . the Narrator!"

"Oh-oh," said Teddy, picking his nose and glancing up at the ceiling apprehensively.

Oh-oh, indeed. This is rather inconvenient. Your faithful narrator wasn't ready to start working on this book, yet. I have too many other things to do. My desk is piled high with papers from my students; I've got to complete some revisions on another novel I've been working on; I'm finishing up work on a graduate degree; my checkbook is hopelessly unbalanced, and the last thing I needed right now was *this*.

"Never mind the excuses," Warrick said, his long white hair framing his chiseled features as he bent over the scrying crystal. Dark red eddies swirled like smoke within the pellucid ball as he concentrated on the crystal, focusing his energies in an effort to achieve resolution of an image. "You've been hiding from me long enough! Now I've tracked you down through the ethereal planes and the time for reckoning has come!"

Reckoning, schmeckoning. I haven't been hiding, I've been *busy*. Look, I've got enough trouble with readers pestering me about when the next book in this series is coming out without having one of my characters start interfering with my writing process. Now get out of my computer and slither back to the depths of my subconscious where you belong. I've got work to do.

"No, you shall not get rid of me that easily," said Warrick, staring intently at the swirling eddies in the crystal. "You have meddled in my affairs for the last time. Your powers are considerable, and I must concede a grudging admiration for your skills in this sorcerous art you call 'narration,' but I, Warrick the White, of the House of Morgannan, Grand Director of the Sorcerers and Adepts Guild and Royal Wizard to the Kingdom of Pitt, will not be trifled with by some upstart demigod from the ethereal planes!"

Oh, please. For one thing, I'm no demigod, I'm just a struggling writer trying to make a living. And you're a fictional character, for God's sake. You don't even *exist* except in my imagination.

"Do not attempt to work your wiles on me, Narrator. I think, therefore I exist."

It's "I think, therefore I am. *Cogito, ergo sum.*" René Descartes. If you're going to quote, get it right. I will not have my readers thinking I'm a sloppy writer. You've already gotten this book off to a really bizarre start, and my editors still haven't recovered from the last time you pulled something like this. They just don't understand how a writer can lose control over his own characters. I had to take some time off from this series and write a serious book just to prove to them I haven't gone totally around the bend. They're still not sure about me, and it's all your fault. This isn't helping any. You're making my life very difficult, you know.

"Not nearly as difficult as it is going to be," said Warrick, concentrating fiercely on the crystal in an effort to bring forth an image of the Narrator, so he would finally know what the mysterious "voice in the ether" looked like.

However, at precisely that moment, Teddy, his little troll familiar, had a slight mishap. Only Warrick was capable of hearing the strange, disembodied entity he called "the

Narrator," so as he watched his master speaking to the crystal ball, Teddy could only hear one side of the conversation. As a result, he wasn't paying very close attention to his work, and the little troll backed into a chair and knocked over a precariously balanced pile of ancient scrolls and vellum tomes. They went crashing to the floor of the sanctorum, making a tremendous racket and upsetting Warrick's concentration.

"Very clever," Warrick said, "but you have only succeeded in delaying the inevitable. I have not attained the highest rank in the Sorcerers and Adepts Guild for nothing. My concentration is not so easily broken." He returned his attention to the crystal ball, willing an image of the narrator to appear.

Unfortunately, that wasn't going to happen, because no matter how hard he concentrated, he couldn't change the fact that this particular crystal ball wasn't equipped for optically correct visual reception. The most it could do was allow him to hear voices from the ethereal planes and see vague, indistinct forms and pretty swirling colors.

"That's ridiculous!" said Warrick. "Of what use is a scrying crystal if one cannot see images within it?"

Not much use at all, apparently. Too bad.

"This is absurd! I have been using this scrying crystal for years and it has never yet failed to serve me properly."

I guess it must be broken, then.

"Nonsense. The scrying crystal is functioning perfectly," Warrick insisted. "And as Warrick redoubled his prodigious powers of concentration, despite all the efforts of the Narrator, the swirling eddies in the crystal started to resolve into an image —"

No, they didn't. And cut that out.

"Despite all his narrative wiles, the voice in the ether could not control the image that started to resolve within the crystal as Warrick concentrated fiercely, and in answer to his will, the swirling mists within the scrying crystal cleared, revealing —"

There was a tremendous crash as Teddy the troll tripped over some ancient vellum tomes that had fallen to the floor and knocked into the table, dislodging the scrying crystal from its ornate pedestal and causing it to roll across the table and plummet to the floor, where it shattered into a thousand pieces.

"Ooops," said Teddy.

"You miserable, misbegotten warthog! Now see what you've done!" Warrick shouted angrily, his chair crashing to the floor as he jumped to his feet and fixed a baleful glare on the frightened little troll.

"Forgive me, Master! I . . . I didn't mean it! It was an accident!"

"I think not," said Warrick, his eyes narrowing suspiciously. "'Twas the Narrator, working his wiles upon you to interfere with me. I begin to see the method in his craft. He strikes at me through you."

"But, Master, I would never betray you!"

"No, not willingly," Warrick replied, "but your will is too weak to resist the powers of the Narrator. So long as you remain with me, he can use you as a weapon with which to thwart my plans. That leaves me with no choice. I must be rid of you."

"Master . . . " the little troll said fearfully. "Master, please! I have always served you faithfully!"

"And in reward for your years of faithful service, I shall not take your life," said Warrick. "But henceforth, Teddy, you are banished from my presence. Go. Leave me. You are free."

"But, Master . . . " wailed the little troll miserably, "where shall I go? What shall I do?"

"I don't know, go hide under a bridge or something. Isn't that what trolls usually do?"

"Under a bridge?" said Teddy. "But, Master, 'tis cold and damp underneath bridges! I shall catch a chill! And however shall I live?"

"Eat billy goats," said Warrick. "Consume the occasional small child. There are plenty of them running about unsupervised, painting graffiti on the bridges. You would only be doing the kingdom a service if you ate them. I'm sure no one would complain. Now get along, Teddy, I have work to do."

"Master, please . . . don't send me away!" wailed Teddy. "I don't even like children!"

"You have a very simple choice, Teddy," Warrick said. "You may either take your freedom and go make something of yourself, or become the subject of my next experiment."

"No, Master, anything but that!" cried Teddy, with an alarmed glance at the strange and frightening apparatus that sat in the center of Warrick's sanctorum.

"Then go. I grant you your freedom. The Narrator shall trouble you no longer. And as soon as I fetch my spare scrying crystal, we shall see who must prevail in this battle of wills."

Warrick turned to get his spare scrying crystal from the carved wooden armoire where he kept his magical supplies, but as he opened it and withdrew his spare crystal ball, a punishing blow struck him from behind. He grunted and collapsed to the floor, unconscious. The crystal fell and shattered into a hundred thousand pieces.

"Oh, no!" said Teddy, staring with dismay at the broomstick with which he had just brained his former master. "What have I *done?*" Dropping the broom, he bolted out of the sanctorum, fleeing in panic.

Okay, that takes care of Warrick for a while. Now, where were we? Give me a minute to collect my wits. This book's already off to a rather rocky start. I didn't really plan it this way. Honest. But those of you who haven't read the first two novels in this series are probably wondering what the hell is going on. If you want to start at the beginning, pick up *The Reluctant Sorcerer* and *The Inadequate Adept* (Warner Books), but if you haven't read those novels yet and want to know what this craziness is all about, I'll try to bring you up to speed. The rest of you hang in there for a while. One way or another, we'll get this sorted out.

It all started when Marvin Brewster, a brilliant but absent-minded young American scientist working at the London headquarters of the multinational conglomerate known as

EnGulfCo International, invented time travel. This could not have come at a worse time for his English fiancée, Pamela Fairburn, a beautiful cybernetics engineer who had already been stood up at the altar on several occasions because Brewster was so intent upon his secret project that he kept forgetting about such mundane things as wedding dates. The wedding guests had even started a betting pool, wagering on how many times Pamela would have to put on her fabulous, white lace designer gown before she actually got married in it. Pamela's father had stopped speaking to her, because the whole thing was costing him a fortune, and her friends were all convinced she'd lost her mind. But Pamela knew Brewster was a genius, and she understood that he wasn't simply toying with her affections. She didn't know what he was working on, but it had to be something terribly important for him to be so excessively preoccupied, something that was liable to be a significant scientific breakthrough that would bring him international acclaim . . . and scads and scads of money. But when he failed to show up for the third scheduled wedding, and no one had heard from him for days, she became concerned and called the EnGulfCo CEO, who happened to be a golfing partner of her father's.

Together with Dr. Walter Davies, executive vice-president for research and development for EnGulfCo International, she broke into Brewster's private laboratory high atop the corporate headquarters building in downtown London, only to discover that her fiancé had disappeared without a trace. Security monitors showed him entering his restricted private laboratory in the penthouse, but they never showed him leaving. He should have been there. But he wasn't.

Pamela was not the only one who was upset at this development. The EnGulfCo CEO was very much concerned, as well. Brewster's research had netted over a dozen very lucrative patents for the conglomerate, and the CEO had recently authorized vast expenditures on his behalf for some surplus military hardware and an unspecified amount of something called Buckminsterfullerine, also known as "Buckeyballs," an incredibly rare and expensive substance that Brewster absolutely had to have for his latest secret project. The only trouble was, nobody had the slightest idea what it was, and Brewster had apparently disappeared off the face of the earth, leaving behind evidence of what appeared to have been a sonic boom inside his laboratory.

Pamela was the only one capable of deciphering his notes and figuring out his filing system, so the CEO authorized her to have complete access to the laboratory in an attempt to find out what Brewster had been working on. And if it had been anyone but Brewster, the CEO would never have believed it when Pamela told him it was time travel, and that he had apparently succeeded in constructing a working prototype of a time machine. The CEO immediately authorized all necessary expenditures for Pamela to duplicate Brewster's apparatus, and at the same time, while reassuring her that he trusted her completely and was only concerned for Brewster's welfare, he put detectives on her tail, had her phone tapped, and set plans in motion to corner the world market on Buckminsterfullerine.

Meanwhile, Brewster had problems of his own. The first prototype of his machine had failed to return from a test run, due to a faulty relay in a timer switch. It's always the little things that screw up the whole works, as anyone who's ever had a British sports car would understand completely. Using up the last of his raw materials, Brewster had constructed a second time machine, programmed with the same coordinates, so that he could go back in time and bring the first one back.

Unfortunately, he not only went back in time, but he crossed a dimensional boundary as well, and crash-landed in a parallel universe where magic really worked. When the time machine's fuel tanks exploded, Brewster was left stranded. His only hope of getting back was to find the first time machine that had failed to return. It should have been at those very same coordinates, but it was nowhere to be found. Unknown to Brewster, three brigands had discovered it sitting in the middle of a road and they had sold it to a nearby adept, who had used a magic spell to activate it. But as we all know from reading owner's manuals, when you don't follow the instructions, things often go awry. The machine remained exactly where it was, but the poor adept wound up being teleported to Los Angeles, where his magic didn't work and he wound up becoming part of LA's homeless population. His apprentice, realizing this was a dangerous piece of enchanted apparatus, loaded it up into a cart and brought it to Warrick Morgannan, better known as Warrick the White, the Grand Director of the Sorcerers and Adepts Guild and the most powerful wizard in all the twenty-seven kingdoms. And that was when your faithful narrator's plot started to unravel.

Now, whenever I teach character development in my writing classes, I always tell my students that it's not enough to say that your protagonist is boldly handsome or that your villain is ugly and malevolent. You need to pay attention to specific detail. So then what do I do? I describe Warrick as "the most powerful wizard in the twenty-seven kingdoms." Nice going, Hawke. Powerful as compared to *what?* How about some perspective here? I could have said something about what the extent of his powers were, and what limitations they had, but noooooo . . . I had to get lazy and throw in a description that had no real specifics. Serves me right, I guess. Now I'm stuck with a villainous wizard who's powerful enough to detect the presence of the Narrator and keeps trying to take over the story. And it's too late to put a limitation on his powers, because he's taken on a life of his own and no matter what I write, he keeps finding spells to counteract everything I do. I really hate it when that happens.

And now he's banished Teddy, his ugly little troll familiar, and the chief weapon in my arsenal against him has neatly been shuffled off the stage. I suppose I could write him back in, but Warrick would only drive him off again, or maybe even kill him, and then Earth First! and the Sierra Club and the Audubon Society would be on my back for eliminating a member of an endangered species. Environmentalists would boycott my books, and all the people who hang those little long-haired rubber trolls off the rearview mirrors of their cars would be writing me angry letters. Who needs the aggravation? I'll just have to think of something else.

Anyway, you're probably wondering what became of Brewster. (Heavy sigh.) How am I supposed to summarize what happened in two novels in a couple of short and cogent paragraphs? If I go on too long, my editors will say it's an "expository lump" and then I'll have to cut it. If I don't cover it well enough, people will write me letters and complain that the first chapter was confusing and they found the rest of the novel hard to follow. I just don't know how guys like Anthony and Asprin do it. They write these series that go on forever and this sort of thing just doesn't seem to bother them.

Sometimes I think maybe I should have listened to my father and become a doctor. Then perhaps I could get the big money, like Robin Cook and Michael Crichton. Or I could've become a lawyer, and then maybe I'd have bestsellers like John Grisham. Or I could have become an actor, like what's-her-name who played Princess Leia in *Star Wars* and wrote *Postcards From the Edge*. If I'd been smart, I would have stayed in radio, and then I could have had monster blockbusters like Rush Limbaugh and Howard Stern. But no, I had to be a *writer*. It seems nobody wants books by writers nowadays. Next thing you know, your garbageman will have a bestseller and I'll still be eating ramen noodles. Oh, what the hell, here goes:

Brewster's crash landing was spotted by a leprechaun named Mick O'Fallon, who pulled our hero out of the flaming wreckage and took him under his wing, because he assumed Brewster was a powerful wizard who could teach him the secret of the philosopher's stone, which in this particular universe had nothing to do with turning lead into gold, but with the manufacture of a much rarer substance known as nickallirium. He set Brewster up in an abandoned keep that had been converted to a mill, complete with a water wheel, and Brewster lost no time in modernizing the crumbling ruin with a complete restoration, including plumbing and electricity. He was assisted in his efforts by the notorious Black Brigands from the nearby town of Brigand's Roost. (Actually, it really wasn't much of a town, more like a couple of shacks and a tavern on the road leading through the Redwood Forest to the Gulfstream Waters.) Black Shannon, the sultry, raven-haired queen of the brigands, cooperated with Brewster in his efforts in return for the promise of significant profits downstream, but as time passed and those profits kept failing to materialize, she started getting antsy.

Meanwhile, Warrick Morgannan was busy trying to find the builder of the time machine, having discovered what it was by eavesdropping on some narrative exposition. To this end, he had employed the infamous Sean MacGregor, alias Mac the Knife, the foremost assassin in the Footpads and Assassins Guild. Together with his hulking, bird-brained apprentices, the brawny brothers Hugh, Dugh, and Lugh, Mac set out to find the builder of the time machine while Warrick emptied out the royal dungeons for "volunteers" in his experiments, putting them into the time machine and using spells to tap into its temporal field, thereby teleporting them into our own universe. This resulted in a number of unusual incidents that provided colorful fodder for the tabloids and alerted a somewhat seedy journalist named Colin Hightower, who was the first to notice a pattern to these strange events. He smelled a story and started to investigate.

Meanwhile, back in the Kingdom of Pitt, in the capital city of Pittsburgh, Warrick had run out of prisoners to use in his experiments, so he had his minions start kidnapping people off the streets. This resulted in a long stream of irate petitions to King Billy, who told Warrick he couldn't simply grab people off the streets and make them disappear, but allowed as how it would be okay to do it with convicted criminals. Unfortunately, Warrick had run out of convicted criminals, so he convinced Sheriff Waylon, the king's ambitious and corrupt brother, to institute a whole slew of new restrictive edicts that would keep the royal dungeons filled. So now, instead of Warrick's minions snatching people off the streets, the Sheriff and his deputies were doing it, and citizens of Pittsburgh kept disappearing without a trace. Needless to say, this displeased the populace. People started packing up and moving like rats fleeing a sinking ship and a revolution was brewing.

Brewster, unaware of all these goings on, had become totally caught up in his efforts to bring progress to the muddy little town of Brigand's Roost. He had showed Mick and the brigands how to forge weapons more efficiently, produce Swiss Army knives, and construct a still to improve their yield of the potent and literally explosive peregrine wine. He had taught them how to construct better housing, and a small settlement had sprung up around the keep. And he taught them how to make aluminum, which turned out to be the same thing as nickallirium, the most precious metal in the twenty-seven kingdoms and the basis for the world's economy. All the coins were minted from it, and the secret of its manufacture was guarded jealously by the alchemists of the Sorcerers and Adepts Guild. And although he didn't know it, Dr. Marvin Brewster had just taken the first steps in bringing about a massive recession in the twenty-seven kingdoms.

Okay, how are we doing? Four paragraphs? Shoot, I didn't think I could do it in two. And there are still a few things I haven't covered, such as Harlan the Peddler's arrival in Brigand's Roost and Mac the Knife's romance with the notorious Black Shannon. Oh, well, we'll just try to cover those bases as we go along. I'll pull it all together one way or another, I promise. Remember, always trust your narrator.

I really would have done a much better job of this if Warrick hadn't gotten us off on the wrong foot. I hope all you people who wrote me letters demanding the next book in this series are happy now. My editors are going to think that living out in the middle of the Arizona desert surrounded by nothing but coyotes and tarantulas and rattlesnakes has driven me right over the edge. I've probably lost all credibility with my students, another novel project has been put on hold until I finish this one, and now I've got one hell of a migraine headache.

But this is it, I swear to God. This is absolutely the last and final novel in this cockamamie series! One way or another, no matter what happens, it all gets wrapped up in this one. And don't write me any letters asking for more sequels. I'm supposed to be a serious writer, for God's sake, and this thing has gotten completely out of hand. Enough's *enough*. I just won't stand for it, I tell you!

Okay. I feel a little better now. The pain in my temples is receding. I'll be all right. I'll have it all back under control by Chapter Two. Bear with me. Remember, always trust your narrator. Now, where were we?

Oh, right, we were still trying to get this story started properly. Damn that Warrick, anyway. I haven't had this much trouble since I wrote those *Battlestar Galactica* novels back in the early eighties. Don't ask. I don't want to talk about it. Just forget I mentioned it, okay? It wasn't me, it was that other guy, what's-his-name. I just got confused there for a moment.

Look, let's just get on with it, okay? Go ahead and turn the page. It'll be all right. I think . . .

Two

"Now remember, luv, no tricks, now. If you try anything funny, I'll scream."

"All right, all right," said Colin Hightower, glancing uneasily at the pretty, blond, and very naked young woman huddled low in the back seat of his rental car. "Just keep quiet and stay out of sight, for God's sake." He sighed heavily. As a reporter, he'd been on the wrong side of the law more than a few times, but he'd never been an accessory in a mental patient's escape from an institution before. And given his less than stellar reputation, he rather doubted the authorities would believe that he had gone along with it under duress.

He opened the driver's side door and walked the dozen or so feet to the front door of his motel room, unlocked it, glanced around, then said, "Okay, the coast is clear."

The blonde jumped out of the car and quickly ran inside the room. He hurriedly followed her in, then closed the door and locked it, mopping his sweaty brow with his handkerchief.

"Oooh," said the naked girl. "What a comfy bed!"

Under other circumstances, Colin would have taken that straight line and run with it like a Heisman trophy winner, but he was far too nervous to think about his slumbering libido. "Megan," he said, in his Liverpudlian accent, "I don't know if you realize this or not, but we're in an awful lot of trouble. By now, they've probably discovered your escape, and if they haven't, they'll certainly know within a matter of hours. I was the last one there to see you. I bribed the orderly to let me in, and he knows who I am. To save his own skin, he'll doubtless claim I forced him to do it at gunpoint or something, and I'm sorry to say most people in my business wouldn't put it past me. Either way, they'll put two and two together and they'll soon have an A.P.B. out on us both."

"What's an A.P.B.?" asked Megan as she bounced fetchingly on the mattress.

Colin had to look away for a moment. There was entirely too much bouncing going on for him to think straight, and he needed to be very clearheaded right now if he was ever going to get out of this mess. "An All Points Bulletin," he said. "That means the police will be looking for us everywhere."

"You mean like the sheriff and his deputies?" asked Megan, with a grimace of distaste.

"And the State Police and Highway Patrol, as well," said Colin. "We've got to get out of town and fast. But the first thing we have to do is get you some clothes. Get up a minute, will you?"

"Why don't you come down here, with me?" asked Megan, stretching out coquettishly and patting the bed beside her with a sly smile.

"Later," Colin said. "But for now, please get up so I can get a good look at you."

"Oh, very well," Megan pouted. She got up and posed for him. "See? You like?"

"Yes, very much," said Colin in a preoccupied tone as he looked her over carefully. "Turn around for me."

She did a slow, seductive pirouette.

"Let's see," said Colin, scratching his chin thoughtfully as he estimated sizes with a practiced eye. "Bra, 32-B; panties, size 5; panty hose, small; dress 4/5; shoes, size 6; and coat, small. I think that ought to do it. And maybe a scarf or something and some sunglasses. The mall should be open until nine tonight, so with any luck, I'll be able to pick everything up in about an hour."

"You're not leaving?" Megan said suspiciously.

"I'll have to," Colin said. "But don't worry, I'll be right back. And I'll bring some brand-new clothes for you."

"New clothes?" said Megan, brightening.

"That's right. Now just stay here, okay? And for God's sake, don't do anything. Just *stay* here. Take a shower and wash your hair or something. I'll bring back some food for us, as well. Then we'll figure out what the hell we're going to do next."

"How do I know I can trust you? What's to keep you from just leaving me here?"

"My own sense of self-preservation, dear," Hightower replied wryly. "I shudder to think what you'd tell the police if they found you here like that. And you need me, so it looks as if we're stuck with each other, for better or for worse. And I'm afraid it's going to be for bloody worse if we don't make tracks out of here real soon, so just sit tight, all right? I'll be back soon."

"Don't take too long," she said.

"Don't worry, I won't. You just behave yourself. Remember, if we get caught, they'll bloody well lock you right back up again. And this time, they'll probably strap you to the bed."

"You could strap me to this one," Megan said coyly.

"I'm tempted to, but not for the reason you think," said Colin, with a grimace. "Now stay put. Watch the, uh, magic box. I'll be back as quickly as I can."

He went out and got back inside his car. As he pulled away, his mind was going a mile a minute. He'd been in tough spots before, and he'd always somehow managed to wriggle out of them, but this one was going to be a real test of wit.

I should've stayed in England, he thought, as he drove toward the mall he remembered passing on his way from the airport. Unfortunately, he had worn out his welcome in London. Even the tabloids, with their notoriously low journalistic standards, had banned him from their pressrooms. Fortunately, however, America's journalistic standards had plummeted even lower, so he had emigrated to the States and secured a job with a major New York City newspaper, thanks to his impressive résumé and the fact that all his former editors were eager to have him permanently on the other side of the Atlantic. Before long, his American employers found out why, and he was now persona non grata with just about every respectable and even quasi-respectable newspaper in the country. It was a considerable achievement that in a profession known for sleaze and sensationalism, Colin Hightower had firmly established himself as the sleaziest, most sensationalistic reporter in the business.

Even his colleagues hated him. Barbara Walters had kneed him in the groin. Pete Hamil had threatened to break his legs. Jimmy Breslin had brained him with a beer bottle and Mike Royko said he knew a guy who knew a guy who could drop him in Lake Michigan if he ever came near him again. Mike Wallace had called him a disgrace to the profession and Bob Woodward had said he was the worst example of irresponsible excess he had encountered since he'd done that book about Belushi. Even *Rolling Stone* had fired him, and Hunter Thompson had actually taken a shot at him with a .44 Magnum. The tabloid news shows on TV were out. Colin simply wasn't very telegenic, with his wide, working-class, ruddy Liverpudlian face, unruly shock of white hair, and red-veined W .C. Fields nose, courtesy of a long and intimate acquaintance with Jack Daniel's. And then there was his taste in clothes, which made him look like a cross between a used-car salesman and an Arkansas real estate broker. The only place left open to him was a well known tabloid based in Florida that ran stories about aliens masquerading as congressmen and WWII airplanes discovered in craters on the moon. And right now, they weren't too thrilled with him, either.

This time, however, Colin was on the track of a *real* story. He could smell it. The only trouble was, he didn't know exactly what it was. All over the world, in widely scattered locations, people were popping up dressed in medieval clothing, apparently all suffering from a similar psychosis. They had no idea where they were; they seemed confused and frightened by modern technology; and they all claimed to come from Pittsburgh. Their stories were all exactly the same. They had been arrested and brought to a white tower, where a sorcerer named Warrick had forced them into some sort of strange device that had magically transported them to this world. And this same Warrick had placed a spell on them, or so they claimed, that compelled them to somehow find their way back to him in the Alabaster Tower and tell him where they'd been and what they'd seen.

It sounded crazy, which was why many of them had wound up in hospitals and mental institutions, but Hightower was starting to wonder. None of these people had any identification on them when they were picked up and not a single solitary individual had a paper trail. It was as though they had suddenly appeared from out of nowhere. Their stories were all remarkably consistent, and none of them displayed any physical signs of having lived in the modern world. No dental work; no surgical scars or inoculation marks; no modern haircuts and not much evidence of personal hygiene. They seemed genuinely ignorant of such things as radio and television, modern plumbing, zippers and buttons, watches, automobiles, and so on, as if they really *had* come from a medieval time. If they were all suffering from the same delusion, it was a remarkably sophisticated and consistent one.

"Jesus, what if it's really true?" Hightower mumbled to himself as he drove. The strange device they all described might be some sort of time machine. And the spell of compulsion they claimed this Warrick had placed on them sounded a great deal like hypnosis. Was it possible that the government had discovered time travel and was conducting tests of some sort? He frowned. No, that made no sense. Even if something like that were possible, they'd surely conduct their tests under strict laboratory conditions, and in utter secrecy. What possible reason would they have for going back into the past, kidnapping people from some medieval time, and transporting them into the present? And then why transport them to so many varied locales and then simply leave them on their own? No matter how he looked at it, there seemed to be no logical explanation. And yet there *had* to be an answer.

Megan was his only solid lead. She claimed to be a prostitute from Pittsburgh who had been arrested because she wouldn't give a freebie to a sheriff's deputy. She had been brought to the Alabaster Tower, which was near the royal palace, and a wizard named Warrick the White had placed her in his magical device and transported her to Pittsburgh, Pennsylvania. Only she denied that it was Pittsburgh, and said it was nothing like the Pittsburgh that she came from, which was in the Kingdom of Pitt, in a land of twenty-seven kingdoms.

He had bribed an orderly at the sanitarium to get an interview with her and a copy of her file, but as he was leaving, she had pushed past him out the door and escaped down the elevator, which they had left keyed open so that Colin could get in and out real fast in case his highly unauthorized visit was discovered.

The orderly's immediate concern had been to get him out of there, and then think up some story to account for the patient's escape. He'd been certain she'd never make it past security in the lobby. However, she hadn't gone down to the lobby, but to the underground parking garage, where she had leaped into Colin's rental car. Under questioning, the orderly would probably break down and tell the truth. Colin didn't dare leave Megan behind. She had jumped into his car, stark naked, and threatened to scream rape if he didn't help her get away. Now he was stuck with her. They'd never believe he didn't plan to break her out. The only way he could see to clear himself was to get to the bottom of this story. And Megan was his only chance to do that.

Some chance, he thought. A bloody crazy nymphomaniac who thought the television was a magic box and the rental car was some kind of magic chariot. "You've really done it this time, Hightower, old sod," he said to himself. "They'll lock you up and throw away the bloody key."

He had to cover himself somehow, account for what he had been doing. As he pulled into the mall, it came to him. He'd file the story. He'd hoped to get to the bottom of it all before going into print, because he didn't want anyone else beating him to the punch, but now he had no choice. And it occurred to him that if he played it right, he could even get the mainstream media to go along. *He'd* become the story.

Reporter investigating bizarre chain of occurrences kidnapped by mental patient. Yes, that was the way to do it. Lay it all out about how these incidents taking place all over the world were somehow connected. Strange Mystery! People From Another Time? Yeah, they'd go for it. Especially with the kidnap angle. He'd claim that Megan was armed and dangerous and was keeping him with her, making him file reports from different locations while they were on the run for the purpose of getting her story out to the world. And once the paper ran the story—and they would—they couldn't deny that he had been assigned to it. It had been his own idea, but his editor had approved it, and once the story ran, he couldn't claim he hadn't known anything about it.

Hightower decided he'd have to phone it in, as soon as possible, and then get out of town, fast. And after that? He'd play it by ear, stringing it out as long as possible until he found out what was behind it all. It would be risky, but it would be worth it. The mainstream media would be sure to pick the story up because of the kidnap angle. And so what if it weren't exactly true? Who were they going to believe, him or an escaped mental patient? He grimaced wryly. Well, given his reputation, it could easily go either way. But it just could be his ticket back into the big time.

"One step at a time, old boy," he told himself. "One step at a time."

Meanwhile, in another space and time (which technically contradicts the "meanwhile," come to think of it, but you get the general idea), on a dirt road winding through the Redwood Forest in the land of Darn, Dr. Marvin Brewster was sitting in a horse-drawn cart with Mick O'Fallon, the brawny little leprechaun swordsmith, and Bloody Bob, the huge nearsighted brigand who had sworn eternal allegiance to Brewster for magically restoring his sight. Actually, Brewster had done nothing of the sort. When he had met Bob, the aging former mercenary's eyesight had grown so bad that he was incapable of seeing anything clearly unless it was about four inches in front of his face. Needless to say, Bob had been forced to retire from soldiering and had joined up with the Black Brigands, who were such a bunch of misfits that they would accept just about anybody. And they knew enough to stay well out of Bob's way when he started laying about him with his sword. Once, he had cleared half an acre of forest before he realized he was surrounded by trees and not human antagonists.

After much trial and error, Brewster had made him a crude pair of prescription lenses, which he had mounted in a helmet visor. The "magic visor" had not quite corrected Bob's vision to 20/20, because Brewster was not a trained optometrist, but it was nevertheless a dramatic improvement and had further added to Brewster's growing reputation as a mighty sorcerer.

At first, Brewster had felt very uneasy about being taken for a wizard, but no matter how much he tried to explain that what he did was science and not magic, nobody believed him. Even after he'd taught Robie McMurphy, a simple farmer, how to grind lenses for some of the other villagers who were having trouble with their eyes, they still thought it was magic, and that Brewster had to be a very gifted mage, indeed, to teach Robie how to work the enchantment so well. To these primitive people, "science" was merely some advanced form of necromancy and Brewster had given up trying to dissuade them from the notion. They called him "Brewster Doc," mistaking his last name for a title, as if he were an alchemist, and mistaking his title (he always liked his friends to call him Doc) for a name. He had grown to like the curious appellation. And if they wanted to believe that he knew magic, he'd finally decided, what was the harm? Besides, having a reputation as a sorcerer brought him a great deal of respect in this strange world and made things considerably easier than they might have been if they thought he was merely an ordinary man.

Initially, Brewster had believed his time machine had taken him back into the past, to England in the ninth or tenth century, but it hadn't taken long for him to realize that he had traveled much farther than he'd thought. For one thing, there had been no dragons in medieval England, nor were there elves or unicorns or fairies. Brewster would never have believed such creatures could exist, yet now he numbered among his friends one gigantic, scaley, talking dragon named Rory, a coffee drinking beatnik vampire elf named Rachel Drum, and a leprechaun armorer and blacksmith named Mick O'Fallon. When he had first met Mick, Brewster had thought he was a dwarf. Now, he was about to meet some *real* dwarves, and he was looking forward to it with both eagerness and a little apprehension.

Brewster tried, without a great deal of success, not to imagine dwarves the way they had appeared in the fairy tales he'd read as a child, because in this universe, the fairy tales were twisted. Here, elves drank human blood—except for Rachel, who was a vegetarian—unicorns smelled worse than skunks, bushes uprooted themselves and wandered about the countryside, and dragons dreamed events in Brewster's universe, somehow tapping into it psychically while they slept. Brewster had no idea what to expect of dwarves.

It was almost dawn, and they had pulled up at a fork in the road leading to the Purple Mountains. As they waited, Brewster smoked his Dunhill pipe. He had long since run out of pipe tobacco, but Calamity Jane, the accident-prone wife of the brigand known as Pikestaff Pat, had concocted a special blend for him made from herbs and wildflowers and some other unspecified ingredients Brewster wasn't sure he really wanted to know about. It was a very pleasant smoke, but ever since he'd seen Jane grinding up some beetles for one of her hallucinatory tea blends, he had decided it was better not to question her too closely about such things. At least the "tobacco" Jane had blended for him didn't make him hallucinate, though it did impart a pleasant buzz.

Sometimes, the life he'd left behind seemed almost like a dream. He had lost track of how long he'd been in this peculiar world. It had to be at least a year by now, perhaps longer. His clothes had all worn out, except for his durable Harris tweed sport jacket, and with his brown leather breeches, high lace-up boots with fringe tops, white cotton tunic and houndstooth sport coat, he now looked rather like a preppie peasant.

He'd never been very good at keeping track of time, and for that matter, he had no idea where he really was in time—or space. Some sort of parallel universe, in another dimension. That was all he knew. He wouldn't have been surprised if Rod Serling suddenly stepped out from behind a rock and started speaking to an unseen television audience.

Unwittingly, he had blundered into the greatest scientific discovery of all time, but unless he found a way to get back home, no one would ever know about it. And since he'd wrecked his time machine, the only way back now was to find the first machine he had constructed and programmed with these same coordinates. The good news was that he had finally learned where it was. The bad news was that it had fallen into the hands of a powerful wizard named Warrick Morgannan, better known as Warrick the White, the royal wizard to the King of Pitt. And from what Brewster had heard of Warrick, getting the time machine away from him would not be easy.

The idea of going up against a real honest-to-God sorcerer was disconcerting enough all by itself, but Brewster had learned that Warrick was already trying to find him. This knowledge had come courtesy of a professional assassin by the name of Sean MacGregor. Mac had been sent out in search of Brewster, but he had met Black Shannon first, and the two bloodthirsty killers had fallen for each other like a ton of bricks. As a result, Mac had turned his back on Warrick, reneging on his contract, and had settled down in Brigand's Roost with Shannon, where he had opened a school for professional assassins. So far, he didn't have too many pupils—just his three hulking, birdbrained apprentices, Hugh, Dugh, and Lugh, and the Awful Urchin Gang, a filthy and unkempt agglomeration of stray children so obnoxious that no one would admit to being their parents.

It had occurred to Brewster that perhaps training the Awful Urchins in the use of weapons was not the smartest idea in the world, but at least it kept them off the streets and out of people's hair, and teaching the only thing he knew gave Mac a feeling of accomplishment. And if Mac was happy, Shannon was happy, and if Shannon was happy, Brewster was relieved, because Shannon basically had three ways of dealing with men—bed them, kill them, or beat them into submission. She had done none of those with Brewster, though there had been several close calls, and Brewster had an uneasy feeling that she was still trying to decide which of the three courses she would take with him. So long as Mac kept her occupied, Brewster felt a whole lot safer. And he felt safer still once he started to bring some profit to the muddy little town of Brigand's Roost. It was to that end that he had come along with Mick on this trip to see the dwarves.

" 'Tis very quiet you've been, Doc," said Mick. "Something on your mind?"

"Oh . . . just thinking, Mick, that's all," Brewster replied, abstractedly.

"About home?" asked Mick.

"How did you know?" said Brewster.

" 'Tis a certain look you get when you start thinking about home," said Mick. "A distant, melancholy sort o' look."

"Ah."

"Are you not happy here, Doc?"

"You know, Mick, the funny thing is, I am happy here. Happier than I can remember being in a long, long time. It's strange. Back home, I was a very wealthy man. I thought I had everything I ever wanted. I had a good home, the respect of my colleagues, and unlimited time to pursue my own research in a private laboratory, funded by a multinational corporation. I even had a charming, intelligent, beautiful young woman who was going to be my wife. I suppose I thought I was happy, but I realize now that there was something missing. I didn't really feel useful. Oh, I'd managed to come up with a few things that made enormous money for the corporation I was working for, and they had practical applications, to be sure, but I never really had the feeling that I was making a difference in people's lives—not the way I am here."

"Aye, things have sure enough changed in Brigand's

Roost since you arrived, Doc. And for the better, too. But tell me, what's a corporation?"

Brewster smiled. "Well, you know all the plans you've been making with Robie and Pat and that peddler, Harlan? That's how a corporation starts. You begin with something that you want to market, like Jane's teas, for instance—"

"Celestial Steepings teas," said Mick.

"Celestial Steepings?" Brewster raised his eyebrows.

" 'Tis what we're going to call the brews," said Mick. "Since Jane has about a dozen different blends by now, we thought each should have its own name, but they should all be known by a trade name, too."

"A brand name," Brewster said, with a grin. "That's called marketing. Harlan's idea, right?"

"Aye," said Mick. "He's got a lot o' fine ideas. We'll be marketing the Many-Bladed Knife, as well, and Doc's Magic Dirt Remover."

"Doc's Magic Dirt Remover?" Brewster asked. "Oh, you mean the soap. You named it after me?"

"We didn't think you'd mind."

"No, I'm very flattered. But that's precisely what I mean. You begin with a plan for goods you want to market, and then you make arrangements for the production of those goods, and for their distribution, and for how you'll advertise them . . . that's mainly what a corporation does. It starts small and as it prospers, it grows bigger and bigger, employing more and more people, accumulating more assets, adding more products, acquiring other companies, selling stock—"

"Stock? What is that?"

"What is stock? Well, basically, it's a way of raising capital. Money to finance your efforts. What you do is you sell small shares of your company to private investors. They give you money in return for those shares, which are pieces of paper that say they own an interest in a small part of your company. By purchasing these shares, they're gambling that your company is going to prosper and those shares are going to be worth more than what they paid for them. And as the company makes money, it pays dividends to shareholders—a small portion of the profits. And that's how corporations grow."

"Interesting," said Mick. "I'll have to mention it to Harlan. But if you say you're happy here, then why do you miss your home so much?"

"Because I don't really belong here, Mick. And because . . . well, mainly because I miss Pamela."

"Ah. Your intended. The beauteous sorceress."

Brewster smiled. Mick and the others naturally thought Pamela was a sorceress, because he'd told them she was a scientist, as well. "I often wonder what she thinks happened to me. I wonder if she believes I ran off somewhere and left her. Or if she thinks I'm dead."

"Perhaps her magic will enable her to follow you and find you here," said Mick.

"Oh, I doubt that very much, Mick. We'd set the date for our marriage three separate times, and each time I failed to show up. It was all my fault, of course; I just became distracted. But who knows, maybe somewhere deep inside, I was afraid of getting married. No, I'm pretty sure Pamela's given up on me by now. It'll probably make her father very happy. He never did like me very much. He thought his daughter could do better."

"Then he's a very foolish man," said Mick.

"Why, thank you, Mick. That was a very kind thing to say."

" 'Tis but the truth."

"Well, I don't know about that. But it was nice of you to say so."

" 'Tis almost sunrise," Mick said, looking up through the canopy of branches overhead. "The dwarves should be coming soon."

"Why couldn't we just go meet them at their village?" Brewster asked.

"I don't think you would enjoy that very much, Doc," Mick replied. "They live underground, you know, in warrens. I might be able to squeeze through their little tunnels, but you're much too big."

"Oh."

"But they come by this way each morning at this time, on their way to the mines up in the Purple Mountains. Whenever we have business to discuss, I always meet them here."

Even as he spoke, Brewster could hear a curious chanting approaching from the distance, down the road. It was a chorus of deep male voices, accompanied by handclapping and foot stomping and percussive mouth noises. A moment later, he could see them coming around a bend in the road, marching in ranks with a curious, bobbing, dancing sort of cadence. As they drew closer, he could make out the words of their rhythmic, sing-song chant.

> "Early in the morning, we rise and shine,
> And haul our asses to the mine,
> Hey, hey, my man! Hi, ho!
> It's off to work we go!

> "We tunnel down hard and we tunnel down deep,
> We keep diggin' that ore until it's time to sleep,
> Hey, hey, my man! Hi, ho!
> It's the only work we know!

> "Rappin' while we work, it's the way to go,
> It keeps the long day from goin' slow,
> Hey, hey, my man! Hi, ho!
> It's the way we run our show!

> "Dig it! Boom-shacka-lacka-lacka!
> Boom-shacka-lacka-lacka!
> Boom-shacka-lacka-lacka!
> Boom!"

Brewster stared with astonishment at the tiny figures as they approached. They were even less than leprechaun-sized, the tallest of them shorter than Mick by at least a foot. Most of them were only about two feet tall, and Brewster was amazed that such deep, basso profundo voices could come from such tiny bodies. They were extremely muscular for their size, mostly blocky torso, with stubby, thick little legs and arms, and large heads crowned with masses of dark, Rastafarian-style dreadlocks. As they drew closer, he could see that their skin was an ash-gray color, and their facial features looked almost Asian. Their eyes were almond shaped and very wide apart, and they had graceful, turned-up noses and pointed chins. Some of them had their hair pulled back in pony-tails and Brewster saw that their ears were pointed as well, and they were even larger than elf ears. They all wore heavy leather boots with thick soles and heels, and baggy leather shorts that came down to just below their knees. But what most struck Brewster were the oversize shirts they wore, in a wide variety of colorful plaids.

"Those shirts . . . " he said. "They look like—"

"Dwarven flannel," Mick said. "Light, warm, and very comfortable. Only dwarven weavers know how to make it, and they will not share the secret with anyone."

"Rapping, Rastafarian, grunge dwarves?" said Brewster.

As the dwarves stopped in front of their wagon, a couple of them detached themselves from the formation and approached. "Hi, ho, Mick," one of them said.

"Hi, ho, Dork," Mick replied.

"Dork?" said Brewster, raising his eyebrows.

The dwarf drew himself up to his full height, though at a full height of only two feet, something about the effect was lost. "I am Dork, headman of my tribe," he said in a surprisingly deep voice. He thumped himself on his chest for emphasis. "And this is Dweeb, my brother."

"Ho," said Dweeb, with a curt nod at Brewster.

"And this is the Brewster Doc, the mighty sorcerer I told you about," said Mick.

The two dwarves looked properly impressed, but not as impressed as they looked when Mick showed them a couple of the Swiss Army knives from the recent production run back at the keep. They went back to the others and were all soon mumbling excitedly as the knives were passed around.

"Dwarves are extremely fond o' tools," said Mick, in an

aside to Brewster. "They love nothing better. The knives will do most o' the work for us, but let me do the bargaining. You just sit there and look important."

"Whatever you say, Mick," Brewster said, and he tried to look as important as he could when Dork and Dweeb came back up to the wagon.

"We *must* have these marvelous knives," Dork said intensely. "Never have we seen such well-made, useful tools. How much will you take for them?"

"Nothing," Mick said.

"But we *must* have them!"

"You misunderstood," said Mick. " 'Tis a gift they are, from Doc to your brother and yourself."

The two dwarves glanced at Brewster with astonishment and Brewster merely nodded, trying to look important.

"Truly?" Dork said with amazement.

"Truly," Mick replied. "Doc would like to make you presents o' them, as a gesture o' goodwill."

The dwarves glanced at each other. "Do you have more knives such as these?" asked Dork.

"They are very difficult to craft," said Mick. "And we require only the very finest materials, such as those you have provided me with in the past, in limited quantities, for certain o' my swords."

The dwarves glanced at each other again. "And if we could provide more?"

"You mean to say you might be interested in an alliance for our mutual benefit?"

"If it is to our mutual advantage," Dork replied cautiously.

"Well then, let's talk some business, lads," said Mick with a wink at Brewster as he got down out of the wagon.

THREE

The muddy little town of Brigand's Roost was no longer a muddy little town, and some of the older residents weren't quite sure what to make of all the changes. Gentrification was a word that was unknown to One-Eyed Jack and Bloody Mary, but as they sat on the second-floor balcony of One-Eyed Jack's Tavern, watching all the new construction, they wondered about the effect all these changes were having on their lives.

Every day, more and more people arrived in Brigand's Roost. Jack had built an addition to his tavern to house the overflow from the rooms he had to let upstairs, and no sooner had the construction been completed than he had to start building yet another addition to accommodate the constant influx of new arrivals. In this manner, the tavern had expanded over the last year until it had become surrounded by a commodious rooming house that had grown to take up an entire block, and was now known as The Brigand's Roost Hotel.

Jack's life had changed completely. A year earlier all he had to worry about was tending bar in his tavern and breaking up the occasional fight on Saturday night, when the brigands would come in to get all liquored up. And every now and then, some traveler would get out of line with one of Bloody Mary's girls and Jack would have to bust a head or two. Otherwise, life had been quiet, peaceful, relaxing, and uncomplicated. Now, everything had changed.

He had found it necessary to hire three bartenders to work in the tavern, which was always full to capacity, even with the wall knocked down and the bar extended. He now had a hotel manager working for him, and a staff of over two dozen employees. He no longer even had the pleasure of breaking up the fights, because Hugh, Dugh, and Lugh were now on the payroll as bouncers, and they kept order with a brutal and direct efficiency. In the twilight of his life, Jack was still fit and strong, if a little creaky, and though he had lost most of his teeth and one eye, he still felt useful and productive. The only trouble was, now he had hardly anything to do. He had become, against all expectation, a wealthy man. And he was having a hard time getting used to the idea.

Bloody Mary was getting on in years as well, but anyone could see that in her prime, she must have been a real heartstopper. She was still beautiful, even though her face was lined with age and she had put on weight, and though it had been years since she had entertained male clients, what she didn't know about the art of love simply wasn't worth knowing. Ten years earlier, she had retired to the country and found her place in Brigand's Roost, where she had become partners with Jack and operated a small and friendly brothel on the upper floor of the tavern. In the last six months, however, she had found it necessary to hire a dozen additional girls and the upper floor of the tavern was no longer enough to handle all the business. Directly across the street, a new building was going up, three whole floors, and a sign in front of it said, "Future Home of Bloody Mary's Gaming and Pleasure Emporium."

Mary wasn't sure about the gaming part, but Harlan had insisted that it would be good for the growth of the town's economy to have gambling on the premises, and as he had bought into her business, he promised he would run the gambling concession and she wouldn't have to worry about anything other than managing her girls. And even there, she didn't have to do much. Saucy Cheryl had taken over most of the managing duties, and Mary had to admit that Cheryl had a real flair for it. She hired only the most beautiful girls and trained them all herself, and there was a list of recently arrived girls waiting to get hired on once the new building was completed.

As they sat on the balcony of the tavern, Mary and Jack watched the constant parade of people going in and out of the offices of Harlan's Townlot Company and Holdings, Ltd., situated next door to the Future Home of Bloody

Mary's Emporium. Within a remarkably short time, Harlan the Peddler had become Harlan the Entrepreneur, a force to be reckoned with in Brigand's Roost. There was even talk of running him for mayor. Brigand's Roost had never had a mayor before, but now they had a Town Council that met in the tavern every Tuesday night, and for the first time in anyone's memory, there were actually ordinances on the books. Before, there hadn't even been any books.

No one had ever actually owned property in Brigand's Roost before. In the past, if someone had arrived in town and chosen for some unfathomable reason to stay, they would simply have homesteaded a little patch of ground and built a shack upon it. Harlan had changed all that. Real estate was now big business in Brigand's Roost. The hawk-faced little peddler had recruited some of the brigands to parcel out all the acreage around the town and survey it, and the ownership was equally divided among all the old-time residents of the town and the environs, which basically meant the brigands and a few of the locals who lived in and around the village. The Townlot Company administered the transfers of the deeds—for a percentage—and Harlan's offices were papered with platted maps indicating all the lots by number. And he had an interest in each and every one of them. When all of the available lots had been sold, they simply cleared more forest land around the town and parceled it out. New lots were sold as quickly as they were surveyed and made available. Suddenly everyone was making money hand over fist.

As Mary and Jack sat on their balcony, they could see the entire main street of the town stretching out before them. It had more than tripled in length in the last few months and would soon quadruple. Where once Brigand's Roost had been nothing more than a curving, rutted dirt street with a few shacks on either side, now it was a full-scale town, with side streets and alleyways, and within a few years—if growth persisted at this rate—it would become a city.

There was now a farmer's market at the end of Main Street, and there were two stables, a blacksmith's shop, two saloons, a hotel, an apothecary shop, four tailors, a dry goods store, a milliner, a leather worker, two construction companies, a soothsayer, three bakeries, two butcher shops, a bank, a jeweler, and even a teahouse, serving a full selection of Calamity Jane's Celestial Steepings teas with homemade muffins and pies. At the edge of town, there was a profusion of market stalls set up—all of whose operators had to pay a trade tariff to the Town Council, of which Harlan was a founding member. A small tent city had sprung up on the edge of town, full of people waiting for housing to become available. And the steady stream of new arrivals showed no sign of letting up.

"Where do you think they're all coming from?" asked One-Eyed Jack, scratching his heavily bearded chin.

"Pittsburgh, mostly," Mary replied, putting her bare feet up on the balcony railing. " 'Tis what the girls say. They're having some trouble there and people are leaving in droves."

"What sort of trouble?" Jack asked.

Mary shrugged. "They say a revolution is brewing, and people want to get out before the fighting starts. There's already been some rioting, I hear."

"How come?" asked Jack.

Mary frowned. "I'm not quite sure. I keep hearing different stories. Some say that King Billy has become a tyrant. Others say he's gone mad and the sheriff is the tyrant and that he has his brother under his thumb. Some say he's even deposed the king and is ruling in his place, while King Billy serves only as a figurehead. But all agree that Pittsburgh has become a miserable place to live, what with all the new ordinances the sheriff has instituted in the king's name. They say a person can't even spit on the street anymore without being arrested. And those who are arrested are taken to the dungeons and never seen nor heard from again. Everyone says 'tis only a matter of time until the people rise up against the king."

"Assuming there's any people left to do it, at the rate they're leaving," Jack replied. "What I don't understand is why they're all coming *here*."

"Word has spread that there's a mighty sorcerer in Brigand's Roost and he's helping people make a better life for themselves here," said Mary. "Everyone who comes to town asks about him. It's that Harlan. He's the one who started it all. Every time a new wagonload of goods goes out to market, he has them take a stack of handbills telling all about the good life and all the opportunities in the booming town of Brigand's Roost. He calls it 'marketing.' "

Jack grunted in assent. "I never saw a man with so much energy. He never stands still. Every time you turn around, he's got some new plan cooking. Things just haven't been the same in Brigand's Roost since he arrived. And I'm not sure all these changes are for the better."

"What are you complaining of?" asked Mary. "You're getting rich."

"True," said Jack. "But for the life of me, I can't reckon what a man's supposed to *do* when he gets rich."

"Work on getting richer," Mary said with a shrug.

"Doesn't seem like all that much work to me," Jack said, scratching his beard again. "Somehow, it just sort of happens by itself."

"That's how 'tis when you have money," Mary said. "It just sort of multiplies. Harlan calls it 'economics.' "

"If you ask me, none of this would've happened without Doc," said Jack, "but 'tis everybody else who's getting rich. What does Doc get out of it?"

"Well now, he's got the old keep, doesn't he?" said Mary. "And he never has to pay for anything in this town. There isn't a man, woman, or child in Brigand's Roost wouldn't give him the shirt off their back if he asked for it. And he gets a cut of all the export business."

"He does?"

"Sure enough he does. Harlan manages it for him. He's not about to bite the goose that gilds the eggs."

"*What?*" said Jack, staring at Mary with confusion.

"Well, something like that, anyway," said Mary, with a scowl. "I don't know, it made sense when Harlan said it."

"But if Doc gets a cut of all the export business, why is it he never has any money?" Jack said.

" 'Tis all in the bank," said Mary.

"Oh," said Jack. He frowned. "You know, I still don't understand this newfangled bank idea."

" 'Tis very simple," Mary said. "You wanted me to handle all our money, right, so you would not be bothered? Well, I took our money and put it all in the bank for safekeeping. In return for holding on to our money, the bank pays us a percentage called 'interest,' so by keeping our money in the bank, we're actually making more. The more money we keep there, the more money we make."

"But what does the bank get out of it?"

"The bank uses our money as an asset, lending it out at interest. There are business loans, and construction loans, and home mortgages, and personal loans, and the longer people take to repay these loans, the more it costs in interest."

"Seems to me I could lend out my own money at interest," Jack said, "and cut out the middleman."

"But then you'd have to handle all the details," Mary said. "This way, the bank takes care of all that for you."

"What happens if people fail to make the payments on these loans?"

"Then the bank takes their assets."

"And then what?"

"It sells them for a profit."

"This was Harlan's idea, right?"

"Actually, I think he got the idea from Doc," said Mary. "But he took to it right quickly."

"I notice that he quickly takes to anything that involves making money," said Jack.

"Well, he's sure enough making money for you," said Mary. "He's making us rich."

"And making himself richer still," Jack replied with a scowl. "If you ask me, putting all that money in one place is just an invitation for somebody to steal it. Wouldn't it be smarter to have our money where we could keep an eye on it?"

"It could be stolen from us, as well. But if we keep it in the bank, then 'tis insured."

" 'Tis what?"

"Insured. That means if someone steals it, the insurance company makes good the loss."

"What's an insurance company?"

"Oh, that's another new idea Harlan got from Doc. 'Tis a business that sells security. You buy an insurance policy that promises to pay you if you sustain a loss. You can buy different kinds of insurance. Fire insurance to protect against your home or business burning down, theft insurance to protect yourself from being robbed, life insurance—"

"*Life* insurance?"

"So if you die, your family gets money."

Jack shook his head. "Sounds like a good reason for your family to murder you, if you ask me."

"Harlan says 'tis protection for your family, in case anything should happen to you. You pay for it in small amounts called 'premiums' each month. And in return for these premiums, if you sustain a loss, the insurance company makes it good."

"But where do they get the money?"

"From the premiums."

"So why not just save the money you'd pay in these premiums and have a nest egg to guard against misfortune? It makes no sense to me. Who runs this insurance company?"

"Harlan," Mary said.

"That figures," Jack replied dryly. "Does Shannon know about all this?"

"Of course," said Mary. "Harlan knows better than to make money in Brigand's Roost without giving her a cut of all the profits. He says 'tis a part of economics called 'extortion.'"

"I'm just too old to understand all this newfangled stuff," said Jack, shaking his head. "I prefer things the way they were."

" 'Tis called 'progress,' Jack. You have to change with the times."

"Why?"

"Why?"

"That's right, why?"

Mary shrugged. "I don't know. You just do, that's all."

"Is that what Harlan says?"

"Right."

"Somehow, I knew that," Jack said sourly.

At that very moment the object of their deliberations was busy conducting a board meeting of The Rooster Corporation, the name they had recently settled on for their fledgling conglomerate. No sooner had Mick told Harlan about Doc's explanation of what a corporation was than Harlan insisted that they form one. They sat around a long table in the executive offices on the upper floor of the Townlot Company, which was now a subsidiary of The Rooster Corporation, along with The First Bank of Brigand's Roost, The Rooster Equity and Assurance Company, and Brigand Exports, Ltd. The corporation also had a strong financial interest in The Brigand's Roost Hotel, Bloody Mary's Gaming and Pleasure Emporium, and over half the other independent businesses in town, including the Farmers Market and the stall concessions in Tent City.

"All right, so the deal with the dwarves went down?" said Harlan.

"A complete and unqualified success," replied Mick. "The moment they saw the knives, they just had to have them. It was clever o' you to suggest giving a couple to their tribal leaders. Now all the others want them, too."

"It was a worthwhile investment," Harlan said, nodding. "Never be afraid to spend money to make money. Especially if it hooks the customer and keeps him coming back for more. So now we've got a supplier for raw materials. That's good. That's very good. So long as Dork's people keep their mouths shut about dealing with us."

"That was part of the agreement," Mick said. "In fact, they insisted on it."

"Why?" asked Robie. "I mean, why should they keep quiet about it?"

"Because they're under exclusive contract to the Sorcerers

and Adepts Guild, that's why," Harlan said. "They're not supposed to be supplying anybody else. So long as we're getting the bauxite and alchemite directly from them, it saves us having to mine it for ourselves. What was it Doc called the alchemite?"

"Cryolite," said Mick. "That's what they call it in the Land of Ing, where he hails from."

"Well, from now on, I think we should call it cryolite, as well," said Harlan.

"Why?" asked Robie, yet again.

"Because nobody knows what the hell cryolite is, you *putz*," Harlan said. (Narrator's Note: He didn't actually say "*putz*," because no one spoke Yiddish in this universe. There were no Jews in the twenty-seven kingdoms, but there was a tribe known as the Hazerai, which roughly translates as "People Who Survive the Guilt," and the Hazerai expression Harlan used was a rough equivalent of "*putz*.") "If we start talking about using alchemite, word will get around that we've got a source. You want the Sorcerers and Adepts Guild finding out we're buying alchemite out from under them?"

"Uh . . . no," said Robie.

"So what do we call it?"

"Cryolite."

"Good boy. You see, you're learning."

"Oh, and there's one more thing," Mick said. "Doc and I had a drink with the dwarves to conclude the deal, and they just went wild for the Mickey Finn. They want to arrange steady shipments."

"Great. You didn't tell them what it was, did you?" Harlan asked.

"No, naturally not," Mick replied.

"Why shouldn't he have told them what it was?" asked Robie, with a puzzled frown.

Harlan sighed. "Okay, kid, let's try this by the numbers. Mickey Finn is our trade name for what?"

"Peregrine wine," said Robie.

"And peregrine wine is made from what?" said Harlan.

"Peregrine bushes," Robie replied.

"And where can you find peregrine bushes?"

"Well . . . just about anywhere. Especially when they migrate. They're all over the damn place."

"Right. And if the dwarves know what Mickey Finn is made from, then they can do what?" asked Harlan.

Robie concentrated. "Try to duplicate the recipe for themselves?"

"Brilliant," Harlan said. "I think he's really coming along, don't you?"

Mick nodded and McMurphy looked very pleased with himself. He had become an unabashed admirer of Harlan and paid very close attention to everything he did. Harlan had a gift, and Robie was anxious to learn as much from him as possible.

"Of course, the dwarves don't have a still," said Harlan. "But we can't expect to keep the knowledge of how to make a still to ourselves. The more the demand for Mickey Finn increases, the more workers we have to hire for the brewery, and sooner or later, one of the brighter ones will figure out how to make a plan for the still and sell it to the highest bidder. We can't control that. What we can control is the recipe, by making sure only the trusted brewmasters have it. Always remember that half the secret of success is staying ahead of the competition. And if you can't stay ahead of them, buy them out."

"Right," said Robie.

"Okay, next item on the agenda," Harlan said. "What are the current distribution figures on the teas?"

Pikestaff Pat went over to the chart he had made up and placed on the easel. His wife Jane was in charge of all the manufacturing, which meant gathering the raw materials and creating the different blends of Celestial Steepings teas, but he kept track of the business end of things. A year ago, he couldn't read or write, but now he had learned how to keep accounts and make flow charts that allowed him to keep track of the inventory and the distribution. He picked up a pointer and stood by the easel proudly.

"We've got three more stores handling our product in Franktown," he said. "Last month they took a shipment of Dragon's Breath Brew and Fairy Mist, and they did so well for them that now they've placed an order for our entire line."

"Excellent," said Harlan. "Go on."

"So far, about half the marketing force has returned for resupply," said Pat. "We've made inroads with our products in eight of the twenty-seven kingdoms, and as soon as the wagons get back from the more distant ones, we should have added at least five or six more. And the earlier complaints from the peddlers about being under exclusive contract to us and handling only our trade goods have all disappeared once they've seen how well our products move. They're all anxious to get out on the road again."

"Just as I predicted," said Harlan, nodding with satisfaction. "And word of mouth from them will make it that much easier for us to expand the marketing force. We'll have to see about stepping up production."

"There's no problem in doing that with the teas, or with Doc's Magic Dirt Remover," Pat said. "The spam ranch is producing plenty of the ugly beasts, so the rendering plant is operating at capacity, but it's going to be tough expanding production on the knives and the Mickey Finn."

"That's true," said Mick. "The dwarves will be buying up most of our supply, and that will ensure a steady source of raw materials from their mine. We can expand the brewery, but if we wait for the migration season every year, we'll run short on peregrine bushes. We'll just have to start raising our own."

"Make a note of that, Pat," said Harlan. "We need to start a nursery. What about the knives, Mick?"

"We're not really in a position to speed up production of the knives without affecting quality," the burly leprechaun replied.

"Okay, let's not rush it, then," said Harlan. "We want to maintain quality, at all costs. The Many-Bladed Knife is our most important product. It has to be first rate. We'll expand production only when it becomes practical. Until then, we'll raise the price. The demand is there; the market can bear it. Now, I'd like to bring up some new business. Brigand's Roost is growing rapidly, and we need to think about the future. Up 'til now, no one's paid very much attention to us here, but all that is going to change soon. A little mud hole of a village that supports a motley bunch of brigands is one thing, but a boom town with a thriving economy is something else again. Sooner or later, someone's going to want a piece of it. And if we want to protect our interests, we've got to make preparations now."

"What sort o' preparations?" asked Mick.

"Well, we're all subjects of the King of Darn," said Harlan, "and at the rate we're growing, it won't be long before His Majesty, King Durwin, decides he's entitled to a share in our good fortune. I don't know about you, but I'm not too thrilled about that idea myself. Durwin's never lifted a finger to help us, why should we have to cut him in for a percentage of the profits in the form of taxes?"

"But we've never been asked to pay any taxes before," said Robie.

"That's because there's never been any money in Brigand's Roost before," said Harlan. "It was too much trouble to send tax collectors to a muddy little hole like this. But now we're no longer a muddy little hole and it's suddenly become worthwhile for His Majesty to take an interest in us."

"So what do you think we should do?" asked Pat.

"I propose we formally secede from Darn and form our own little kingdom," Harlan said.

Silence fell upon the room. For several moments no one spoke as the full import of Harlan's audacious proposal sank in.

"Our own *kingdom*?" Robie said with disbelief.

Mick gave a low whistle. "That would sure enough get us noticed."

"If we form our own kingdom, we get to make our own rules," said Harlan. "And nobody gets to put their hands in our pockets. Nobody."

"King Durwin would never sit still for that," said Pat, shaking his head. "He's always left us pretty much alone before, but if we start our own kingdom within his lands, he's liable to take exception."

"Let him," Harlan said. "We've got our own sorcerer, and at the rate people are arriving, we'll soon be able to have our own army, as well. And it will be a very well-paid army, which should attract the finest mercenaries. With Doc's knowledge and our skills, Durwin won't be able to do anything to stop us."

"I don't know," said Mick, dubiously. " 'Tis an awfully big step. And a dangerous one. Who would be our king?"

"Why not a queen?" asked Harlan.

Their eyes got very wide. "*Shannon*?" Pat said.

"Why not?" said Harlan. "The famous leader of the Black Brigands would make a formidable queen, and her consort would be the former top-ranked assassin of the Footpads and Assassins Guild. What better man to train an army? He's already got the school for it. And with Doc as royal wizard, we would be invincible. No other kingdom would dare to interfere with us. We'd also have our economy to back us up. If anyone decided not to recognize our right to rule ourselves, we'd simply cut them off from our exports. And people are going to *want* our exports. What we've done so far is only the beginning, my friends. Before long, Brigand's Roost is going to be a thriving city, with small towns and villages springing up around it. There's already a small village around Doc's keep, and it's growing every day. There are only a few miles separating it from Brigand's Roost, and soon, it will all be one town. Doc's keep would make a perfect royal palace—once we expanded it, of course. Doc would still have his tower, which we could designate as the official wizard's residence, but we could extend the old walls and build the palace on the grounds where the rendering is being done now. I'm sure Doc wouldn't mind the new construction if it resulted in a renovation of his tower and the rendering operation being moved. He's never complained, mind you, but the smell is enough to stun a unicorn."

"It has gotten pretty bad," Mick agreed. "We could easily clear some land and move it."

"My point is, before long, this is going to be the richest city in all the twenty-seven kingdoms," Harlan continued. "And if we want to determine our own destiny, we're going to have to become number twenty-eight."

"Queen Shannon," Mick said thoughtfully. "Have you spoken to her about this yet?"

"I wanted to be certain we were all in agreement first," Harlan replied. "I think we should present the idea to her together."

"Queen Shannon," Pat said, trying out the sound of it. "But queen of what? What shall we name our kingdom?"

"How about . . . Brigantium?" asked Robie.

"Brigantium," said Harlan, raising his eyebrows and nodding. "Now that has a ring to it. I like it."

"Queen Shannon of Brigantium," said Mick. "It does sound rather impressive, doesn't it? But I'm not sure how Mac will feel about being a common consort to a queen."

"Leave Mac to me," said Harlan. "He'll be no common consort. He'll be Commanding General of the Royal Army of Brigantium and First Minister of Defense."

"Impressive," Mick said, glancing at Harlan with respect. "I find it hard to believe that only a short while ago you were a mere peddler."

"I was never a *mere* peddler," Harlan replied. "I was a visionary. All I needed was the right opportunity. And this, my friends, is it. All we need is the courage to take it. All in favor?"

"Aye," said Robie, immediately.

"Aye," said Pikestaff Pat after a moment.

Mick nodded. "Aye," he said softly. " 'Tis a bold and risky step, but I can see the reasons for it."

"That makes it unanimous," said Harlan, pouring them all drinks of Mickey Finn. "I think this calls for a toast. Gentlemen, I give you . . . the Kingdom of Brigantium! Long live the queen!"

"Long live the queen!" they echoed, and tipped their goblets back.

Harlan gasped and turned purple as the potent brew went down.

"Count of three," said Mick.

"Two," said Robie.

Harlan stood swaying for several seconds, then his eyes rolled up and he collapsed senseless on the table.

"Four," said Pat, impressed. "He's getting better."

"Since the chairman is unconscious, I declare this meeting adjourned," said Mick. He wrapped Harlan's fingers around the gavel, raised it, and let it drop onto the table. "We'll go see Shannon first thing in the morning, after he sleeps it off."

"What?" said Shannon, staring at them with astonishment. "Have you all lost your minds?"

"Think about it," Harlan said. He still looked a little green around the gills. "We've got a pretty good thing going here. You're making far more money now than you ever did when the brigands were plying their outlaw trade, and for a lot less effort, too. But at the rate things are going, it won't be long before King Durwin or one of the rulers of the other kingdoms decides to move in on us. When there's fresh meat on the road, the carrion begin to gather. If we want to hold on to what we've got, we have to take steps to protect ourselves. We must seize the initiative."

"He's got a point, my love," said Mac, nodding in agreement. "Warrick is already searching for Doc. And that mercenary who tried to take you in for the bounty on your head has doubtless reported to him long since. I am surprised nothing has come of it yet. Warrick the White is not one to sit idle for long. He may be gathering forces against us even as we speak."

Shannon nodded. "Aye," she agreed, "but making preparations to defend ourselves is one thing, forming our own kingdom is quite another. It would be an open invitation to King Durwin to send troops against us."

"All the more reason for us to have a standing army,"

Harlan said. "And Mac is just the man to lead it. A general needs troops, but he also needs a king. Or, in this case, a queen. After all, who is better suited to the task than you? No one would question your leadership."

"But how could I possibly be a queen?" asked Shannon. "I am a commoner, not someone of royal birth."

"Royal birth is merely an accident of fate," said Harlan. "It has never rendered anyone fit to be a king or queen; it has merely allowed them to be born into the position. Keep in mind, however, that before any royal lineage was ever established, *someone* had to be first to assume the title, and more often than not, they assumed that title by virtue of overpowering all the other aspirants. I don't happen to see any other aspirants about at the moment, but even if there were, I have little doubt that you could overpower them quite easily."

"True enough," said Mac with a smile. "We would have ourselves a warrior queen."

"After all," continued Harlan, pressing the point, "you have always ruled Brigand's Roost in all but name. We would merely be making it official. We are a thriving town now. 'Tis only right that we should do things in a manner that was proper and respectable."

"Respectable," said Shannon, mulling it over. "I had always wondered what it would be like to be respectable. A proper lady."

"A proper *queen*," said Mick. "First lady o' the realm."

"And you all want this?" Shannon asked.

" 'Twas unanimous," said Robie.

"All that's left is an official proclamation," Harlan said. "And the small matter of appointing ministers and recruiting a palace guard and an army. Mac is eminently suited to that task. After all, he has already founded a school to train assassins. It could easily be expanded to train an army, as well. With Mac's training and Doc's knowledge, we could have an army that would be unsurpassed in might."

"Would I not need a king?" asked Shannon with a side-long glance at Mac.

"Well, that would be your royal perogative, if and when

you should ever choose to marry," Harlan said quickly. "However, the Commanding General of the Army of Brigantium and the First Minister of Defense would certainly make a fitting royal consort."

"General MacGregor," said Mac. "It does sound rather more impressive than 'Mac the Knife,' does it not?"

"Have you spoken with Doc about this?" Shannon asked.

"Not yet," said Harlan, "but I feel certain Doc will go along with whatever we decide. He doesn't seem to care a great deal about such things, one way or the other. You've all known him longer than I have, of course, but from what I've seen, it appears that Doc's concern is solely for his craft. He is not what I would call a terribly ambitious man."

"Unlike some people I could mention," Shannon said wryly. "What's in this for you, Harlan?"

"A fair question, to be sure," Harlan replied. "What's in it for me is a considerable measure of security, the ability to conduct my business—*our* business, I should say—without having to concern myself about anyone trying to muscle in and take things over. Or cut themselves in for a substantial percentage of the profits."

"And if they did, then you could always claim you had no choice except to go along with the new regime," said Shannon. "No, I think not, peddler. If we secede from Darn, then my head, as well as Mac's, and anyone else's who becomes part of our new regime is on the block. I think I'd feel much better if you were to share in the risk, as well as in the profits."

"There has been talk of running him for mayor," said Robie.

"Not nearly risk enough," Shannon replied. "If you want me to be queen, then you, peddler, are going to be my prime minister."

"Well now, I'm not so sure that's such a wise decision," Harlan said uneasily. "After all, I am a businessman, not a politician. I lack the talent for statemanship."

"Oh, I think we have yet to plumb the depths of your talents," Shannon said. "If we are to form our own kingdom, then you, my friend, are going to play one of the key roles. If you share equally in the responsibility, then you shall also share equally in the blame if we should fail."

Harlan looked decidedly uncomfortable. "I feel 'tis only fair to remind you that I already bear considerable responsibility. I am a member of the Town Council, and chairman of the board of The Rooster Corporation. I am also the chief executive officer of the First Bank of Brigand's Roost and Rooster Equity and Assurance. And I am also president of the Townlot Company and a silent partner in The Brigand's Roost Hotel and Bloody Mary's Gaming and Pleasure Emporium. Surely, that is more than enough responsibility for any man. After all, I am only human, and there is only so much I can do."

"Then learn how to delegate responsibility," said Shannon. "If your new duties as prime minister of Brigantium start to interfere with your ability to operate your various enterprises, which you would never have developed had I not permitted it, then I suggest you find someone else to run them. I know nothing about being a queen. If you expect me to accept the title, then you shall have to advise me on the proper way to rule."

"But I know nothing of such matters!" Harlan protested.

"I am certain you know a great deal more than I," said Shannon. And with a lightning motion, she drew her sword and placed the point against the peddler's throat. "You *will* be my prime minister. I am afraid I must insist."

Harlan swallowed hard. "Well . . . since you put it that way . . . I accept your gracious offer of the post."

"A wise decision," Shannon said, sheathing her blade. "And your first duty as prime minister will be to inform Doc of our plans, and ask for his support. I suspect that we are truly going to need it."

"As you command . . . Your Majesty," Harlan said with a courtly bow.

"Your Majesty," Shannon said. And then she smiled. "I must admit, I like the sound of that."

FOUR

It was a warm night, and the full moon bathed the grounds of the keep in a silvery glow. It would have been nice to say there was a perfume of heather on the evening breeze, or something equally poetic, but unfortunately, your faithful narrator must report that the only "scent" on the air was the stench rising from the rendering pots in the courtyard. It would be difficult to convey the precise sense impression, but if you've ever driven through Elizabeth, New Jersey, on a warm and muggy summer day, you'll get the general idea.

No matter how he tried, Brewster just could not get used to it. He had no one but himself to blame. He had wanted to have something to wash with, and at the same time do something about the personal hygiene of the brigands, most of whom had smelled like bears in heat, so he had taught them how to render spam fat into soap. The wild spam was a rather loathsome scavenger, a hairless, pink speckled creature that looked like a particularly ugly cross between a wild boar and a rat. They were so inedible that even starving hunters would pass them by. Rendering them into soap was the only practical use anyone had ever found for them. Now, the brigands washed enthusiastically, the better to be walking advertisements for the soap they marketed under the name "Doc's Magic Dirt Remover," and the two or three rendering pots in the courtyard had multipled into a veritable sea of huge black cauldrons, bubbling away throughout the day and night, producing huge quantities of spam soap and a stench that made the eyes water.

The soap had become such a profitable commodity that to keep up with the demand, the former brigands had become spam ranchers and the pens of domestically raised spams just beyond the walls of the keep meant that Brewster had to live not only with the stench of the rendering operation, but the constant grunting and squealing throughout the day and night. It wasn't exactly what he had in mind when he had set about bringing some progress to the muddy little town of Brigand's Roost. On the other hand, it did keep most of the villagers at bay, as they thought the "sulphurous fumes" coming from within the crumbling walls were part of his wizardly arts.

Since he had moved into the keep and started renovating it, adding plumbing and electricity, the little settlement that had sprung up outside the walls had grown from a few tents and shacks into a small village of identical two-bedroom frame cottages, all painted in bright and cheery colors. And though Bloody Bob's construction company kept putting up new homes according to a simple plan Brewster had drawn up for them, they still could not keep up with the demand. Every day, more land was being cleared and more homes were going up and soon the little village spreading out beyond the keep would meet the town of Brigand's Roost, about four miles away. The roads between the houses were all dirt, which made things rather messy when it rained, and the sanitation was appalling, especially with the spam pens so close to the homes.

Brewster made a mental note to see what he could come up with for paving the streets. Cobblestones would work, but asphalt or something like it would be more efficient. They would need some sort of steamroller. Perhaps the internal combustion engine he was working on, powered by the explosive peregrine wine, could be adapted to the purpose. And something simply had to be done about the sanitation, before disease began to spread. Not knowing any better, the people simply threw their refuse out into the streets. It was how the plague had started in medieval times on Earth, and Brewster had no wish to see it happen here. He would have to speak to Harlan about putting together some sort of sanitation department.

"The aroma in the courtyard tonight is rather piquant," Rory said as he perched on the parapet of the tower. As usual, fairies buzzed around the huge dragon like flies around a sweaty mare, their bright glow reflecting off his iridescent scales.

"It is getting pretty bad," said Rachel Drum as she sat cross-legged on the flagstones, absently tapping her bongos with her fingertips. "It wouldn't be a bad idea to consider moving the rendering operation."

"Like, to another kingdom," added Brian, the Werepot Prince. Since the moon was full, he had reverted to his human form, which had remained magically youthful despite the fact that he was well over sixty years old. He didn't look a day over eighteen, and he was a very handsome prince, indeed. Unfortunately for him, he only looked this way on nights when the moon was full. The rest of the time, he was a talking chamberpot. It was the result of an enchantment placed upon him by a wizard whose daughter the irrepressible Prince Brian had knocked up, along with half the other young girls in his kingdom. What became of all the other children he had fathered was anybody's guess, but the wizard's daughter had produced a son who had now grown into a man and become a wizard in his own right—none other than Warrick Morgannan.

"I'd feel awkward asking them to move the rendering operation," Brewster said. "The whole thing was my idea in the first place. And it seems the soap is really selling well. It's given them a great sense of accomplishment. I'd hate to put a damper on their enthusiasm."

"So why can't they be enthusiastic somewhere else?" asked Brian sourly. "Each day, the stench grows worse."

"I don't know, I rather like it," said the dragon.

"You would, you great worm," said Brian wryly.

"Look, we did not come here to argue," Brewster pointedly reminded them. "I'll see if I can convince them to move the rendering operation somewhere else, but meanwhile, we have much more important things to discuss. We have to do something about Warrick."

"The time is not yet propitious," said Rory.

Brewster sighed with exasperation. "You always say that. Meanwhile, Warrick continues to teleport people to my world, using *my* machine. I feel responsible. What's going to become of them all? They'll never be able to cope in a modern technological world. What's happening to them is all my fault. I can't just sit by and do nothing!"

"But you are doing something," the dragon replied. "Each day, you are weakening Warrick's base of power. He is the Grand Director of the Sorcerers and Adepts Guild, royal wizard to the richest of the twenty-seven kingdoms, yet each day, that kingdom grows weaker and more unstable. And all because of you."

"He's right, you know," said Brian. "People are leaving Pitt by the score and coming here to make better lives for themselves. Warrick's abuse of power has brought about civil unrest in Pittsburgh, and a revolution is coming. As the economy of Brigand's Roost grows stronger, that of Pitt grows weaker. All this serves to undermine Warrick and make him appear ineffective not only to the people of Pitt, but to his fellow sorcerers in the guild. And if he is perceived to be ineffective, he shall also be perceived as vulnerable."

"What I can't understand is why he hasn't moved against me yet," said Brewster. "By now, he certainly knows who I am, and where I am. So what's he waiting for?"

"Don't ask me," said Rachel. "He's Brian's son."

"Thanks for reminding me," said Brian with a sour grimace. "He may be my son, but I've never even laid eyes on him, so how should I know what he's thinking?"

"Well, the apple never falls far from the tree," said Rachel. "What would you do if you were in his place?"

"You know, that's an interesting question," Brewster said, gazing at Brian thoughtfully. "Fathers and sons often have similar character traits. And you do know a great deal more about the workings of the guild and the politics of this world than any of us. Seriously, Brian, if you *were* Warrick, what do you think you would do?"

Brian raised his eyebrows. "Well . . . I don't know. Let me think a moment." He frowned, trying to picture himself in Warrick's place. "If I were the Grand Director of SAG, and I stumbled upon a magical device that was beyond my comprehension, such as your machine, then I think that I might easily conclude it had been made by a sorcerer who could be more powerful than I." He nodded to himself. "And if that were the case, then I would have to wonder why I didn't know about him. The obvious answer would be that he wasn't a member of the guild. But *why* wasn't he a member of the guild? It is against the law for anyone to practice sorcery unless he is a certified member of the guild. So . . . whoever this sorcerer might be, he's apparently not afraid of the law."

"But Doc didn't know about the law," said Rachel. "He isn't from this world."

"Yes, but if I'm Warrick, I don't know that, do I?" Brian said. "And a sorcerer who's not afraid of the law probably has enough power to set himself above it. If I were Warrick, I'd find that very disturbing, I should think. So whatever I decide to do, I'm certainly not going to be hasty."

"Good point," said Rachel. "But you'd have to do something."

"True, and so far, we know that Warrick has placed a bounty on Doc," said Brian, "and sent Mac and others like him out to find him. That mercenary, Black Jack, was one such. Well, Mac has not returned, but if I were Warrick, I would not know why. As a wizard of considerable power and repute, I would certainly be adept at the art of scrying with a crystal ball, but the question is, would I risk it in this case? It could mean opening an astral channel through which a more powerful adept could strike back at me. Doc would not be able to do that, of course, but if I'm Warrick, I have no way of knowing that. I think I would err on the side of caution, at least until I knew more. I would probably assume that Mac had found Doc and that Doc had defeated him, or else suborned him to his will."

"What about Black Jack?" asked Rachel.

"Good question. If we assume he made his way back to Warrick, then that means Warrick certainly knows who Doc is, and where he is. So, if I were Warrick, what would I do with that information?" Brian paused to think a moment. "I'd know that Doc was in Brigand's Roost, and by now I'd know that Brigand's Roost is a town in the Kingdom of Darn that is growing by leaps and bounds, and producing marvelous products said to be the result of sorcerous handiwork. So clearly, my rival is not making any attempt to hide. Quite the opposite. It would seem almost as though he were taunting me, daring me and the rest of the guild to do something about him."

"It would?" said Brewster, uneasily.

"Oh, aye, I think it would, indeed," said Brian as he paced back and forth across the parapet. "That would make me very angry. Furious, in fact. But I'm not the Grand Director of the Guild for nothing. I am not a fool. I have worked long and hard to gain my present position. I did not succeed by acting rashly. Someone who so openly defies the guild . . . defies *me* . . . must be a very powerful adept, indeed. I would need to learn more about him before I attempted to take him on. I would need to be very cautious and discover if he has any weak points, and if so, what are they? I would need to plan my course of action very carefully, because this is a conflict I could not afford to lose. Every day, I see that time machine in my sanctorum, and I know that I cannot divine how it was made, nor even how to operate it properly. Perhaps I am even a little afraid of it. And it daily serves to remind me that I am facing the most powerful adept I have ever encountered. So . . . how would I proceed?"

Brian stopped his pacing.

"I would send spies to Brigand's Roost," he said, nodding to himself. "And at the same time, I would prepare for war."

"War?" said Brewster, with alarm.

"It would seem the perfect solution. I would go to King Billy and tell him that Brigand's Roost is stealing our citizens and our trade. I would tell him that they prosper at our expense. There have been riots in the city and revolution is in the air. Our treasury is being depleted. Our tax base is being undermined. Something must be done. And what better way to unite a kingdom in a common cause than war? Take all the anger and frustration our subjects are feeling and redirect them at the outlaw sorcerer in Brigand's Roost. He is to blame for everything. Aye, if I were Warrick, I think that is exactly what I'd do. Why risk taking on a powerful sorcerer all by myself when I can do it with an army?"

"You know, I hate to admit it," Rachel said, "but that makes sense."

"You really think that's what he'll do?" asked Brewster with concern.

"It would certainly explain why he has not moved against us yet," said Brian. "He has probably been making preparations, and waiting 'til the time is right. For all we know, he has already planted spies among us. They would blend easily with all the new arrivals coming in. Doubtless, he has also been seeking support from the other wizards in the guild, and that would take some time. They all tend to look after their own interests first. A threat to Warrick would not concern them overmuch, but if there was a threat to all of them, then that would be another matter."

"But I'm not threatening anyone," Brewster protested.

"I fear 'tis not how they would see it," Brian replied. "A powerful sorcerer who practices his craft in open defiance of the guild? I think I would certainly consider that a threat. To say nothing of the fact that you are producing nickallirium."

"I am?" said Brewster with a frown. "What's nickallirium?"

"The substance that you call aluminum," said Brian. "The secret of its manufacture is jealously guarded by the guild, because 'tis the most precious metal in the twenty-seven kingdoms. All the world's coinage is minted from it."

"Good Lord!" said Brewster, aghast. "Why didn't anybody tell me?"

"We thought you knew," said Rachel.

"I never even had a clue!" said Brewster. "You mean to tell me that all this time we've been producing aluminum, or nickallirum, and devaluing the currency?"

"I don't understand," said Rachel with a frown. "What do you mean, devaluing the currency?"

" 'Tis simple," Brian said. "Doc taught Mick to make

nickallirium for use in the manufacture of the Many-Bladed Knives. Each knife goes out to market with handles made of nickallirium. Harlan and his sales force will only accept coins of nickallirium for the purchase of the knives. No barter. Since we can manufacture nickallirium, the knives can be priced very attractively, and the purchasers are getting not only a useful tool, but a valuable commodity, as well. Craftsmen in the other kingdoms, such as jewelers and armorers who make precious ornaments of nickallirium, are unable to compete. The knives are worth more than the goods that they produce, yet they are priced more cheaply. And as the demand for the knives increases, more coinage flows into Brigand's Roost. Since we do not import any goods from any of the other kingdoms, that coinage remains here, which means there is an imbalance of trade. People follow the money. Our population increases, more craftsmen come to Brigand's Roost, jewelers and the like, and they can purchase nickallirium from us more cheaply than they could back in their own kingdoms, where the available supply was limited and the price reflected that accordingly. So, since they can buy it from us more cheaply, they produce more ornaments of nickallirium here than they ever could back where they came from. All these goods are exported, and since they bought the raw material more cheaply, they can also price their goods more cheaply, thereby undercutting the craftsmen in all the other kingdoms. This means the demand for our products increases even more, while the demand for local products in the other kingdoms continues to decrease, because they cannot compete. And still more coinage flows into Brigand's Roost."

Rachel frowned. "But will this not eventually create a shortage of coins?"

"Indeed, it will," said Brian. "And the treasurers of the guild will have no choice but to mint more. However, that will not change the fact that the other kingdoms cannot compete with us on the price of goods made from nickallirium. To keep the worth of nickallirium high, they must control the available quantity. But so long as we keep on making more, they cannot control it. The more we make, the less theirs is worth. And they cannot simply keep on minting more coins, because the more coins they mint, the more they devalue their worth. Meanwhile, the flow of coinage into Brigand's Roost continues. We get richer; they get poorer. And if it goes on long enough, their economies will simply collapse. So I would say the guild would certainly regard Doc as a significant threat. They will regard all of us as a threat. Aye, war seems a very likely possibility."

Brewster swallowed nervously. "This is terrible. I never even considered anything like this." He shook his head. "I only wanted to help people, but instead I'm destroying the balance of trade and bringing about a recession in all the kingdoms we do business with. Why didn't anybody *tell* me about this?"

"You never asked," said Brian with a shrug. "You mean to say you've never even seen a coin?"

Brewster frowned. "Now that I think of it, I guess I haven't. I've never really paid too much attention to such things. No one has ever asked me to pay for anything." He sighed and ran his fingers through his hair. "I had no idea. Well, we'll simply have to stop making aluminum, that's all."

"At this point, I don't know if you can," said Brian. "Things have changed too much. Brigand's Roost is well on its way to becoming a thriving city. The brigands are actually working for a living and enjoying it. They're all becoming wealthy and even starting to dress like gentlemen. And what about all the people who have come here to make new lives for themselves? No one here will give up what they have, what *you* have given them. There is probably more wealth in Brigand's Roost now than in all the other towns and cities of this kingdom combined. And one way or another, sooner or later, someone's going to try and take it."

"But if Warrick convinced King Billy to send an army against us, then wouldn't that be an act of war against the entire kingdom?" Rachel said.

"Oh, I doubt that would concern Warrick very much," said

Brian. "King Durwin could never match his resources against those of Pitt. Of course, if we had our own army, then Durwin might grant us his support, but I wouldn't count on that too much."

"Why not?" asked Brewster.

"Darn is a poor little kingdom," Brian replied. "And if Warrick gains the complete support of his guild, then he would effectively have the support of all the other kingdoms. Of course, he may not get their complete support, but even if he only musters partial backing, those are still odds King Durwin would be foolish to confront. The smart thing for him to do would be to wait it out and see what happens, then throw in with whichever side seems strongest."

"What can we do?" asked Brewster with chagrin.

"Make ready to defend ourselves," said Brian. " 'Twould seem the prudent course."

Brewster sat down on a bench and put his head in his hands. "What have I done?" he said miserably. "This wasn't what I intended at all. I only wanted to help people."

"But you have," said Rachel. "They owe you a great deal. You've given them knowledge, but they're the ones who have put it to work and they owe it to themselves to fight for what they have achieved, if it should come to that."

"It should not prove difficult to raise an army for defense," said Brian. "There is no shortage of mercenaries seeking employment, and it would provide an occupation for many of the people coming in."

"And you already have an air force," the dragon said, thumping his chest with a massive claw.

"You mean you'd help?" said Brewster.

"Of course," said Rory. "What are friends for? Besides, life has been singularly uneventful lately. I haven't burned down a village in years. Terrorizing an army would be ever so much more entertaining."

Brewster swallowed nervously. "I don't think 'entertaining' is a word I'd use in that context." He bit his lower lip. "Surely, there has to be a way to avoid violence."

"Peace through superior strength is what my father always used to say," said Brian.

Brewster shook his head. "I need to think," he said. "I'm the one who got us into this mess. It'll be my responsibility to think of a way to get us out."

"It's too bad you're not a real sorcerer," said Brian. "Of course, we're the only ones who know that. That could be a marked advantage."

"Only until someone calls my bluff," said Brewster glumly.

"You were going to have to face Warrick sooner or later," Brian said. "I must admit, it will be interesting to see what happens when science goes up against magic. But don't worry Doc, we'll be with you every step of the way!" Brian's remark was punctuated with a clang as the moon went down and he turned back into a chamberpot, clattering down onto the flagstones of the parapet. "Oh, *bollocks*!"

"A phony wizard, a vampire elf, an existential dragon, and a talking chamberpot," said Brewster wryly. "How can we lose?"

Meanwhile, somewhere in Pennsylvania:

"Hightower! You crazy son of a bitch! What in God's name are you up to?"

Colin winced and held the receiver away from his ear, waiting until his editor stopped screaming. "Jack, calm down, for Christ's sake," he said, when the torrent of invective ceased.

"Calm down? Are you kidding me? I just got through talking with the Pittsburgh police, for crying out loud. The phone's been ringing off the hook ever since we ran your story. They tell me you broke that girl out of the sanitarium at gunpoint!"

"Jack, will you listen to me? You know perfectly well I wouldn't have the faintest idea how to use a gun. Guns frighten me. I've been terrified of them ever since that maniac, Thompsen, almost blew my head off with that cannon of his. I didn't break anybody out of anywhere."

"Hightower, goddamn it, you'd better start telling me the truth and you'd better talk fast!"

"Okay, okay, just calm down, will you? Look, this is exactly how it happened. I bribed an orderly to get me a copy of the girl's file and sneak me in there to interview her. When he was letting me back out of her room, she bolted out the door and went down in the elevator. He thought she went down to the lobby, but she went to the parking level, where she jumped into my car, stark naked, and made me drive her out of there."

"Made you? How?"

"Jack . . . she was naked. Think about it."

"Oh. I see. Where are you calling from?"

"I'm calling from a public phone booth. I won't say where. Now I've got another story to file. I'm going to fax it to you in about an hour, from another location, but meanwhile, I need you to back the police off for me."

"How the hell am I supposed to do that?"

"Get onto the lawyers. Look, the girl hasn't broken any laws so far as I know. And she's not crazy. She was never formally committed. She doesn't want to be there. You can't just stick someone in a sanitarium against their will. They have to go be committed by their doctor or a family member. It's a complicated process. They were just holding her there for observation until they could find out who she was. Only they're not *going* to find out who she is."

"What are you talking about?"

"Jack, just listen to me, all right? I'll be faxing you all the details. That bastard little orderly just lied to save his own skin. How else could I have gotten a copy of her file if he didn't get it for me? I'll fax you a copy of the file, too."

"All right, Colin, what's going on? What are you on to?"

"I'm going to need your help, Jack. This is too big for me to handle all by myself. But it's my bloody story. And if you screw me out of the credit for this one, so help me, I'll break your bloody neck."

"Okay, okay! Jesus, I never heard you talk like this. I'll call the lawyers. But I need something more to go on."

"I'll be faxing you a list of people, Jack. People that have been cropping up in odd corners of the world, all telling the same fantastic story. Megan knows many of them. They're all from her hometown. None of these people have a paper trail, Jack. Officially, they simply don't exist. It's as if they suddenly appeared from out of nowhere."

"Jack, you're not seriously telling me you believe this nonsense about—"

"Somebody's discovered *time travel*, Jack," Colin interrupted him. "I know it sounds incredible, but it's the only explanation that makes any kind of sense. There's a machine ... I'm going to get an artist's rendering of it based on Megan's description, and I'll be faxing that to you as well. Get some of our people to follow up on some of these other cases. You'll find they're all telling the same story. None of them know anything about modern technology. They won't know about anything that's happened within the last several hundred years, at least. They're all from a medieval time, Jack. Someone named Warrick has transported them here for some reason."

"Colin, have you absolutely lost your fucking mind?"

"Don't take my word for it, Jack. Check it out. I'm telling you, this is the biggest story of the century. Possibly of all time, no pun intended. Somebody's built themselves a time machine and gone back into the past, and now they're sending people here, God only knows why. I just need to find out who's behind it. If you print what I send you, it might shake things up a bit and someone might come crawling out of the woodwork."

"This is the nuttiest thing I've ever heard."

"Jack ... have you read your own paper lately?"

"Yeah, all right, but you're telling me this stuff is actually on the level, fahchrissake!"

"Just run with it, Jack. You won't regret it, I promise you. I'll bring you a bloody Pulitzer for this, I swear to God."

"I ought to have my head examined. Or maybe you ought to have your head examined. But what the hell, it's boosting circulation."

"There's my boy," said Colin with a grin. "I'll be in touch."

He hung up the phone.

"So what happens now?" asked Megan, sitting on the bed across from him in the motel room.

"We keep moving," Colin said. "Somebody's got to know something about all this. If we make enough noise, maybe they'll try to get in touch."

"It's ever so nice of you to help me, Colin."

"I'm trying to help both of us, my dear. I just hope somebody crops up to give us another lead. At the moment, I'm fresh out."

"You look tired, luv. Why don't you take your shirt off and let me rub your back?"

Colin raised his eyebrows.

Megan got up off the bed. She smiled and a moment later her dress slipped to the floor.

"God, I love this job," said Colin, stretching out on the bed.

FIVE

All right, I've avoided it long enough, I suppose. I've dealt with Harlan and all his machinations in Brigand's Roost; I've covered what's happening with Brewster, and I've done some work on the subplot with Hightower, but even though I was going to open this chapter with Pamela, Brewster's brilliant bride-to-be (assuming he ever survives this story), the fact is I'm never going to get through this book if I keep ignoring Warrick.

"I was wondering if you would ever work up the courage to confront me once again," Warrick said, sitting back in his chair and glancing up toward the ceiling with a smug little smile.

Look, don't tell me about courage, all right? *You* try making a decent living as a writer. I wrote a book connected to a popular television series about a starship and its crew, and it's been months since I delivered it, but I *still* haven't been paid. Meanwhile, the bills keep piling up. You think magic is tough? Try dealing with publishers.

"So, it would appear as if the omnipotent narrator is not as powerful as he seems," said Warrick.

Powerful? Don't make me laugh. I can't even control the characters in my own novel. Well, one character, at least. Still, I created you, so I suppose I'm going to have to deal with you, one way or another.

"You *created* me?" said Warrick, raising his eyebrows. "What monumental arrogance! You dare ascribe to yourself the powers and virtues of a deity?"

Hey, not me. I'm just a simple storyteller. Whereas you, my friend, are nothing but a royal fictional pain in the ass.

"Well, deity or not, I could easily say the same of you. I have many important matters to occupy my attention, yet since you have chosen to descend from your ethereal plane to plague my existence, I have been able to think of little else. You have caused me to banish my familiar, and while Teddy left much to be desired, I was still rather attached to him. I had him since I was a child."

I know, numbnuts. I wrote that.

"And as for this . . . time machine," Warrick continued, getting up and walking over to the device, "I have deduced that you were the guiding force behind its creation, and do not bother to deny it. You may not have constructed it, but you provided the inspiration. You see, I know a great deal more than you may think."

You do, huh? All right, just what exactly do you think you know?

"The sorcerer who had constructed this device," said Warrick, walking around it slowly, "the one through whom you work . . . thanks to a freebooter by the name of Black Jack, I know his name now. 'Tis Brewster Doc. I know he is an alchemist who resides in the Kingdom of Darn, in a town called Brigand's Roost. I also know he has acquired his knowledge of the sorcerous arts without sanction from the guild, and that he has the secret of the philosopher's stone. He has been making nickallirium, in violation of the law, and he has taught the secret to mere peasants, an even grosser violation. He apparently seeks to dominate the trade of all the twenty-seven kingdoms. Shall I go on?"

By all means. I could use some interesting dialogue at this stage of the story.

"I have not been idle, as you can see. I have my spies."

Of course, you have your spies. You think this is news to me? I covered that in Chapter Four.

"Do you wish me to continue, or not?"

All right, go ahead. But let's not get into a long and detailed summary, okay? The reader already knows all this stuff.

"Very well, then, I shall be brief and come right to the point. I want the secret of this time machine. And I want this outlaw sorcerer."

I already know that. So?

"So, since we seem to be working at cross purposes, perhaps there is some way to settle this conflict between us. After all, I am not an unreasonable man. There must be something that you want."

How about casting a particularly nasty spell at a certain editor who's been holding up my check?

"That might be arranged," Warrick said. "Anything else?"

You could stop interrupting the flow of my narrative, or would that be asking too much?

"Aye, if you expect me to bend to your will," Warrick replied. "Rest assured that in the long run, I shall prevail, despite your narrative arts. For if you were truly as powerful as you pretend, then you would not hesitate to smite me down. And yet, you cannot, else you would have already done so."

Don't tempt me. About the only thing that's stopping me is the fact that it would be very awkward to bring in a new villain at this point in the story. But if you push me hard enough, I just might do it anyway. After all, readers who have stayed with me this long know by now that anything could happen. And it might be an interesting challenge, come to think of it.

"You are merely bluffing."

Really? Are you so sure about that?

"There are limits to your powers. You can but influence events in this world in small degrees. You cannot alter them. For all your boasts, you have not the ability to do away with me and replace me with someone else."

Oh, yeah? Watch this, wise guy . . .

Suddenly there was a loud popping noise and three figures materialized out of thin air in the center of Warrick's sanctorum. They were two men and a woman, dressed identically in black fatigues with military insignia. On their collars were little golden pins, stylized symbols for infinity bisected with the number one.

"What the hell?" said Finn Delaney, glancing around. "Where *are* we? This isn't Pendleton Base!"

Andre Cross tossed her blond hair out of her eyes and

unholstered her sidearm with a quick, smooth, practiced motion.

"Take it easy," Lucas Priest said, holding his hand out. "Something's gone wrong. I think we've clocked into the wrong series."

"Hey, Delaney, take a look at this," said Andre, pointing to Brewster's machine.

"What is it?" the burly time commando asked. "Some kind of helicopter?"

"No, I think it's a crude temporal translocation device," said Andre, approaching it with curiosity.

"That?" Delaney said. "It looks like something H. G. Wells cobbled together from spit and baling wire."

Andre sensed a movement behind her and spun around, leveling her weapon. "What was that? Come out of there, you!"

Slowly, Warrick peeked out from behind his desk.

"Careful, Andre," Lucas cautioned her. "He looks like a local. We don't want to cause any temporal contamination in this period."

"Seems to me like somebody's already done that," Delaney said, glancing at the time machine.

"Who are you people?" Warrick demanded.

"Colonel Lucas Priest, First Division, United States Army Temporal Corps," said Lucas, stepping forward. "And who might you be?"

"I am Warrick the White, of the House of Morgannan, Grand Director of the Sorcerers and Adepts Guild and Royal Wizard to the Kingdom of Pitt. What is the meaning of this intrusion?"

"Get him," Delaney said, looking him up and down. "For a guy who dresses in a bedsheet, he's got more names than a Mexican softball team."

"Careful, Lucas," Andre said. "I don't like the looks of this character." She raised her plasma blaster. "Keep your distance, mister." She fired a warning shot that struck Warrick's desk and vaporized it in a blinding flash of light.

"All right!" cried Warrick with alarm. "All right, Narrator, you have made your point!"

There was a loud popping noise and the Time Commandos disappeared.

Now . . . you were saying?

Warrick looked shaken. He swallowed hard. " 'Twould seem that I have underestimated you. Your powers are more extensive than I had believed possible. Who were those . . . those beings? Demons from the ethereal planes?"

Hardly. They were characters from another series I wrote a few years back. Though demons might be interesting, actually . . .

"No, no, never mind," said Warrick quickly. "There shall be no need for any other demonstrations. What is it you wish?"

Your promise . . . no, your *solemn oath* to stop interfering with the narrative.

Warrick scowled. "Very well. You have my solemn oath that I shall not interfere with your narrative arts."

Just go on about your business and let me get on with mine.

"As you wish," said Warrick in a surly tone.

Good. Now that we've got that settled, you can see about getting yourself a new desk while I get on to the next scene.

Pamela Fairburn was tired. More than tired, she was bone weary. Every muscle in her body seemed to hurt and there was a pain in her lower back that wouldn't go away.

"Good Lord, Pamela, what are you doing to yourself?" her chiropractor asked on her third visit. "You're storing up an amazing amount of tension. You must be under enormous stress."

"I've had an awful lot of work to do, Lynn," she said, grimacing as the chiropractor manipulated her.

"You'd better take some time off, and soon. I've never seen you like this before. You need a vacation, girl."

"I can't afford it," Pamela replied. "I'm working on a very important project."

"What's more important than your health?"

"Some things are," said Pamela, getting off the table. "Thanks, Lynn. That feels much better. I appreciate it."

"I'm going to give you a prescription for some muscle relaxants," the chiropractor said. "But take it easy with them. They're very strong."

"Thanks, Lynn. You're a lifesaver."

"Pamela . . . Look, it's really none of my business, but maybe you should just get on with things, you know? Stop driving yourself so hard. Go out on a date or something."

"A date?" said Pamela. "What do you mean, a date? I happen to be engaged, or have you forgotten?"

"How could I forget? You invited me to three of your weddings. Unfortunately, the groom failed to show up each time."

"What are you saying?"

"Pamela . . . he's been gone for over a year now. Don't you think it's about time you accepted reality? Marvin ran off on you. And he isn't coming back."

"You don't understand, Lynn. It isn't like that."

"Isn't it? You can't go on carrying a torch for the guy, Pamela. Look at what you're doing to yourself. He isn't worth it."

"Yes, he is," said Pamela. "And don't ask me to explain, Lynn. I can't get into it. Thanks for the scrip."

"You're welcome. But at least think about what I've said. And stop pushing yourself so hard. Burying yourself in work is not the answer. You'll only give yourself a nervous breakdown. Get some rest, for God's sake."

"I will. And thanks again, Lynn."

On her way home, Pamela stopped off to get her prescription filled. As she came up to the cash register to pay for the pills, her glance fell on the racks of tabloids and she froze with astonishment. She grabbed the paper from the rack and stared at the photo and the headline.

"TIME MACHINE INVENTED?" the headline proclaimed. The photograph on the front page was an artist's rendering of a device that looked almost exactly like Brewster's sketches in his notes. Pamela paid for the paper and hurried outside. She found a bench under a streetlamp and sat down to read the article. And as she read, she felt her stomach tightening into knots.

The author of the article was a reporter named Colin Hightower. The name meant nothing to her. She couldn't wait to get back to her apartment. She ran to the nearest pay phone, pulled her electronic organizer out of her purse, and punched up the home number for an editor she knew on *The London Times*.

"Howard? This is Pamela."

"Pamela! This is a pleasant surprise. Not setting another wedding date, are you?"

"Howard, I need your help. Does the name Colin Hightower mean anything to you? He's a reporter for —"

"Hightower!" The reaction was immediate. "Good Lord! What on earth can you possibly have to do with a character like him?"

"I need to get in touch with him. It's very important. But it has to be handled discreetly. Can you help?"

"Well, yes, I imagine I can, but for heaven's sake, *why?* Are you aware of the man's reputation?"

"No, I don't know anything about him."

"Well, perhaps I'd best enlighten you before you decide to pursue this any further. The man is a walking blot on the profession of journalism. He is the worst sort of Fleet Street muckraker, and there's nothing he won't stoop to for the sake of a story, the more lurid and sensational, the better. He's an unethical and utterly unprincipled scoundrel who's been run out of every newspaper job in London. Even the tabloids won't have anything to do with him. Last I heard, he was working for some sleazy little rag based in the States, which sounds like the perfect place for him. What could you possibly want with a lowlife like him?"

"I really can't get into it right now," said Pamela, "but it's extremely important. I must speak with him as soon as possible."

"And you can't tell me why?"

Pamela took a deep breath and bit her lower lip. "Howard, I . . . " She hesitated. "I really shouldn't say anything, but I know that if I don't, you'll only start digging and I can't have you doing that. It's an extremely sensitive matter. I'll need your word that if I do tell you what this is all about, you won't breathe a word of it to anyone, under any circumstances."

"Well, now I'm dying of curiosity," said Howard. "All right, you have my word."

"I can't speak about this over the phone," she said. "Is there someplace we can meet?"

"How about down by the Thames, across from Parliament near the Archbishop of Canterbury's residence?"

"Perfect. I'll meet you by the souvenir stands in one hour."

"I'll be there."

She hung up the phone and started walking quickly back toward her apartment. It was growing chilly and it looked like rain. She wanted to get her raincoat and umbrella, as well as take some time to read the article again and figure out just what she was going to say to Howard St. John. She had no intention of telling him the truth. He'd probably think she'd slipped a cog or two. And if he believed her, it would be even worse. She couldn't risk exposing Marvin's discovery. Not only for his sake, but because she knew exactly what would happen to her if she did.

Technically, even though she didn't really work for them, she had become an employee of EnGulfCo International ever since she started trying to piece together the details of what Marvin had been working on from his notes. She'd had to sign a raft of legal forms—"purely as a formality"—which made her liable for prosecution if she revealed any details of Marvin's work. Even if she managed to survive the crushing lawsuit that would follow if she told St. John the truth, her career as a scientist would be finished.

However, she didn't see how St. John could possibly believe her. The truth was simply too incredible. She had a hard time believing it herself, even with access to Marvin's files. No, she would have to come up with a convincing story to tell Howard, something he could accept that would still fit the situation. As she walked briskly back to her apartment, she turned the matter over and over in her mind, trying to work up a plausible scenario.

Hightower's story was immaterial. He had stumbled onto the truth somehow, but it made no difference. Judging from what Howard had told her about Hightower, he'd have no difficulty believing it was just some outrageous story the reporter had concocted. So she would have to find some element of it that she could connect to the story she'd give Howard. The artist's rendering. She could show Howard some sketches she had made at home from memory based on Marvin's notes, which of course she had not been allowed to remove from the laboratory. That would show that Marvin's machine and the artist's rendering in the paper were similar enough to cause her great concern, though coincidence was not out of the question. She nodded to herself. Yes, that would add some plausibility to the story. It could just be a coincidence, and she wanted to contact Hightower to satisfy herself on that point. But she still had to tell Howard something about what the machine was supposed to be.

What could she tell him? The time machine looked vaguely like a helicopter. In fact, the bubble and part of the body, as well as the skids, had been taken from a military helicopter, though she could not recall which one in particular. It didn't matter. If Howard researched it, he could easily find that out himself and that would add further plausibility. So, something similar to a military helicopter. But what? There were no rotors, no guns were mounted, and part of the body was missing. Plus there was that unusual looking torus that surrounded it, the accelerator for the Buckminsterfullerine that created the time warp. So the machine looked somewhat similar to a helicopter, only it clearly wasn't one. What could it be?

A simulator. Yes, that was it. A sophisticated military helicopter simulator designed for . . . what? Some top-secret, super-advanced model of military helicopter, obviously. Her firm had done some work on the original Visually Coupled Aircraft Systems Simulators, fully enclosed, computerized helmets that were the basis of the Virtual Reality simulators that were currently all the rage. She knew enough about that to throw around some convincing technical details that would hold up under scrutiny in case Howard decided to investigate. But if she made the story convincing enough, there was no reason why he should. She knew Howard St. John was a man of his word. He had promised to keep this to himself, and if he believed that national security was at issue, he'd act responsibly. He was a journalist, but not of the Hightower sort.

All right, she thought, what was special about this particular simulator that it should be so highly classified? VCASS technology was nothing terribly new, after all. It had to be the next generation. What could that be? Something sufficiently advanced—and perhaps just a little outrageous—to convince Howard of the need for absolute secrecy.

Brain/computer interface. She stopped as the thought popped into her head. Yes, that was perfect. It was all still in the realm of theory in reality, more the province of science fiction than science fact, but it was just outrageous enough to sound believable, though nowhere near as outrageous as time travel. The simulator was something Marvin had designed as a complement to an implantable microprocessor designed to decrease pilot reaction time and allow him to operate the new helicopter with the speed of thought. Hightower had obviously made something even more outrageous out of the story, but the question was, had he seen a copy of the top secret plans? Had the security of the EnGulfCo lab been compromised somehow? Was there the possibility that Hightower was part of an espionage network and this ridiculous story he'd concocted was nothing more than an excuse to run the drawing in the paper and in that way transmit it to some foreign power? Yes, that was a nice touch. Howard already had a very low opinion of Hightower, and that would fit right in. She started walking again, then stopped, wondering if perhaps that last touch was a bit much.

And that was when she heard the footsteps.

The street was practically deserted at this hour, except for the occasional passing car, and the sound of footsteps might not have struck her at all had they not stopped as soon as she stopped. She almost turned around, but caught herself just in time. She continued walking, suddenly on the alert, the hairs prickling on the back of her neck. She was being followed. She was certain of it.

She continued walking toward her apartment without looking back, but listening intently. When she paused, the footsteps paused. When she sped up, the footsteps sped up. She ducked inside the lobby of her building and ran to the elevator. She pushed the button and the doors opened immediately. She was thankful for that. She quickly went inside the elevator and pressed the button for her floor, then ducked back out again before the doors could close. Then she hid behind some of the lush, potted plants in the lobby.

No sooner had she concealed herself than a man wearing a trench coat and an Irish tweed walking hat came into the lobby. He approached the elevator and watched the indicator lights until the elevator stopped at her floor. He did not press the button to summon it. Instead, he merely nodded to himself, turned around, and went back outside.

That clinched it. She waited until he'd left, then took the stairs, running all the way up to her floor. She went into her apartment, closed the door behind her, and leaned back against it, breathing hard. She checked her watch. Still about forty minutes left before her meeting with St. John.

Who could be following her? Who knew what she was working on? Only three people, herself included. The other two were the CEO and the vice president of R and D for EnGulfCo. She exhaled heavily. Of course. They didn't trust her. They were having her watched. It occurred to her that the man following her could have been a stalker, but she dismissed the idea immediately. No, that would have been too much of a coincidence. Given the nature of Marvin's project, it made perfect sense that they would have her followed. They probably even had her phone tapped. She cursed herself for not thinking of that before. Stupid.

Fortunately, she had called St. John from a pay phone. Of course, that was no guarantee the call had not been monitored. She knew only too well what kind of sophisticated electronic surveillance devices were available to people with resources like EnGulfCo had. But she hardly ever used pay phones. And if they had her apartment wired, which was likely, then there would be no reason for some sophisticated bolometric mike. There was a good chance the call had not been overheard. If it had been, then they already knew about the meeting and it was too late to do anything about it.

She'd have to proceed on the assumption that they hadn't overheard. She grabbed her raincoat and umbrella and took the stairs back down, going past the lobby to the basement level. She took the maintenance corridor to the back entrance and carefully slipped outside, then walked several blocks in the wrong direction, taking side streets and checking to see if she was being followed. When she was satisfied that there was no one on her tail, she hailed a cab and drove to her meeting with St. John.

She got there a little late. St. John was already waiting for her. She gave him the story she'd concocted, including the bit about Hightower possibly being a foreign agent, which she said with just enough paranoia to convince St. John that she was seriously alarmed and even slightly hysterical.

"Take it easy, Pamela," he said, patting her lightly on the back. "I suspect you're overreacting just a bit. Hightower may be a lowlife, but he's not that much of a lowlife. And I can't imagine any foreign power employing someone as unreliable and unpredictable as him. Still, I must admit the drawings look remarkably similar. Perhaps it's only a coincidence, but I can certainly understand your concern. Still, don't you think this sort of thing is a matter for SIS? I mean, if military secrets are involved . . ."

She hadn't thought of that. She improvised quickly. "We can't risk involving SIS at this point," she said. "I mean, they have been compromised before, you know. The Philby case and all that. The security on this project is so tight that only a handful of people are even aware of its existence. You can appreciate why I had to swear you to absolute secrecy. They don't even trust the intelligence service. If anyone knew I'd spoken to you about this, we'd both go to prison for violation of the Official Secrets Act."

St. John nodded gravely. "Yes, I can see that. All of which makes it sound that much more incredible that someone like Hightower could have gotten hold of the drawings. Especially in America. I mean, it just sounds so bloody improbable. It has to be a crazy coincidence, that's all."

"Howard, that paper's just come out," she said. "If the intelligence service was in on this, they would already be investigating. But the handful of people who know about the project aren't really the sort to read the tabloids, if you know what I mean. They probably don't know about this yet. What worries me is . . . well, it's Marvin. You know how he is. He's brilliant, but when it comes to things like this, he can be hopelessly naive. And you know how absent minded he is. They always search him before he leaves the lab, not because they don't trust him, but because it's just like him to slip something into his pocket and forget about it. And he doodles constantly. He might have made a drawing and lost it, or perhaps left it somewhere . . ." She sighed heavily. "The thing is, he's disappeared. He's done this sort of thing before, as you well know, but this time he's been gone for a long time, and we're concerned that something may have happened to him. We've got people looking for him, but the company is trying to keep the whole thing very low profile, because there's a great deal of money at stake, and, well, you know how it is."

"Yes, quite," said St. John, nodding several times. "They don't want the government boys to know they've lost track of their pet genius. It does sound like a rather sticky situation. You poor dear, no wonder you're so frantic."

"It's possible Marvin may have gone back to the States for some reason," she said, quickly following up. "It would be just like him to take off to consult with one of his old colleagues back home and become so caught up in work that he's utterly lost track of time. That's why I've got to speak with this Hightower person and try to find out if he knows anything about this."

"But how do you intend to do that without tipping him off?" St. John asked. "He's a cagey bastard."

"I don't know," said Pamela. "I'll think of something. I think I can throw enough technical jargon around to utterly confuse him. Can you put me in touch with him? Discreetly?"

St. John nodded again. "Yes, of course, I'll get on it right away. It shouldn't take more than a telephone call or two. How do you want to handle this? You want him to call you, or do you want to call him?"

"We need to be very careful about this," she said. "I think it would be best if we arranged a time for him to call me, but not at home or at the office. That would be too risky."

"You could use my place," St. John offered.

"You're a lifesaver, Howard. Thank you. But don't call me. I'll call you and check in periodically, to see if it's been arranged."

"Right. But this whole thing sounds so farfetched . . . it's probably only a bizarre coincidence."

"If it is, then it will be a great relief to me," she said. "But I have to know for sure. And it's all got to be kept strictly on the Q.T."

"Mum's the word," said St. John. He checked his watch. "It should be about noon in New York. I've got a friend at *The New Yorker*. I'll give her a call as soon as I get home. She should be able to track down Hightower without too much trouble. I won't tell her why, of course. She owes me a few favors."

"I don't know what I'd do without you, Howard. I owe you one."

"Nonsense, old girl. Glad to help. Now go on home and try to get some rest. No need to worry yourself into a state. Just leave everything to me. Give me a call tomorrow."

"I will. And thanks again, Howard."

He stayed with her until she flagged down a cab, then waved good-bye as it pulled away. She settled back in the seat and exhaled heavily. He'd bought it. Now, all she had to do was figure out how to handle Hightower.

SIX

While Pamela Fairburn was eluding the detectives on her tail and Colin Hightower was eluding the police, not to mention half a dozen collection agencies and his ex-wife, Marvin Brewster wasn't eluding anything. He had started this entire mess and now the weight of it rested squarely on his slender shoulders.

They all sat together in the great hall of the keep, around a long wooden table, while Calamity Jane served breakfast and dodged Thorny, who kept trying to help, but only wound up getting in the way. The peregrine bush that Brewster had adopted when it was just a little shrub had grown alarmingly in the last year and now stood over seven feet tall, which meant it could no longer follow Brewster all around the keep, the way it used to do. It would no longer fit through the narrow stairwells or the doorways of the smaller rooms, so it had been relegated to the lower floor and the great hall, where it resided like an ambulatory Christmas tree and visitors had to keep careful track of its movements for fear of getting impaled on its large and spiky thorns.

Thorny didn't seem to understand that it was capable of hurting people. It was just a bush, after all. Actually, at this point, it more closely resembled a mesquite tree on steroids, but the point is that shrubbery doesn't think. It simply reacts—to sunlight, to moisture, and in Thorny's case, to Brewster's kindness. Mick had intended to brew wine from its roots, but Brewster had intervened and made a sort of pet of the plant. On some primitive level, the bush had sensed that and had bonded to him. During the last migration season, it had disappeared, and Brewster thought he wouldn't be seeing it again, but when the peregrine migration season was over, Thorny had returned to the keep—only it had grown another three feet. Now, with its much larger thorns, the plant was dangerous, but Brewster couldn't bring himself to bar it from the keep. Like a cat, it went out each night to burrow its roots into the soil and came back again each morning.

"Watch it, you overgrown weed!" said the chamberpot as Thorny brushed against the table and accidentally swept Brian off. Brewster just managed to catch the chamberpot before it struck the floor.

"Thorny!" he shouted.

The plant responded to his tone and backed away, its branches drooping.

"I just hope you all know what you're doing," Brewster said, glancing around at the others sitting around the table as he set Brian down. "Raising some troops for defense is one thing, but actually breaking off and starting up your own kingdom is inviting trouble."

"Our kingdom, Doc," said Mick. "You're just as much a part o' it as we are."

"Mick's right," said Harlan, nodding emphatically. "After all, you started all this. We owe everything we have accomplished to you."

Brewster looked uncertain. "Well, maybe I provided some ideas and technical help, but I never considered the political implications. When it comes to things like that, I'm out of my depth."

"I'll handle the politics, don't worry," Harlan said. "We just wanted your support on this. And we wanted to ask if you would accept the title of Royal Wizard."

"But I've told you, I'm *not* a wizard!" Brewster protested. "I've tried and tried to learn how to do magic, but it's simply hopeless. Ask Mick."

" 'Tis true," admitted Mick with a shrug. "But then I am not a very good teacher. I have some ability with magic, but only because I am a leprechaun and it comes to me naturally. I am not a trained sorcerer. 'Tis not that you have failed, Doc, 'tis that I lack the knowledge to instruct you properly."

"It makes no difference," Harlan said, dismissing the whole debate with a wave. "People believe you are a sorcerer, Doc, and your science *is* a sort of magic. 'Tis merely a different form of knowledge. In any case, the title is what counts. Every kingdom has a royal wizard. The office would be merely a formality."

Brewster turned to Shannon. "Are you sure this is what you want?" he asked her.

"Doc, you and I have had our differences," she replied. "In the beginning, I had little faith in your abilities, but you have proved me wrong. I have learned to trust your judgment. And if I am to be queen—strange as that may sound— I would like the benefit of your advice. I would be honored if you would accept the title."

"Well, if that's what you all want, then I'll accept, of course," said Brewster, "but I'm not sure you really understand the implications of what you are proposing to do. I had no idea that when I taught Mick and the others how to make aluminum, I was actually showing them how to make nickallirium. I didn't realize what that meant. In my world, gold is what the currency is based on and aluminum has little value by comparison. Here, gold is worthless because it is so plentiful." He shook his head. "Everything is different here. You'd think I would have learned more by now. Producing products for the market is one thing, but manufacuring nickallirium is something else entirely. By manufacturing nickallirium, we are threatening the economies of the twenty-seven kingdoms, and if we continue, they will have no choice but to go to war against us."

"All the more reason for us to be prepared," said Shannon.

"Shannon, you're talking about taking on the whole world!" said Brewster. "Don't you see that our producing nickallirium is the one thing that will unite the other kingdoms against us? And by forming our own kingdom, we would be announcing to the world that we are a power unto ourselves."

"What's wrong with that?" asked Robie. "Why shouldn't we have the right to determine our own destiny?"

"Excuse me," said the chamberpot in Brian's usually sarcastic tone, "I'll admit it's been a few years since I've formally fulfilled any of my functions as a prince, so perhaps I've missed something, but since when have peasants had any rights?"

"They shall have rights in *our* kingdom," Shannon said.

"I see," said the chamberpot. "And how do you suppose the other monarchs will respond to that? They'll see it as a challenge, a threat to their power and their way of life. 'Twould be yet another compelling reason for them to go to war against us."

"What if we entered into formal negotiations with the other kingdoms," Brewster suggested, "and promised to stop making nickallirium if they recognized our right to rule ourselves?"

"I do not think that would help, Doc," said Mac, entering the hall. He was carrying a bulging sack over his shoulder. "Forgive me for being late, but I was unavoidably detained." He swung the sack off of his shoulder. "Look what I found," he said. He untied the sack and dumped it out onto the table. With a frightened cry, Teddy came tumbling out.

"*Eeeuuw*, a troll!" said Rachel.

"Ah, but not just any troll," said Mac. "Observe his collar."

Teddy tried to scramble back out of the way, but Mick grabbed him and pinned him to the table. Teddy struggled to break free, but though trolls are not much smaller than leprechauns and surprisingly strong for their size, Mick was no ordinary leprechaun. The years he'd spent at his forge had given him a powerful physique, and he clamped a muscular arm across Teddy's throat while he read the little metal tag on his collar. "Property of Warrick Morgannan, Alabaster Tower, Royal Mile, Pittsburgh."

"A spy!" said Harlan.

"Warrick's own familiar, no less," said Mac. "I caught him outside in the bushes, scouting out the grounds."

"Well, we know how to deal with spies," said Shannon, drawing her sword.

Teddy cried out in fear and kicked Mick in the stomach, breaking free and leaping up to run down the length of the table with surprising speed. Shannon swung her sword, but missed, and Teddy jumped down to the floor and bolted toward the door. However, Thorny happened to be in the way. As Teddy tried to dodge around the bush, Thorny scuttled to one side to get out of his way, inadvertently blocking his path. Teddy darted in the other direction, but Thorny moved that way as well, blocking him once again, and before Teddy could dart around the bush, Mick brought him down with a flying tackle. They thrashed on the floor until Robie and Pikestaff Pat came running up and grabbed Teddy by his arms, holding him between them.

"Don't kill me, please!" the little troll wailed. "I am not a spy, I swear it! I truly meant no harm!"

"You lying little hairball!" Mick said. "You deny that you are Warrick the White's familiar?"

"Aye, 'tis true I was, but no longer! He has banished me!"

"A likely story," Harlan said. "Do you take us all for fools?"

" 'Tis the truth, I swear it on my life!" said Teddy. "Have your wizard place me under a spell of compulsion if you do not believe me and you shall see that I speak truly!"

"Warrick could have warded you against such spells," said Mick.

"Then surely your wizard would detect the wards, if he is as powerful as they say," said Teddy. "Please, you must believe me! I serve Warrick no longer!"

"Then why are you here?" asked Shannon.

"I came to offer my services to the mighty Brewster Doc," said Teddy. "I have been a sorcerer's familiar all my life. 'Tis all I know. And no other sorcerer in the guild would accept a familiar who's been banished by the Grand Director. I had nowhere else to go." He sniffled miserably.

"That's the most ridiculous story I have ever heard," said Harlan. "You expect us to believe that?"

" 'Tis the truth!" insisted the troll. "I swear it! And I can prove it to you, if you will but allow me."

Shannon narrowed her eyes suspiciously. "How?" she asked.

"Before I left, I stole some items from my former master," Teddy said. "Magical items he never would have parted with willingly."

"What items?" Shannon asked.

"In the satchel," said Teddy. He glanced at Mac. "He took it from me."

"You mean this?" said Mac with a derisive snort. He removed a small leather bag from his shoulder. It did not look big enough to contain much of anything. He tossed it to Shannon.

She caught it and looked inside. "It contains nothing but a few scraps of food." She tossed it aside.

"Only because you do not know the secret of the satchel," Teddy said. "The satchel, itself, is one of the magical items that I took."

Brewster picked up the bag and examined it. "What secret?" he asked.

"Take me to Brewster Doc and I shall reveal it to him," said the troll.

"You're speaking to him," Shannon said.

The troll's eyes grew wide. *"Him?"* he said with disbelief. *"He* is the mighty wizard of Brigand's Roost?"

"Well, I don't know about the mighty part," said Brewster, "but I guess that is my formal title."

Teddy looked skeptical. "You do not look much like a wizard."

"Say the word, Doc, and I'll slit the little warthog's throat," said Shannon.

"No, don't," said Brewster. He crouched in front of Teddy, setting the bag down on the floor. "Look," he said, "I don't want to see you hurt, but you're in a rather difficult position. If there's some way you can prove you're telling us the truth, I advise you to do so now."

Teddy glanced at the two men holding him, then looked uneasily at Shannon, standing there with her sword drawn. He swallowed hard. "Very well," he said. " 'Tis a Bag of Holding. Place your hand upon the satchel and say, 'Open wide and open deep, reveal the secrets that you keep.' And then open it."

"Be careful, Doc," said Harlan. "It could be some sort of trick."

"Allow me," said Mac, picking up the satchel and carrying it over to the table.

"Hear me, troll," said Shannon. "If he opens it and anything happens to him, I will make sure you die a very slow and lingering death."

Teddy merely swallowed hard and nodded that he understood.

Keeping an eye on Teddy, Mac placed his hand on the satchel and repeated the words, "Open wide and open deep, reveal the secrets that you keep." And then, cautiously, bending back away from it, he opened the satchel. Nothing happened. He glanced back at the troll, then carefully looked inside the satchel. "Well, I'll be damned," he said.

"What is it, Mac?" asked Brewster.

Mac reached into the pouch and pulled out a sword. The blade was much too long to have been contained inside the small satchel, and yet, it nevertheless came out of the bag. It had a hilt wrapped with silver wire and a round, flat pommel with the symbol of the sun carved into it. The curved crossguards were artfully twisted and the well-oiled leather scabbard was hand-tooled with intricate designs. Mac unsheathed the blade and it gleamed as it caught a shaft of sunlight shining through one of the windows of the great hall. The entire length of the blade was etched with cursive runes.

"An elven blade!" said Mac. "I recognize the style of the runes, but I cannot read them."

"Let me see," said Rachel.

Mac handed her the sword.

The elf held the blade across her hands, so that she could read the runes. Her eyes grew wide and she inhaled sharply.

"What is it, Rachel?" Shannon asked.

"Dwarfkabob!"

"*Gesundheit*," Brewster said.

"No, *Dwarfkabob*!" said Rachel. "'Tis the enchanted Sword of the Shaman!"

"HOLD IT! CEASE! STOP EVERYTHING!"

Warrick! Damn it, what are you doing interrupting this scene? I thought you and I had made a bargain!

"Dwarfkabob?" said Warrick. "You named an enchanted sword *Dwarfkabob*?"

It dates back to the days when elves and dwarves were deadly enemies. Actually, they still don't like each other very much and . . . why am I explaining this to you, anyway? Who's writing this thing, you or me? Besides, it was your sword. Teddy stole it from you.

"Nonsense. Teddy would never have had the gumption to steal anything from me. What is more, he knows that all of my valuable personal possessions are spell-warded against theft."

No, he doesn't. I mean, he didn't.

"Yes, he *did*. You think he would have been my familiar for most of his life and not known something like that? You think I would leave magical talismans lying around unprotected? Not even a sorcerer's apprentice would be so stupid. *I* certainly would not be. That would be completely out of character. You cannot have things happen simply for the convenience of your narrative. That sort of thing lacks believability."

Look who's talking. I don't believe this. I am just totally losing control. Look, I thought we had an understanding. You promised not to interfere and now you've broken your word.

"Of course, I've broken my word! I'm the *villain* of this tale, remember? I am wise to your design now, Narrator. I finally understand that this narrative art of yours is merely a form of sympathetic magic. You are observing events here from your ethereal plane and setting down a chronicle of what you see, and by doing so, you seek to influence the outcome."

What?

"Aye, you are very clever in your application of this art,

but the principles are rudimentary. I should have realized this before, but you worked your tale in such a way that you prevented me from seeing it before. However, by trusting me, you have allowed your guard to slip, and now I know what you intend. Well, I am afraid that I shall have to disappoint you."

All right, that's it. You've messed with this story for the last time. I don't care if it screws up the plot, I've had it! You're history, my friend. You're toast. You are *out* of here.

"Unfortunately, what the Narrator failed to realize was that while he was busy chronicling the events in Brigand's Roost, Warrick had prepared a powerful warding spell to protect himself against being written out of the story."

Oh, is that right? Well, we'll just see about that. How would you like to go? A heart attack? No, not suitably dramatic. And not nearly satisfying enough. For all the grief you've given me, I think I'll give you a particularly nasty, gruesome death. Let's see . . .

"I am waiting."

Keep your shirt on, I'm thinking.

"Do let me know when you have hit upon an interesting idea."

Oh, you'll be the very first to know, trust me.

"Aye, I know. Always trust your narrator."

Shut up! You're distracting me.

"By all means. Take your time."

I could . . . no. That's been done. Or else . . . nah, that wouldn't work. Hmmm, let's see, now . . .

"You know, I believe I will take a nap," said Warrick. "Be sure to wake me whenever you are ready. I would hate to sleep through my own death. That would hardly be very dramatic, would it?"

I'm gonna kill him. I swear, I'm gonna kill him . . .

I give up. I guess it's just one of those days when I should have stayed in bed. Yes, I know I've been telling you to trust your narrator, but narrators are human, too, you know. We have bad days, just like the rest of you. And this has been a *really* bad day. It's now about three in the morning as I write these words, twelve hours since I wrote that last paragraph, and I haven't been able to come up with any way to write Warrick out of this damn story without having the whole thing fall apart. Let me tell you, it's been pure hell.

Believe me, for a writer, there is absolutely nothing worse than hitting the wall. You feel like a spent marathoner. No matter what you do, nothing seems to work. The brain simply refuses to function. No matter how hard you try, the words just won't come. So you get up and take a walk, or else go out and work in the yard, or try to read a book, only that doesn't work because you're too worried about your own writing to get into someone else's story. So you wash the dishes that have been piling up in the sink all week, then you clean the house, change your sheets and do the laundry, maybe shop for groceries, straighten all the pictures on the walls and rearrange your bookshelves, and when you're done with all of that and can't think of anything else to do, you try calling your friends.

If it happens to be a weekday afternoon, all your friends are working, because they have *real* jobs, so then you call your writer friends, on the principle that misery loves company. Except the ones that are having trouble writing, just like you, aren't home. They're out taking a walk, or working in the yard, or doing the laundry, or shopping for groceries . . . and the ones who are home have their answering machines on because *they* are busy writing, damn it. So you succumb to the ultimate degradation and sit down to watch TV with a bag of Doritos and a six-pack of beer.

You tell yourself that you've just been trying too hard and you simply need a break. You just need to take your mind off writing for a while. Maybe there's a good movie on HBO. Of course, with my luck, it turns out to be *Throw Momma From the Train*, where Billy Crystal plays a writer who spends the entire movie trying to come up with an opening sentence for his novel. So you switch the channel in frustration and you get *The Owl and the Pussycat*, where Barbara

Streisand spends the entire movie making George Segal feel inadequate because he's a failure as a novelist. In disgust, you switch the channel yet again and it's an episode of *Murder, She Wrote*. Five minutes into the show, you've figured out who the murderer is and you spend the rest of the show wondering how J. B. Fletcher got to be such a famous mystery novelist when she never actually seems to do any writing. She's too busy solving murders in Cabot Cove or visiting relatives, who immediately start dropping like flies whenever she shows up. You'd think when people saw her coming, they'd start locking their doors and putting on bulletproof vests. And there's another thing, publishers are always wining and dining her. The closest *I've* ever come to being wined and dined by a publisher was when an editor took me to a Brewburger about ten years ago. Screw it, change the channel.

Oh, great. It's Barbara Walters interviewing Judith Krantz at home in her luxurious, multimillion-dollar mansion in Beverly Hills, complete with three swimming pools. Yech. Back to channel surfing. Okay, here's something. *Entertainment Tonight*. That's probably safe. Nope. They're doing a feature on Michael Crichton, who's become so damn successful he could probably sell his shopping list. It would, of course, become a bestseller, get made into a movie, and he'd get to direct. Jesus, there's no getting away from it! Okay, the hell with it. I'll go cook dinner and then settle down to watch Letterman.

"On the show tonight, ladies and gentlemen, the master of horror, Mr. Stephen King —"

Gyahhhh! Quick, switch to Leno.

"Our first guest tonight is a genuine movie legend, an honest-to-God superstar, ladies and gentlemen. You know him as Spartacus, but now he's embarked on a new career as a bestselling author. Please join me in welcoming Mr. Kirk Douglas —"

I shut off the TV and sit there in the dark with my empty, jumbo size bag of Doritos and the crushed remains of a sixpack scattered on the floor around me, thinking, "God hates me."

Around one A.M., I slink back to my office, where Archimedes, my Apple Mac computer, sits malevolently on my desk, and I just stand there in the doorway, glaring at it. It glares back. There's nothing much to do at one A.M. in the Sonoran desert. The nearest town is Tucson, a forty-five-minute drive away, and by the time I get there, the bars will all be closed. And, of course, I can't go to sleep, because I've got insomnia. It's either face that damn computer or watch the Home Shopping Network or those late night commercials with bimbos in lingerie moaning and pouting into the camera, exhorting you to call their 976 numbers. I actually consider it for a moment. What the hell, I haven't even had a date in months. I imagine how the conversation might go . . .

"Hi, is this Stormy? Listen, if you had to knock off an evil wizard, how would you go about it?"

"Huh? What kind of fantasy is *that*?"

"It's not a fantasy . . . Well, yeah, actually it is, but not like you think. See, I'm a writer and I'm working on this book and —"

"You're a writer? Really? Hey, you know, I do a little writing. I mean, this phone sex thing is only temporary, something to tide me over, you know? Actually, I'm working on this romance novel and it's pretty hot. My friends all think it's great, you know; they say it's got real commercial potential. As a matter of fact, I just happen to have it here with me and since you're a real writer and all, maybe I could read you a few chapters and you could tell me what you think. . . . "

God, even my fantasies are depressing.

"How utterly pathetic."

Leave me alone, Warrick. Just . . . go away.

"I could have told you this would happen," Warrick said, "only you refused to listen. You think you can turn my own familiar against me with impunity? You think you can conjure up spirits to threaten me in my own sanctorum and I will submit meekly to your will? I, Warrick the White, of the House of Morgannan, Grand Director of the—"

Yeah, yeah, yeah, I know already. Spare me the résumé. I *wrote* it, remember?

"As you wish. Perhaps now you are prepared to discuss matters reasonably."

I'm too tired to argue. And I can't just go back to the last scene in the keep. You've completely screwed up the continuity of the story now. Okay, screw it, I give up. What do you want?

"I have told you what I want." He walked over to Brewster's time machine and stood staring at it. "I want the secret of this infernal magical device. None of the subjects I have transported with it have returned, despite the spell of compulsion I had placed upon them. I want to know why. I want to know where they have gone. I want to know the purpose of this damnable machine and the secret of its operation. I want to know everything about it."

Okay, you win. It's a device for traveling through time, as you have already surmised. Except that it does not merely travel through time, but through a dimensional portal, as well.

"A dimensional portal?" Warrick frowned. "What is that?"

A warp in the fabric of time and space. Sort of a passageway to another world, another plane of existence.

"A gateway to the ethereal planes?"

Something like that, yeah.

"To the world where you reside?"

Well . . . yes, I suppose so. In a manner of speaking.

"Then this sorcerer, this Brewster Doc, is not of this world? He is, like you, a creature of the ethereal planes?"

Well, he's ethereal, all right, but he's not like me. At least, I didn't think he was like me, but so far all my friends who've read pieces of this thing have said he's *just* like me, so maybe you're right, I don't know. I'm just not up to explaining it.

"I see," said Warrick, rubbing his chin thoughtfully. "So then Brewster Doc is a projection of you, an avatar, and this device is a gateway to the ethereal planes? Fascinating. So that is why none of my subjects have been able to return. There is no gateway for them on the other side."

Right.

"And this outlaw sorcerer, Brewster Doc, cannot return to his own world unless he possesses this machine?"

Correct.

"Excellent. Now we are getting somewhere. So then, for this machine to work properly, it must not only transport whoever is inside it through the gateway it creates, it must also pass through that gateway itself?"

Now you've got it.

"Of course, it all makes perfect sense," said Warrick. "I simply did not know the secret of its proper operation. So . . . what is the secret?"

I'm too tired to argue. First, you've got to get into the machine.

Warrick frowned suspiciously. "And then?"

Well, nothing can happen unless you get into the machine. You have to be inside to work the controls.

"I see," said Warrick. Carefully, he got into the machine and sat in the pilot's seat. "Now what?"

You have to strap yourself in.

Warrick examined the safety restraints carefully, then strapped in. "Very well. What next?"

You see that box in front of you, the one with what looks like a small dark window in it?

"Aye?"

That's the trip computer. You have to set it for time and destination.

"How?"

There's a little red button on the box, see it?

"Aye, I see it."

Press it.

"What will happen when I do?"

The computer will be activated and the window will light up, along with all the instruments. When that happens, you have to set the temporal translocation chronometer for the month, the day, the year, and the time of day.

"And how do I perform this task?"

You use the keyboard.

"What is a keyboard?"

Oh, jeez. This could take forever. Look, let's just do it the easy way. Step by step, the Narrator patiently explained to Warrick how to use the computer keyboard to enter the temporal chronometer settings, as well as the location coordinates. There. That ought to save some time.

"Very well, now what?" asked Warrick when he was done.

Look to the right of the box. You see a switch with a dial above it?

"Aye."

Push it down.

Warrick clicked the toggle switch down. A high-pitched whine came from the machine.

"What is that noise?" asked Warrick, alarmed.

Just the engine warming up. Don't worry. It's normal. Now throw the switch right next to it.

As Warrick did so, the Buckminsterfullerine in the torus surrounding the machine began to accelerate. The sound of the whine increased, and over it a rhythmic, whooping, pulsing sound ensued. All the indicators on the instrument panel started registering. Warrick's face lit up with excitement.

" 'Tis working!" he shouted over the noise. "It lives! The machine lives!"

Okay, now you see that lever beside your right knee?

"Aye!"

Watch the indicators on the dials. When the needles start pointing into the red, pull it back.

The noise became deafening. Warrick watched the dials carefully, then pulled the lever back. The whooping whine built to a screaming pitch, then the air around the time machine began to shimmer. Bright blue electrical arcs played all over the surface of the machine as the warp began to open up, then a sonic boom crashed through Warrick's sanctorum and the time machine disappeared.

Heh, heh, heh. Sucker. Mess around with me, will he? Okay, now let's see if we can't get this story back on track. When last we left Brewster and his friends, Mac had captured Teddy, Warrick's little troll familiar, who had made his way to Brewster's keep with an aim to offering his services to the mighty sorcerer of Brigand's Roost. Since Teddy didn't have a proper résumé, he did the next best thing. To demonstrate his good intentions, before leaving the Alabaster Tower, he stole some of Warrick's prized magical possessions, which, as Warrick pointed out before when we were so rudely interrupted, were spell warded against theft. (Picky, picky, picky.) However, having been Warrick's familiar for so many years, Teddy had learned the wards, and so before he stole the items, he spoke the spell to take the wards off. So there.

The little satchel Teddy brought with him was called the Bag of Holding, and most of the time it looked and functioned just like an ordinary leather shoulder pouch. However, when one placed his hand upon the bag and recited the proper spell, the bag could release its treasure trove. It was capable of holding a limitless number of items, the only limitation being that whatever was placed into the bag had to fit through its opening.

Now, how could this possibly work, you ask? Well, it was magic. Whatever was placed into the bag temporarily went into another dimension, where it remained until the spell was spoken once again and the item could be retrieved from the bag. You know how sometimes you put your keys down and then you can't find them anywhere, no matter how hard you look, and then they turn up inexplicably in the most obvious place? Well, it's sort of the same principle. This was how the Bag of Holding was capable of containing an elven sword with a thirty-three inch blade.

Now, as Rachel has already revealed, this was no ordinary elven blade. Its pommel was engraved with the figure of the sun, and the entire length of its blade was etched with magical elven runes that identified the sword as Dwarfkabob, the legendary Sword of the Shaman.

"What is the Sword of the Shaman?" Brewster asked. (There, you see? We're back on track again. I told you, always trust your narrator.)

"Long ago, in the days of the great wars between the elves and the dwarves, there lived a mighty elven wizard known as the Shaman," Rachel said, beating out an accompanying tattoo on her bongos as she spoke. "He was of no tribe, and he lived all by himself deep in the Redwood Forest, in a small clearing by a brook. The leaders of all the elven tribes went to him for counsel, for in those days, there were many rivalries among the different tribes, and they were hindering the struggle against the dwarves. One day, the Shaman called all the tribal leaders together and he brought out a wondrous sword—this sword—and he called it Dwarfkabob. With this sword, he said, no opponent could prevail against its wielder, for it was enchanted, and the nature of the enchantment was such that it took the skill of the opponent and transferred it to whoever wielded the sword. Each of the elven tribal leaders advanced their claim for it, but the Shaman said the sword would only go to him who could compose the finest poem, because whoever carried Dwarfkabob would be the warlord of the elves, and such an elf needed to display cleverness and wisdom.

"So each of the elven leaders were sent back to their own tribes, to work on composing their poems. In a month's time, they were to return and perform their compositions before the Shaman, to decide who would win the right to own the blade. Each tribe wanted their leader to win the sword, so they all participated in the composition of the poems. One elf would contribute a phrase, another would alter it and make it better, still another would follow it with a rhyme, and so forth, until over the course of the month, these poems had been written and rewritten and rewritten, until each tribe was certain they had attained the finest composition possible. And at the end of the month, when the moon was full, they all gathered together to meet with the Shaman and perform their poems to see who would win the sword.

"It was the largest convocation of elves the world had ever seen. All the tribes were present to support their leaders, from the oldest members of each tribe down to the youngest child. And the Shaman listened gravely and attentively as each tribal leader stepped forth in turn and performed his composition, which was in fact the composition of the entire tribe. From this convocation came the tradition of elven poetry, which has continued to this day, and each year, at the time of the Summer Solstice, the elven tribes gather once again to perform their compositions and choose which is the best. So it has been, ever since that day."

Rachel finished with a flourish on the bongos, and the others waited, expecting her to go on. The silence stretched. Shannon glanced at Mac and frowned. Mac raised his eyebrows. Mick scratched his head. And finally, Brewster asked, "So . . . who won the sword?"

"Oh," said Rachel. Then she shrugged. "No one won it."

"What do you mean, no one won it?" Shannon said.

"How could that be?" asked Mac. "Was that not the point of the entire convocation?"

"Aye, 'twas," said Rachel. "But while everyone was gathered around the great bonfire, listening to the compositions, someone stole the sword. And it has never since been seen, until today."

"You mean, it's been lost all this time?" asked Brewster.

"Aye," said Rachel.

"But how did Warrick come into possession of it?" Shannon asked, picking up the sword and turning toward Teddy.

"He purchased it from a notorious dealer in stolen talismans in Pitt," said Teddy. "The dealer told him he was sure 'twas enchanted, but as he could not read the elven runes, he was unable to discern the nature of its magic. So Warrick bought the sword from him and set about looking for someone to translate the inscription. Only when he found someone to translate it, it turned out that the inscription was a riddle which Warrick was never able to solve."

Rachel chuckled.

"What's so funny?" Shannon asked.

"There never was any riddle to solve," Rachel replied. "The inscription tells nothing at all about the nature of the blade's enchantment. The Shaman was a very spiritual elf, who loved poetry and found it everywhere in the world around him. The inscription on the blade is merely a testament to that."

"What does it say?" asked Brewster.

"The words of the inscription are, 'I think that I shall never see a poem lovely as a tree,'" said Rachel.

Brewster shut his eyes. "I had to ask," he said.

"The point is that even if Warrick knew the secret of the blade's enchantment, it would have done him no good," said Rachel.

"Why not?" asked Shannon.

Rachel shrugged. "It only works for elves."

"Well, in that case," Shannon said, handing the sword to Rachel, "let's try it out."

"Oh, no," said Rachel, shaking her head. "I couldn't."

"Mac," said Shannon. "Draw your sword."

"Against *her*?" said Mac, with astonishment.

"I want to see if the story of this enchantment is true," said Shannon.

"But . . . I am no fighter," Rachel protested. "I cannot even use a sword!"

"All the better," Shannon said. "That will make it a fitting test. Mac . . . engage her."

Mac sighed. "As you wish, my love." He drew his blade and smiled. "Fear not, I shall not hurt you."

Swallowing heavily, Rachel drew the sword. With a condescending little smile, Mac took a fighting stance. Rachel nervously did her best to copy him. But as soon as their blades touched, Rachel suddenly underwent a transformation. She drew herself up, standing more erect, and shifted her fighting stance, holding the blade with confidence. And as they engaged, her blade whipped around so quickly that no one was able to see exactly how she did it, but in the next instant, Mac's sword was flying aross the room.

Both their jaws dropped simultaneously.

" 'Strewth!" said Mac, with amazement.

"I did that?" Rachel asked, wide-eyed.

" 'Twas my father's own technique for disarming an opponent!" Mac said. "He taught it to me when I was but a lad!"

"Interesting," said Shannon. "And you say the magic only works for elves?"

Pikestaff Pat ran to pick up the sword and return it to Mac.

" 'Tis what the story says," Rachel replied.

"Pity," Shannon said. "Mac, let Pat try."

Pikestaff Pat took the blade and hefted it experimentally, nodding with satisfaction at its balance. He took a fighting stance facing Mac. They engaged, and though Pat was a competent swordsman, he was not even remotely in Mac's class and it only took moments for Mac to disarm him and have his swordpoint at Pat's throat.

"Well, the legend appears to be true," said Shannon. "I suppose that means the sword should go to Rachel, since she is the only elf among us."

"To *me*?" said Rachel, with disbelief.

"I guess that makes you the warlord of the elves," said Brewster with a smile. "Good thing we're friends."

Shannon pursed her lips thoughtfully. "Hmmm. I wonder. How do you suppose the elven tribes will react when they learn that Dwarfkabob has been found once again?"

"You mean, would they follow Rachel and support Brigantium?" said Mac. He grinned. "Well, if they do, then 'twould make us the first kingdom with elves among our army."

"But we don't even have an army yet," said Brewster.

Shannon took the elven sword and handed it to Rachel, who stared at it with awe. "Not yet," she said with a smile. "But this could make a good beginning." She turned to Teddy. "What else is in the Bag of Holding?"

"Warrick's Cloak of Darkness," Teddy said.

"You mean this?" said Mac, pulling out a long, black hooded cloak. "It looks like a perfectly ordinary cloak. What's so special about it?"

"Put it on," said Teddy.

Mac shrugged and slipped into the cloak. And promptly vanished from everybody's sight.

"Well, now what happens?" he said.

"Good Lord!" said Brewster.

"What?" said Mac. "What are you all staring at?"

"Mac," said Shannon, "you have become invisible!"

Mac raised his hand in front of his face, though of course, the others couldn't see that. "But I can see myself perfectly well."

"Aye, but we can't see you!" said Mick.

"Really?" Mac said. A moment later, Shannon cried out and jumped, spinning around as Mac came up behind her and gave her a pinch. She looked all around, but couldn't see any sign of him. "Mac! Stop that! Where are you?"

"Right in front of you, my love," he said, and there was a smacking noise as he kissed her on the lips.

Shannon reached out quickly and snatched the black cloak seemingly out of thin air, pulling it off Mac and revealing him.

"Well, now that's what I call a useful item of apparel," Mac said. "But whoever wears it will have to be quick on his feet, to make sure it is not snatched away from him like that."

"You see?" said Teddy. "You think Warrick would have parted with such items willingly, merely to make you believe I was sincere in wishing to join you?"

" 'Tis possible," said Shannon, with a frown, "but I rather doubt it. Does the bag contain anything else?"

Teddy shrugged. "I do not know, Mistress. I only placed the sword and the cloak inside it. But there is no telling what else might be hidden within. The Bag of Holding can contain many, many things."

"We should explore the contents of this bag," said Shannon. "Pat, Mick, see what else it holds. Meanwhile, troll, I am not yet completely satisfied that you are earnest in your intentions."

"But what more could I do, Mistress, to convince you?" Teddy asked anxiously.

"You could tell us of Warrick's plans, for a start," she said.

"How much does he know about us, and what does he intend?"

And as Mick and Pat explored the contents of the Bag of Holding, Teddy told Shannon and the others everything he knew. He told them about Brewster's time machine, and how Warrick was obsessed with learning the secret of its proper operation. He told them of Warrick's concern about the "outlaw sorcerer" of Brigand's Roost, and of how Warrick had convinced the royal sheriff to draw up a comprehensive list of new repressive edicts, the better to keep the dungeons stocked with "volunteers" for his experiments.

He told them of Black Jack's arrival in Pittsburgh, and of how the villainous mercenary had reported everything he'd learned to Warrick. Black Jack had apparently recovered from being shot by Brewster, and he had told Warrick how the sorcerer known as Brewster Doc commanded a dragon and threw thunderbolts, which was apparently how he had interpreted his gunshot wound. He also told Warrick that Brewster Doc was now allied with the infamous Black Shannon and her brigands, and that Mac had betrayed him and gone over to the opposition. The only thing Teddy failed to mention was the "voice in the ether," the demonic spirit from the ethereal planes that Warrick called "the Narrator," for while Teddy had never actually seen or heard this disembodied spirit, he had felt his power and was afraid to tempt fate by mentioning him. And finally, he gave them the most alarming news of all, though it was not entirely unexpected.

"Warrick has also told King Billy that 'tis Brewster Doc who is responsible for the recent unrest in Pittsburgh," Teddy said. "Between him and Sheriff Waylon, they have the king convinced that the outlaw sorcerer of Brigand's Roost has sent secret agitators into Pittsburgh, so that while he undermines Pitt's trade on one hand, he seeks to foster revolution on the other. Now King Billy is a decent sort, but he isn't very bright, while his brother, the sheriff, is crafty and ambitious, a fitting minion for Warrick. Between them, they have convinced King Billy that the only way to prevent a revolution is to muster an army to defend the kingdom and attack the outlaw sorcerer before he grows too powerful. To that end, Lord Kelvin, Grand Marshal of the Army of Pitt, has begun recruiting more soldiers and mercenaries to bolster the strength of King Billy's troops. And Warrick has petitioned the Sorcerers and Adepts Guild, in his post as Grand Director, to lend aid and sanction to this enterprise."

Shannon glanced at Brewster, Mac, and Harlan. "Brian was right," she said. "There shall be war."

"Only they will be expecting a motley bunch of brigands and some peasants armed with pitchforks, not an army," Mac said. "That means there is no time to lose. We must declare ourselves a sovereign state and set about raising troops at once. I will see to it that announcements are made throughout Brigand's Roost, Keep Village, and the Tent City that every ablebodied man who wishes employment is urged to join the Army of Brigantium."

"And I will make certain handbills go out with every member of our sales force, advertising for soldiers and mercenaries," Harlan added.

"What about King Durwin?" Brewster asked.

"Leave King Durwin to me," said Harlan. "I have been thinking about this problem and I believe I may have a solution. I will send a delegation to Durwin's court, informing him of our decision to form the sovereign state of Brigantium and thanking him for his support."

"But . . . he has not given us any support," said Shannon.

"Of course not, but that's beside the point," said Harlan. "My message to King Durwin will be printed up in all the handbills we shall distribute throughout the other kingdoms. By officially thanking him for his support, we will be giving the impression that he has, in fact, supported us from the beginning. And as a gesture of goodwill, and to commemorate our alliance, Darn will be given favored nation trading status, which means that they will be able to purchase all of our export goods at a significant discount, and that any goods imported from Darn will be admitted free of tariffs."

"But they are not exporting any goods to us," said Mac with a frown. "And since when have we had import tariffs?"

"Since about a minute ago, when I thought of it," said Harlan. "You see, by publically thanking Durwin for his support, as well as giving him a discount on our trade goods and exemption from import tariffs, we will be making it appear as if Durwin has been giving us his official backing all along. And it might not be a bad idea to open a brewery in Franktown, Darn's capital city. We shall need to expand our production facilities anyway, to compensate for our contract with the dwarves, and we've been talking about moving the rendering plant, as well, which we shall need to do in order to expand the keep and build a fortified palace. We shall let Durwin have a brewery and a rendering operation, which our people shall establish and run, but which will employ the poor citizens of Franktown. In this manner, we shall be helping Durwin's economy and cutting him in for fifty percent of the profits. It will expand our operations, and at the same time, give Durwin an incentive not to interfere with us."

"And, coincidentally, establish an alliance in the eyes of all the other kingdoms," Brewster said. "That's very clever, Harlan. You have the makings of a brilliant politician."

"*Politician*?" Harlan blanched. "Sir, I am a respected businessman! There is no need to be insulting."

"Sorry," Brewster said. "But you are the prime minister, after all."

Harlan looked crestfallen. "I know. I have reached a new low. I *knew* I should have been a bard."

"Well, if you had been, I'm sure you would have been a very successful one," said Brewster.

Harlan brightened. "You really think so?"

"I know so," Brewster said.

"Well, perhaps in another life," said Harlan with a sigh. Then his gaze fell on the table where Mick and Pat were exploring the contents of the Bag of Holding. *"Yipes!"*

The table was piled high with ancient, rolled-up scrolls and leather-bound vellum tomes and glittering amulets and silver chains and gem-encrusted bracelets, several crystal balls on ornate pedestals, rings with hidden compartments, golden goblets inscribed with eldritch runes, daggers etched with mystical designs, carved wooden staves, human skulls turned into candleholders, glass vials containing potions of all sorts, ceramic pots storing magical powders and incense, and several dozen sets of keys.

"All that came out of there?" asked Brewster, in astonishment.

"There seems to be no end to it," Mick replied.

"You still think Warrick would have surrendered all that voluntarily?" asked Teddy smugly.

"What's this?" asked Pat, reaching inside the bag and grunting. " 'Tis heavy enough." He pulled out a large book that barely made it through the opening of the bag. It was at least four inches thick and handsomely bound in old black leather with silver fastenings.

"Let me see that," Brewster said, impressed by its appearance. He read aloud the ornate script stamped into the cover in silver letters. "The Grimoire of Honorious."

"That's it!" cried the chamberpot excitedly in a muffled voice. "That's it, by the gods, that's it! Get me out of here!"

"Brian?" Brewster said, looking around. "Where are you?"

"I'm underneath all this bloody trash!" Brian's voice came from beneath the pile on the table. "I took a nap and these stupid fools have buried me!"

They started rummaging through the treasure trove on the table until they found the chamberpot and pulled it out.

"Honorious!" said Brian. "That's the wizard who enchanted me, curse his black, unlamented soul!"

"Then . . . if this is his grimoire," said Shannon, "that could mean—"

"The spell! The spell he used on me is in there! It *has* to be!"

"Then maybe the spell to reverse it is in there, too," said Mick.

"Open it! Open it and see, quickly!" the chamberpot cried.

Brewster unfastened the silver clasps and opened the grimoire to its table of contents. "Let's see . . . Spells of Compulsion, Love Spells, Spells of Repulsion, Spells to

Raise Demons, Spells to Cure Headaches, Spells to Cause Headaches, Spells to Ensure Regularity, Spells to Cause Constipation, Spells to Make Noses Run . . . what kinds of spells *are* these?"

"Go on, keep reading!" the chamberpot urged him.

". . . Spells to Cause Night Terrors, Spells to Attract Wealth, Spells to Enhance Sexual Performance . . . hmmmm, page 362." Brewster started leafing through the pages.

"Later! Later!" the chamberpot shouted. "Go back to the listing!"

"Oh, okay," said Brewster, turning back to the table of contents. "Let's see now, where was I? Oh, right. Spells to Bring About Unbelievable Orgasms . . . wait a minute, I want to see this one . . . ."

"Will you forget about that?" cried Brian. "You've got all day to browse! I've been a chamberpot for sixty some odd years, for crying out loud!"

"Okay, okay," said Brewster. "Ah, here we are. Spells of Transformation, page 593."

"Aye, that's the one!" cried the chamberpot excitedly. "Turn to that one, quickly!"

"Hold on, I'm getting there," said Brewster. "Okay, here we are. Now let's see . . . Spell to Transform People into Newts, Spell to Transform People into Toadstools, Spell to Transform People into Footstools . . . footstools?"

"Honorious had dozens of them," Brian said. "He liked having his enemies under his foot."

"Right," said Brewster, wryly. "Okay, here we go. Spell to Transform People into Chamberpots."

Shannon grinned. "I suppose he also liked his enemies to catch—"

"Never mind," said Brewster, interrupting hastily. "We get the point."

"Does it say how to reverse the spell?" asked the chamberpot, anxiously.

"Hold on, I'm skimming it," said Brewster. "The writing's a bit hard to read. It's rather florid. Honorious seemed to go in for lots of purple prose and his script is really elaborate—"

"Will you forget about his penmanship and get on with it?" cried Brian.

"Ah, here it is," said Brewster. He read aloud. "To reverse the spell, repeat the words, 'Abracadabra, change back.' "

About one third of the items on the table clattered to the floor as the chamberpot suddenly disappeared with a popping sound and Brian materialized in its place, sitting on the table in his normal human form.

"Abracadabra, change back?" he said with disbelief. "Sixty miserable years of being a lousy chamberpot and *that* was all it took to break the spell?"

"I guess it looks that way," said Brewster, raising his eyebrows.

"Aaaaarrrrrrggggggh!" Brian screamed, kicking out his legs and sweeping most of the table clean as items went crashing to the floor.

While Prince Brian, finally freed of his enchantment, tears his hair and hammers his fists against the table in frustration, we will diplomatically take our leave and pay a visit to the Kingdom of Pitt, to check in on Bonnie King Billy and his luscious queen, the lovely and ever-so-sultry Sandy. Thought your faithful narrator forgot all about them, huh? Well, just because they're only minor supporting characters and we haven't seen them since the last book in the series (*The Inadequate Adept*, Warner Books) doesn't mean they've been entirely neglected. They simply haven't had their lines come up yet. But we're about to get to their scene, don't worry. Remember, always trust your narrator. Now, where were we? Oh, right. Cue King Billy.

"_____"

I *said*, cue King Billy.

"_____"

Billy, you nitwit!

"Huh? What? Sandy, my dove, did you just say something?"

Sandy turned from her vanity, where she sat holding a

mirror and brushing her lovely, long blond hair. "No, I said nothing."

"I thought I heard someone call my name," said Billy with a frown. "And rather disrespectfully, too."

"And you naturally thought it was me?" said Sandy, raising her delicate eyebrows. "Really, William, you are developing a persecution complex. You are starting to see conspirators everywhere."

" 'Tis because there *are* conspirators everywhere," said Billy in a surly tone. "First 'twas petitions, then 'twas demands, now I am faced with public denunciations, with riots and demonstrations . . . they have even defaced my statues!"

"Well, the statues didn't look anything like you, anyway," Queen Sandy said, resuming her brushing.

" 'Tis not the point! The point is that the people are losing respect for me!"

"That implies they had respect for you in the first place," Queen Sandy said laconically.

"There, you see?" said Billy, pointing an accusatory finger at her. "Not even my own queen respects me! How can you say such a thing to me? I have always been a good king! I have always been good to my people! Do I not feed the poor?"

"Aye, but you feed them with spam," replied Queen Sandy.

"So what's wrong with that?"

"Have you ever eaten spam?"

"No."

"I didn't think so."

"Well, what should I feed them then?"

"William, we have had this conversation countless times before," Queen Sandy said, putting down her hairbrush and turning toward him. "I tell you that the people need bread, and vegetables, and meat, and you always say that it would be too expensive. I tell you the people need jobs, and you always say there are not enough to go around."

"Well, there aren't," King Billy said in a sulky tone.

"Especially since that outlaw sorcerer in Brigand's Roost has started stealing all our trade. Warrick warned me about him, and Warrick was right, as he usually is."

"Warrick has you twisted around his little finger," said Queen Sandy with disdain.

"He has not! Waylon says the same thing. Something must be done about that man! He is ruining my kingdom!"

"Your brother Waylon's first allegiance is to Warrick, not to you," said Sandy. "He resents you because you were born first and you got to be the king while he only gets to be the royal sheriff."

"Nonsense! Waylon is loyal and true! Has he not been constantly engaged in putting down the riots and raising an army to defend my kingdom against this upstart sorcerer?"

"Give an army to an unscrupulous man whose ambition knows no bounds and what do you suppose he will do with it?" asked Sandy. "Waylon has always wanted your throne, and now you are giving him the means to seize it."

"I do not want to listen to that kind of talk! You are only trying to upset me! You are always treating me as if I were a child! Well, I am not a child!" King Billy said, stamping his foot. "I'm not! Now leave me alone! I have important strategy to plan."

He went over to a large table on which a relief map of the Kingdom of Darn had been constructed with sand and dirt. Rows of little lead soldiers and cavalry squadrons were set up on the borders, and Billy started moving them about, making galloping sounds and bugle noises with his mouth.

Queen Sandy sighed and rolled her eyes, then got up and left the royal bedchamber. She knew there was no reasoning with Billy when he got like this. She was married to a moron, and a childish one at that. And the worst thing about it was, she had no one in the palace in whom she could confide. She had ladies in waiting, of course, but she could not trust any of them. Warrick always knew everything that went on in the palace. She had married Billy when she was just fifteen, an arranged marriage to cement an alliance between her kingdom and Pitt, and though she was well loved by her subjects, she often felt like a stranger in her own house.

Billy had never mistreated her in any way, quite the opposite; he doted on her, and that made it all the worse. If he had been a cruel and unfeeling husband, it would have been easy to resent him, but he was rather lovable in his own goofy way. What she resented was his relentless stupidity. She realized he couldn't help it, and that was the most frustrating thing about it. He would always be a pawn for men such as Warrick and Waylon. Billy was simply a born follower. Unfortunately, he had also been born king.

She went down the hall to her own private apartments and told the guards on duty that she was retiring early because she did not feel well, and was not to be disturbed. This did not surprise the guards at all. They knew the queen often retired early when she did not feel well, which really meant that she and the king had argued once again and Billy would be spending the night alone. The guards simply nodded and looked at one another knowingly.

"And stop looking at one another knowingly," Queen Sandy said irritably. "I hate that."

The guards looked properly contrite, but she knew they would be smirking as soon as they closed the doors behind her. She smiled. They wouldn't smirk if they knew what was about to happen.

She quickly changed out of her dressing gown and slipped into a pair of brown leather breeches, high boots, a white tunic, and a brown doublet. Then she tied her long blond hair back in a ponytail and tucked a long dagger into her belt. She knew there was no chance that Billy would feel bad about their argument and come to her apartments to apologize. Billy never admitted he was wrong. He was the king, and the king could not possibly be wrong about anything. What Billy preferred to do was wait until the next day and then simply pretend the argument had never happened. And since only the king could countermand her order to the guards that she was not to be disturbed, she knew that she could count on complete privacy until morning.

She slipped on a long black hooded cloak and went into her bedroom. She pressed a hidden button behind the head-board and a panel in the wall slid open, revealing a secret passageway. Billy had no knowledge of this passageway. She had discovered it quite by accident the third year of her marriage. When she first found the secret panel and opened it, she discovered a note inside. It said, "Don't tell anyone about this. It's just a little secret between us girls."

Thinking about the interesting dynamics of past royal marriages, Sandy lit a candle and ducked inside the passage-way, then the panel slid shut behind her.

SEVEN

The private Lear jet landed at Heathrow Airport as Colin Hightower polished off the last of the Jack Daniel's in the well-stocked bar. The stewardess was amazed at his capacity, but being a professional, she kept her opinions to herself. Her passengers were a decidedly odd pair. She had flown private flights with everyone from corporate VIPs to rock stars and she thought she had seen it all, but this couple was definitely unique.

The man looked like a seedy racetrack tout and the young woman with him, well, the stewardess had no idea what to make of her. She was a lot like the groupies rock stars often brought along on their travels, but this one was a real case of arrested development. She seemed to have the mind of a child. She acted as if she had never even been on an airplane before. During takeoff, she had acted frightened—which was not unusual, lots of people were afraid of flying—but once they were airborne and the captain had turned off the seat belt sign, she had flitted from window to window, marveling at the view and exclaiming with wonder that they were flying like birds. Undoubtedly, she had to be on drugs. It was probably the only way a guy like that could get a pretty young girl like her. Maybe he was a dealer, but he sure as hell didn't look like one. He certainly didn't look like anyone who could afford flying on a private jet. His clothes were cheap and tasteless. But then again, rich people had their eccentricities. It was not for her to judge. She was glad she'd soon be rid of them now that they were landing.

"Oooh, look, Colin, we're coming down!" Megan exclaimed excitedly.

"Just stay in the seat, luv, and keep your belt fastened until the plane has stopped moving," Hightower replied. It felt strange being back in London once again. It had been a long time. He wasn't sure what to expect, but his instincts told him he was really on to something. He had a feeling he was shortly going to find out what this whole thing was all about.

He had checked in with his editor and was told that there had been a call for him, from someone on the staff of *The New Yorker* magazine, no less. The caller said it was urgent that he get in touch with her and left a number. Several cautious phone calls later, Colin was on the line with somebody named Pamela Fairburn, and she had given him a real earful. He had a feeling there was someone else present on her end, and that she could not speak freely, because she had been somewhat evasive with her answers, but she had told him enough to really pique his curiosity. She arranged to send a private jet for him, to meet him at whatever location he chose, and told him she would put him up at company expense, carte blanche, at the Mayfair Hotel. It was extremely urgent, she had said, and concerned national security, high-level defense contracts and all that, and it was extremely important that she meet with him in person. And by all means to bring Megan.

Hightower was naturally suspicious, but he couldn't resist such a come-on. It certainly wasn't the police. They wouldn't spend that kind of money. This had all the earmarks of large-scale private enterprise. The jet had been chartered by EnGulfCo International, one of the largest multinationals on the face of the earth. Yes, he had rocked somebody's boat, all right. Whatever was behind this curious story, he was definitely on the right track.

The jet had met him at a small private airfield outside Scranton, Pennsylvania, and the landing was practically a touch and go. They had stayed on the ground only long enough to take him and Megan on. Now, as they landed, they taxied not to the terminal, but to a private hangar, where a stretch limousine was waiting for them. The driver held the doors open for them and they drove off as soon as they had entered. No going through customs or anything. And the bar in the limo was well stocked with Jack Daniel's. Hightower decided he could definitely get used to this sort of treatment.

They arrived at the Mayfair Hotel a short while later and found a suite reserved for them on the top floor. Ordinarily, Hightower would not even be able to get through the front doors of a place like the Mayfair, but the treatment they received was red carpet all the way. "Yes, Mr. Hightower, your suite is ready, of course. And if there is anything that we can do to make your stay more comfortable, please do not hesitate to let us know."

The bellman took them up to their room and Colin started rummaging around in his pockets for a tip, but the man only smiled and shook his head. "Thank you, sir, but that will be quite unnecessary. Everything's already been taken care of. Have a nice stay, sir."

"Right," said Colin, shutting the door behind him.

"Oooh, what a lovely room!" said Megan. "It looks like a room in the royal palace!"

Colin frowned, then realized she wasn't talking about another hotel. And then the bedroom door opened and a woman came out dressed in an elegant, dark blue suit and navy pumps. And she was carrying a gun.

"Bloody hell," said Hightower. "I knew this was all too good to be true."

"Please sit down, Mr. Hightower," said Pamela. "And you, too, miss. And don't make any sudden moves, please. I've been shooting competitively since I was a little girl, and I'm really very good with this."

"Dr. Fairburn, I take it?" Colin said.

"Pleased to meet you. Do sit down. We have a great deal to discuss. I hope you had a pleasant flight. Would you care for some refreshments?"

"We had some on the plane," said Hightower. "But I sure could do with another drink."

"The bar's over there," said Pamela, gesturing with the gun. Colin didn't know very much about guns, but he knew enough to recognize a semiautomatic with a silencer when he saw one.

"Is the gun really necessary?" he asked, slowly heading

over to the bar and taking care to make no abrupt moves. "Or did you bring us all this way only to shoot us?"

"If I wanted you dead, Mr. Hightower, I could have accomplished that with a great deal less trouble," Pamela replied. "EnGulfCo has enormous resources. I could have hired a professional for a lot less money than it would have taken to charter that private jet. No, the gun is for my own protection. You see, I don't know you, and you do not exactly come highly recommended."

"Ah, I see," said Hightower, relaxing somewhat. What she said made perfect sense, of course. "Yes, I am well aware of my considerably less than sterling reputation. However, I have prided myself on always getting the story, regardless of what it took. I may not be upper crust, like you, but I am a competent professional."

"Very well," said Pamela. "In that case, why don't you prove it to me? And forget all the fanciful speculation in your story. Tell me exactly what it is you think you know."

"Well, that's rather difficult to do without speculating," Colin said, "because I have no proof, you see, but here goes. I think someone—probably EnGulfCo, given your rather intense interest—has invented time travel. I think you've got yourself a top secret working prototype of some sort of time machine, only something has gone wrong."

"Go on."

"What I think must have happened," Colin continued, "is that whoever took this machine into the past has either deviated from the plan or else has suffered some sort of mishap and lost control of the machine, because somebody named Warrick now has it and is sending people from his time into ours, for reasons I can't fathom. Perhaps he is experimenting with the machine, trying to figure out how it works. Perhaps he thinks it's some sort of device for execution, because apparently he's using prisoners as his subjects. In either case, Megan here insists that he lives in an Alabaster Tower close to a royal palace of some sort, and that he is a sorcerer. I'm not quite sure what to make of that, but she obviously believes that he is literally capable of casting spells and such."

"Interesting," said Pamela. "Keep going."

"He seems to have a rather highly placed position in the government of his nation, which Megan tells me is called the Kingdom of Pitt," Colin said, pouring himself a drink. "She is from its capital city, which is known, coincidentally, as Pittsburgh. From what she tells me, the period sounds definitely medieval. Now I've done a little research, but I can't find any reference to any Kingdom of Pitt, nor a land of twenty-seven kingdoms or a city known as Pittsburgh. Except for the one in Pennsylvania, of course, and its history hardly goes back to medieval times. This initially led me to suspect that Megan comes from a time period about which very little is known, possibly the England of Celtic times. However, there's one thing that doesn't quite fit. She speaks a very modern sort of English, with only a few out of place expressions and constructions."

"And what conclusion do you draw from this?" asked Pamela.

"That she wasn't genuine, but after spending some time with her, I am convinced she is exactly what she claims. Either that, or she's one of the best actresses I've ever seen. If it's a performance, it has absolutely no inconsistencies. What's more, I've interviewed several other people who claim to have come from this same kingdom, and their stories are all the same, down to the last detail, with only one variant. Some of them claim that before they were transported here, this Warrick placed a 'spell of compulsion' on them, which sounds rather like a posthypnotic suggestion. This suggestion, or compulsion, drives them to seek a way to return to him in the Alabaster Tower and tell him where they've been and what they've seen. However, I've also spoken to at least one person who claims that no such compulsion was placed upon him."

"And is that all you have?"

"Not quite. After the first story ran," Colin went on, "my paper received a rather interesting call from a young musician in New York. When I called back and spoke to him, he told me a fascinating story, after first informing me that if I used his name, he would say that it was only a publicity stunt to get his band's name in the paper. He said he was from this same time period, only unlike the others, he was not from the Kingdom of Pitt. He claimed to have come from a kingdom known as Darn, where he worked as an apprentice to a sorcerer. I asked him some questions pertaining to certain details I had left out of the story, and except for the spell of compulsion, his answers matched what I knew. Or at least what I'd been told by Megan and the others.

"One day, he said, some brigands brought a curious apparatus to the sorcerer to whom he was apprenticed. They claimed to have found it sitting abandoned in the middle of a road. This sorcerer proceeded to use every spell he could think of to divine the purpose of this machine and figure out how it worked. One of them was apparently successful, because while he was sitting in it and casting his spell, he suddenly disappeared, but the machine remained. This so-called apprentice then realized that it was a dangerous device, so he took it to Pittsburgh and delivered it to Warrick the White, whose title is—get this—the Grand Director of the Sorcerers and Adepts Guild and Royal Wizard to the King of Pitt.

"Warrick questioned him about the spells his master had used, then forced him to get into the machine while he spoke the same spell. The next thing this young man knew, he was in New York City. He managed to survive by living on the streets for a short time, until he met a girl who took him in. Soon afterward, he got a job as a vocalist with a rock and roll band. He seemed quite happy with his lot and had no desire whatsoever to return to his own time. Like Megan and the others, he insisted that where he came from, magic really works. However, it apparently doesn't work here, because although he was a sorcerer's apprentice and knew some magic, none of his spells would function since he had arrived. This didn't seem to bother him, though. He was enjoying a considerably upgraded lifestyle as an up-and-coming young musician and said he'd take electric guitars and MTV over magic anyday. He told me he was confident no one would ever believe this story, except perhaps whoever had made the machine in the first place, and if I knew what was good for me, I'd drop the whole investigation, because the government was probably behind it all."

Pamela raised her eyebrows, but said nothing, waiting for him to go on.

"All in all, it was quite an interesting conversation," Colin said. "Under ordinary circumstances, I would have dismissed him as a drug-addled young neurotic, but then these aren't exactly ordinary circumstances, are they? So," said Colin, as he finished off his whiskey and poured himself another, "what I think is that either this whole thing is the nuttiest and most complicated hoax I've ever heard of, or else this time machine or whatever it is has enabled you to discover the existence of a parallel universe. How am I doing?"

Pamela had lowered her gun. "A parallel universe!" she said. "Jesus, I hadn't even thought of that." She took a deep breath and exhaled heavily. "Why don't you pour me one of those? I think I could use it."

"My pleasure," Colin said, reaching for another glass. "Now, turnabout is fair play, Dr. Fairburn, if that is really your name. I realize you're the one with the gun, but don't you think I'm entitled to some answers after all the work I've done? How close was I?"

Pamela took the drink from him and tossed it back in one gulp. "Entirely too close," she said, and told him everything.

"Marvin Brewster, eh?" said Colin when she'd finished. "I've heard of him. We used to call him 'the nutty professor.' Little did we know."

"He happens to be my fiancé," Pamela said.

"Sorry. No offense. So, where do we go from here?"

"I wish I knew," said Pamela. "I've been working on duplicating Marvin's machine, and it's almost complete, but without a fresh supply of Buckminsterfullerine, there's no way to make it work."

"And you can't get your hands on any more of this Buckminster-whatever-it-is?" asked Hightower.

"It's not exactly something you can buy over the counter," Pamela said, wryly. "Marvin got his supply from a meteor that fell to Earth on some Pacific island. We have the capability to manufacture it now, but not nearly in the same density. EnGulfCo's working on it, but in the meantime, unless they can locate some more from another meteor fragment somewhere, there's nothing more that I can do."

"Which means that Brewster's stuck . . . wherever he is," said Colin.

"I don't even know if he's still alive," said Pamela disconsolately.

"Well, it's some terrific story, that's for sure," said Colin. He took a small tape recorder out of his pocket. "This thing's gonna win me a Pulitzer."

There was a chuffing sound and the tape recorder flew out of Colin's hand, smashed by a .38 caliber hollowpoint bullet. Hightower glanced at Pamela with shock as she lowered the semiautomatic.

"Are you crazy?" he shouted. *"Look what you just did! You could have killed me!"*

"She's a sorceress!" said Megan.

"She's a bloody nutcase, is what she is!" said Hightower.

"Relax, Mr. Hightower. I've been shooting clay pigeons and grouse hunting with my father most of my life. If I had wanted to kill you, rest assured, I would have. And believe it or not, I just did you a favor."

"A favor!"

"That's right. If the chairman of EnGulfCo even *suspected* I'd spoken to you about this . . . well, to be quite honest, I'm not really sure how far he'd be willing to go, but at the very least, he'd make absolutely certain you never published your story anywhere."

"If you people think you can suppress a story like this—" Colin began, but Pamela interrupted him.

"Look, I'm taking a tremendous risk telling you all this. You have no idea. I've had my phone tapped and I've been followed ever since I started on this project. I'm reasonably sure I wasn't followed here, but it's only a matter of time before your part in this becomes exposed. I chartered that jet on an EnGulfCo account, and that same account is paying for your room."

"Well, that wasn't very smart, was it?" Colin said.

"It makes no difference, Mr. Hightower," Pamela replied. "The chairman of EnGulfCo is not in the habit of reading the tabloids, but it's only a matter of time before your story comes to his attention one way or another. And if you think he can't suppress it, think again. He could easily buy your newspaper and have you fired. Or, for a lot less money, he could simply have you disappear."

"Are you serious?" said Colin.

"I'm not sure I'd put it past him," Pamela replied. "Think about it. A discovery like this would mean a fortune to whoever controlled it. Think of the power it would place into their hands." She shook her head. "I'm afraid Marvin's really done it this time. He's gotten himself, and all of us, into one hell of a mess."

"So what were you intending to do?" asked Colin.

Pamela shrugged. "I don't know. I hadn't really thought it all through. Right now, all I can think about is Marvin. He's in trouble, and there doesn't seem to be anything I can do to help."

"Well, perhaps there's something I can do," said Colin. "Look, so long as this discovery remains a secret, EnGulfCo is holding all the cards. Granted, I want to write the story, so I have a vested interest. However, getting this whole thing out into the open is your best chance to help Brewster. So long as EnGulfCo remains in control, they can call the tune. But if you were in control, then it would be a different story, wouldn't it?"

"What do you mean?" asked Pamela.

"Right now," said Hightower, "all that's happened is a couple of pieces have appeared in an American tabloid that has printed stories about Elvis being spotted in convenience stores. In other words, no one's likely to take any of this very seriously. Especially given my rather less than savory reputation. However, while I might be easily dismissed, that wouldn't be the case with you. Especially if you had some sort of proof, such as detailed notes and diagrams of the machine. If we were to approach, say, *The London Times*, and you could convince them this whole thing was on the level, then EnGulfCo could no longer control the situation. Now, what's in it for me, you may well ask? Well, I get to write the story. And I'm on record as the guy who broke it, and my career is made. What do you say?"

Pamela moistened her lips. "I have a good friend on the editorial board of *The Times*. The difficulty would be in getting the proof from Marvin's laboratory. I'd never get it past security."

"You have access to the lab, right?"

"Yes, of course. But I'd never get out with Marvin's notes."

"Well then, we'll simply have to think of something," said Colin. "Are you allowed in after hours?"

"Yes."

"Good. That means fewer people will be about. Do you have a pencil and a piece of paper?"

"There should be some paper in the desk there. And I've got a pen."

"We'll need a rough layout of the place. The route to and from the lab. How many guards, how many cameras, elevators, flights of stairs, and so forth. I need to know as much as you can tell me about what sort of security they've got. Can you do that?"

"Yes, I think so."

"All right, let's get to it."

"You sound as if you've done this sort of thing before," said Pamela.

"Dr. Fairburn, you wouldn't believe some of the places I've gotten into."

"Well, if we're going to be partners in crime, you might as well call me Pamela."

Colin grinned. "All right, Pamela." He glanced over his

shoulder at Megan. "Why don't you watch the magic box awhile, dear? Pamela and I have got some work to do."

Queen Sandy made her way through the dark and winding streets to a part of town where even a strong and well armed man out walking alone after sunset would be taking his life in his own hands. However, if she felt afraid, she showed no sign of it. She headed purposefully toward the corner of Cutthroat Avenue and Garotte Street, and a raucous alehouse known as The Stealers Tavern. As she walked with her cloak billowing out behind her, she watched the shadows and steered clear of the mouths of alleyways, staying in the middle of the deserted street. But in this part of town, caution was not necessarily a guarantee of safety.

As she approached the corner where the tavern stood, three figures detached themselves from the shadows and moved out into the street to block her way.

"Well, well," one of them said, "what have we here?"

"Is that the best you can do?" Sandy replied.

"What?"

" 'Well, well, what have we here?' What a cliché. Was that the most original line you could think of?"

"What's a cliché?" asked one of the other alleymen, for that is what they were, the term "mugger" not having been invented yet.

"Shut up!" the first alleyman said.

Sandy glanced over her shoulder. The street behind her was clear. "You mean you didn't even think of blocking my escape?" she said. "Have you three ever done this before?"

"Don't try running away," the first alleyman said. "We'll chase ye down."

"Aye, we're very swift, ye know," the third alleyman added.

"Fleet of foot," said the second alleyman, nodding emphatically. "Very, very fast."

"Shut up!" said the leader. He pulled out a dagger. "Right, now, lady, hand it over."

"Hand what over?" Sandy asked.

"Your purse, of course! Don't be a twit!"

"I haven't got a purse."

"What do ye mean ye haven't got a purse? Every woman's got a purse!"

"Well, I don't."

"Come on, do ye think we're stupid?"

"Incredibly," said Sandy.

"Ey, did you hear what she just said?" the third alleyman said, turning to their leader.

"Of course, I heard, ye idiot! I'm standing right here, ain't I?" He turned back toward Sandy. "Now don't go making this any harder on yourself, lady. Let's have the money."

"I don't have any money," Sandy said. "And if I did, I certainly wouldn't give it to the likes of you. Now stand aside and let me pass."

"Look, lady, we've got knives," said the leader of the alleymen. He held his up so she could see it clearly, then nudged the other two and they held theirs up, as well.

"How nice for you," said Sandy. "It so happens I have one, as well. See?" She pulled her dagger out.

"Aye, but there's three of us," the first alleyman said.

"I'm astonished you can count that high," Sandy replied wryly.

"Look, lady, what the bloody hell's the matter with ye? Ye don't want to get hurt, do ye?"

"No. Do you?"

The three alleymen glanced at one another, perplexed. "Ain't ye even a little bit afraid?" their leader said.

"Not really," Sandy said. "I am getting a bit impatient, though. If you're going to do something, I wish you would just get on with it. I have other things to do."

"I don't get it," the second alleyman said uncertainly, looking to the leader of the trio. "She ain't afraid. Why ain't she afraid?"

"I think she's bluffing."

"Maybe she's an assassin?" said the third alleyman.

"Don't be stupid," said the leader. "There ain't any female assassins in the Guild."

"Well, maybe she's a mercenary?" said the second alley-man.

"She don't look like no mercenary. Mercenaries carry swords. And she ain't got a sword."

"Well then, maybe she's—"

Sandy rolled her eyes in exasperation and gestured at the three men, mumbling a spell under her breath. The three alleymen froze as if rooted to the spot and she simply walked past them.

". . . a sorceress," the third alleyman finished. "She's a bloody sorceress!"

"Shut up!" the leader said as Sandy walked away.

"She could've turned us into toadstools, ye damn fool!"

"Who're ye calling a damn fool?"

"I'm calling you a damn fool!"

"Shut up, or else I'll bust yer face in!"

"Can ye move?"

"No, I can't bloody well move! Does it look like I can move?"

"Fool, fool, fool!"

"Shut up!"

Sandy left them arguing, frozen into immobility in the middle of the street behind her. They would remain frozen until morning, at which point they would recover their mobility with no ill effects, except possibly sore joints, assuming no one would do anything to them if they were found that way during the night. However, that wasn't Sandy's responsibility. They had brought it on themselves, and all things considered, they had gotten off easy. If Sandy were a sorceress, they might easily have been turned into toadstools, or something worse, but she wasn't a sorceress. If she were, then she would have been a member of the guild and both Warrick and her husband would have known she had ability with magic. They didn't, and she preferred to keep it that way, because she was a witch.

Now, there were two kinds of witches in the twenty-seven kingdoms, licensed witches and unlicensed witches. Licensed witches were registered with the Sorcerers and

Adepts Guild, but they weren't really full members because they had not formally apprenticed with a sorcerer, only paid half dues, and had no voting privileges. They were found primarily in the larger towns and cities, where they operated small businesses out of garish storefronts with signs advertising such things as psychic readings, palmistry, phrenology, astrological forecasts, tarot fortune telling, crystal therapy and past life regressions. They usually adopted fanciful names, such as Lady Starfire, Dame Isis, or if it was a male witch, something like Lord Woodchuck Dragonlance. They often formed groups with ranking systems, sold mail order courses in witchcraft, and taught classes at the local extended university.

Unlicensed witches, like Sandy, could be found almost anywhere, but it was difficult to tell who they were, because they looked and acted pretty much like anybody else. Most of them practiced witchcraft quietly as a religion, some practiced it as a system of ethical philosophy. Some met in small groups, others followed a solitary practice, but none of them made a commercial activity of what they called "the Craft." They shared their beliefs only with those who were honest and sincere in their desire to learn, refused to perform spells that would cause harm to any living being, and never charged money for anything they did. As a result, all the licensed witches claimed that they weren't real witches at all, and denounced them in their newsletters when they weren't busy denouncing one another. And since unlicensed witches were not registered with the guild, they were technically in violation of the law each time they practiced magic.

As queen, Sandy had tried to use her influence to change things, not only for other witches like herself, but for all the downtrodden citizens of Pitt. However, it would have been unethical for her to cast a spell to make her husband change the laws. She had tried subtle persuasion, but soon found that subtlety was completely lost on Billy. And with Warrick as the royal wizard and Billy's crafty and ambitious brother, Waylon, as the Royal Sheriff, any direct action on her part would have been dangerous and quickly neutralized. So she had done the only other thing that she could do. She played her part as the aloof and pampered queen, while secretly being a member of the Underground.

Now, unlike the various underground, politically subversive groups in Earth's history, the members of this particular band were not guerrilla fighters. They were strictly nonviolent in their actions, and did what they could to embarrass King Billy's regime, thwart the activities of the Royal Sheriff, and support the downtrodden lower classes of the city, which included practically everybody. They published inflammatory manifestos, scrawled political graffiti on the walls, and tried to interpose themselves between the sheriff's deputies and anyone they attempted to arrest unjustly. In other words, they were a sort of medieval Greenpeace.

In the course of her clandestine activities with the Underground, Sandy had made a number of interesting and unusual acquaintances, not the least of which was Lady Donna, known simply as "La Donna" to the members of The Stealers Guild and as "The Lady" to the members of her local, the Sluts And Strumpets Sisterhood, or SASS for short. As Sandy came into The Stealers Tavern, she pulled her hood up around her face and quickly made her way toward the back, where La Donna was at her usual table in a secluded, candlelit booth. She was sitting with several of "her girls," as she referred to her sisters in the local that she headed, and with a tall and dapper-looking, dark-haired dandy who wore a rather threadbare doublet of faded green brocade and a brown velvet coat with worn-through elbows. He looked like an aristocrat who had fallen on hard times, but in fact, he was a low-born peasant named Gentlemanly Johnny, head of the Swindlers local of The Stealers Guild.

Now one might think that thieves, assassins, cutthroats, alleymen, pickpockets, and the other assorted criminals who made up the membership of The Stealers Guild would have more sense than to hang out in a bar known as The Stealers Tavern. It did seem a little bit obvious. However, the laws of Pitt were such that while it was illegal to commit a crime, it was not a crime to belong to a guild for criminals. (Don't ask me to explain it, I don't really understand it either. It has something to do with the complexities of labor negotiations and PAC funding.) Anyway, since the sheriff and his deputies all knew where The Stealers Guild hung out, they were always on the lookout for any crimes committed in The Stealers Tavern. As a result, The Stealers Tavern was at the same time the biggest hangout for criminals in Pitt and the safest bar in Pittsburgh.

"I need to speak with you," said Sandy as she approached La Donna's table.

Rumor had it that when she was young, La Donna was a svelte and sultry beauty who turned heads everywhere she went. But that was just a rumor, and as rumors often go, it happened to be false. La Donna started it herself. However, since La Donna was fairly advanced in age, to put it diplomatically (or to put it undiplomatically, she was a pretty old broad), no one recalled what she had looked like when she was young, so her secret was safe. As a girl, La Donna had been rather plain and very pudgy. Now, she was still plain, only she had grown from pudgy to immense. Despite her size, however, and her age, La Donna was extremely sexy. What made her sexy was the fact that she believed that she was sexy, and one's self-image has a great deal to do with how one is perceived. She looked up at Sandy and languidly raised one eyebrow, then made a dismissive motion with her heavily beringed hand and her girls got up from the table and went off to mingle. Gentlemanly Johnny stayed, however.

"I need to speak with you," said Sandy.

"Sit down, then," said La Donna. "Have a drink."

"No, thank you," said Sandy, joining them at their table. They bent low over the table and put their heads together, speaking in low voices so as not to be overheard, which may have drawn attention to them because it made them look as if they were plotting something. However, in The Stealers Tavern, almost everybody sat that way. There was more complex plotting going on in The Stealers Tavern than in a dozen Agatha Christie novels.

"So, what can I do for the Underground?" asked La

Donna. She did not recognize Sandy, of course, and did not even know her name. One would hardly expect to find the queen visiting The Stealers Tavern, much less being a member of the Underground, and commoners never got close enough to the queen to recognize her. Granted, her face was stamped on all the coins, along with King Billy's, but it was a very poor likeness. It looked a great deal like King Billy, in fact, which was not surprising because the mint used the same stamping for them both as a cost-cutting measure.

"I cautioned you that your people were going too far, inciting riots," Sandy said. "I told you that violence is not the way. Now the army is mobilizing. The call has gone out for mercenaries to augment the troops and they have already started arriving in the city."

"With all due respect, my dear," said Gentlemanly Johnny, without suspecting whom he was addressing, "your concerns are groundless. The troops are not being recruited to put down the revolution, but to march against the outlaw sorcerer in Brigantium."

"Brigantium?" asked Sandy, frowning. "What is Brigantium? My information was that the outlaw sorcerer was in Darn, in a town known as Brigand's Roost."

"Then your information is somewhat out of date," said La Donna. She pulled out one of Harlan's flyers. "They have broken off from Darn and created the Kingdom of Brigantium, forming an alliance with King Durwin. It is against them that King Billy sends his army."

"And as for the mercenaries," added Johnny, "only the dregs have been answering King Billy's summons. All the best ones are going to Brigantium, because they are offering much better pay."

"Be that as it may," said Sandy, "once the troops defeat the outlaw wizard of Brigantium, they will be returning home, rich with plunder and seasoned from battle. And then they shall make short work of your revolution."

"Oh, I think not," said Gentlemanly Johnny with a smile. "For one thing, you are assuming the Army of Pitt will be victorious, and that is by no means a certain thing. For another, this war could not come at a better time. While King Billy sends his troops against Brigantium, there will be only the sheriff's deputies and the palace guard remaining behind, with perhaps a squad or two of archers. It will be the perfect time to stage an assault upon the palace."

"And assuming you succeed, what then?" asked Sandy. "You will have captured the palace, and perhaps the king and queen, though they will doubtless have ample time to escape while the deputies and the palace guard repel your assault, and then you will only be in possession of the palace. The army will return and displace you easily. Meanwhile, the revolution's leaders will have been revealed, and they shall hunt you down."

"Oh, not us," said Gentlemanly Johnny. "You think *we* are the leaders of the revolution?"

Sandy frowned. "The Stealers Guild has been behind all of the riots that have taken place."

"To be sure," La Donna said. "But we are not fools. We have merely provided the spark to light the powder trail. We have not taken credit for any of our actions. By now, the revolution has gathered its own momentum among the people of the city, and they have chosen their own leaders. We are privy to their plans, of course, because our members do attend the secret meetings, but none of us are among the actual leaders. We merely work behind the scenes, so to speak. It is much safer that way."

"I see," said Sandy dryly. "So if the revolution fails, all of you are safe, because they will arrest the leaders. And if it succeeds, then you shall benefit."

"We benefit either way," said Gentlemanly Johnny. "Think of all the opportunities that will arise when the revolution starts. We are expecting record profits."

"So then you don't care about the people at all," said Sandy. "You don't care about ridding the kingdom of corruption. All you care about is money."

"That's not true," La Donna said. "King Billy might not be a bad ruler if he had good people to advise him, but he has Warrick the White and Sheriff Waylon and their cronies.

If we are rid of them, then life in the kingdom will improve for everyone. We would like to see the revolution succeed, for everybody's sake."

"But if it should fail," Johnny added, "then is that any reason why we cannot make some money on the venture?"

"I see I have wasted my time," said Sandy, getting up. "The Underground has been struggling to improve life for the people of the kingdom. But you are only going to doom them."

"A word of caution, my dear," said Gentlemanly Johnny. "We would welcome the support of the Underground. However, if you are not with us, then we must assume you are against us."

"Is that a threat?" asked Sandy.

"Consider it a word of sage advice," said Johnny, giving her a level stare. "If you will not support us, then stay out of our way. Interference is something that will not be tolerated."

"I will pass on the message," Sandy said. She turned on her heel and left.

Gentlemanly Johnny made a small hand signal to a large man sitting at the bar. He glanced up as Ferret Phil, the leader of the Burglars local, came over to the table. "Follow her," said Johnny. "Find out who she is and where she lives, and who her friends are. And be discreet."

"I always am," said Ferret Phil with an ugly grin. "Consider it done." And he hurried off on Sandy's trail.

EIGHT

If Brewster had thought his courtyard was a place of frenetic activity before, then it was in absolute pandemonium now. Bloody Bob had pulled all the workers off their other construction jobs to work full-time on the palace of Brigantium, and since none of the laborers were unionized, Brewster was amazed at how quickly things got done. Harlan had offered Bloody Bob a bonus for each day they came in under the construction deadline, and as a result, the huge work force labored literally around the clock, toiling through the night by torchlight to get the job done.

It was the home improvement project to end all home improvement projects. The spam rendering operation had been moved out of the courtyard to a forest clearing several miles away, until it could be moved to Franktown, and now what used to be the courtyard was rapidly shaping up as the new palace of Brigantium. Having worked as a top-rank mercenary for much of his life, Bloody Bob had seen his share of royal palaces, and with Brewster's help, he had drawn up a complete set of plans to ensure that the palace of Brigantium would outshine every other he had seen. The sprawling courtyard in front of the keep was going to be the new great hall of the palace, and the ruins of the outer walls had been knocked down to make room for the new walls of the palace, which would be surrounded by an inner and an outer bailey. There would be a well fortified barbican and drawbridge, crenellated towers with cruciform loopholes, sally ports, hoardings, and machicolations and all sorts of neat medieval stuff. It was going to be really cool.

The walls of the outer and the inner bailey were going up rapidly, because fortifications were the most important part of any castle. After studying some of Bloody Bob's designs, Brewster had made some modifications, so that the outer and the inner bailey were not simply square or circular, but star-shaped. Initially, Bob thought there could be some magical significance to this, but Brewster had explained how the points of the star, with fortified towers and walkways at the top, enabled the walls to be better defended by affording a much wider field of fire. Any assault force attacking the walls would be vulnerable not only from the front, but on their flanks, as well. Bloody Bob was deeply impressed. He was puzzled by the large embrasures Brewster added for the cannon, because he did not know what a cannon was. Brewster tried explaining the concept to him, then finally gave up and realized that nothing short of a scale model demonstration would suffice.

With Mick's help, he had forged a small cannon that he christened the "water gun." Actually, the name was some-thing of a misnomer, because the gun did not use water. The design was meant to use the highly explosive peregrine wine as a propellant. When Brewster set it off for the first time, the explosion, even for a small model, was deafening, and the range of the tiny cannon balls he'd made was truly impressive.

"Now, imagine the same thing," he'd said, "only about ten times this size, with one emplaced at each embrasure on the walls, facing every possible avenue of approach."

" 'Strewth!" said Bob. "The castle would be impregnable! No army would even dare approach the walls!"

"Oh, they might get close," said Brewster, "but it would cost them. Still, in case we should be attacked by a large enough force where the commanders wouldn't mind signifi-cant casualties, I've come up with another idea that should help, if we can get them built in time."

He took Bloody Bob, Pikestaff Pat, Harlan, Mac, and Shannon down to Mick's shop, where Mick and his appren-tices had been hard at work producing a crude internal com-bustion engine from sand castings Brewster had designed.

"I had initially envisioned this engine driving a sort of steamroller," Brewster explained, "so that we could pave the streets, but then it occurred to me that it could just as easily drive a tank."

The tank itself was not yet finished, but the frame was ready with the engine mounted. Brewster fired it up, using the peregrine wine as fuel. The noise alone would have been enough to rout an army, but when he shifted into drive and the tank rolled out across the meadow on crude but effective iron caterpillar treads, their reaction was one of pure astonishment.

"Of course, this just gives you an idea of how it moves," said Brewster, after he'd put it through some simple paces and shut off the engine. "We can mount an armored turret on it, with a smaller version of our water gun, and it would make a practical assault vehicle to use against foot soldiers or cavalry. Each tank would require a crew of two. One to drive it and one to be the gunner. Of course, they would be most effective supported by a squad of foot soldiers."

"Doc," said Mac, " 'tis you who should be the general and not I. With this tank of yours, we shall be invincible! Thirty or forty of these would make cavalry charges obsolete!"

"Well, we'll be lucky if we can get just this one built in time," said Brewster. "And it still may have some flaws. I don't know how much time we'll have to test it. And I'm still not entirely happy with the way the engine's running. It's almost as temperamental as Pamela's antique Jaguar."

"A jaguar?" Shannon said. "What sort of creature is that?"

"Uh . . . a very finnicky one," said Brewster. "If you don't grind the shims just right . . . oh, well, never mind. The point is, I'm still working out the bugs."

"Bugs?" said Mac.

"Nagging little problems," Brewster explained. "It's just an expression."

"Sometimes, Doc, I don't think we speak quite the same language," Shannon said with a frown.

"Mmmm. I know what you mean. 'Strewth, and all that. Anyway, I've thought of another application for this engine design, on a rather smaller scale. If we can get it working right, I might be able to come up with something else you might find useful. It all depends on how much time we'll have."

"Word has it that the troops are massing in Pitt," said Mac. "King Billy has recruited more soldiers from among his populace and sent out a call for mercenaries. However, we have the jump on him there, as our call went out first, thanks to Harlan's distribution network. We're offering a much higher salary, and we've been attracting some of the best fighters. I've been housing them at the Assassins School. A few of them have even guest lectured some of the classes. I think we're in good shape there."

"When do you suppose Pitt's army will march against us?" Brewster asked.

" 'Tis difficult to say," Mac replied with a shrug. "The new troops must be organized and drilled, and outfitted as well. They have been busy making preparations for the past few months, however, so 'tis possible that they may move against us anytime. How long do you think it will take to get the palace and the fortifications completed?"

"At the rate they're going, if they keep up this pace, the outer walls and the exterior of the castle should be complete by the end of the next month," said Brewster. "Bloody Bob's got all his crews working around the clock, in shifts, and they're making amazing progress. The castle won't be ready to move into for another several months, but it'll be a place where we can make a stand."

"That's the important thing," said Mac.

"How are we doing with arming the troops?" asked Shannon.

"Well, Mick's been busy with Doc's projects, but we have all the smiths and armorers in town producing weapons. And many of the troops we have recruited already have their own. Our biggest problem is with training them, appointing officers and so forth. It is there that King Billy is ahead of us. He has had more time. What is more, his spies have doubtless been reporting to him and he knows by now that we are preparing for war, and that the longer he delays, the better it is for us. I do not think he will wait much longer, and I cannot see how our army will be as well prepared as his."

"About those spies," said Brewster. "You think there's any chance they might have learned about what we're doing here at the keep?"

" 'Tis possible, but I strongly doubt it," Mac replied. "Only our most trusted friends have been admitted through the inner walls, and no one has seen anything you are preparing here save us and Mick's apprentices. And they have been camped out here on the grounds as a condition of their service, the better to ensure the secrecy of the work in which they have been engaged. We may not have succeeded in unmasking Warrick's spies, but neither have they succeeded in discovering what goes on here at the keep."

"Good," said Brewster. "If their army is going to be better trained than ours, then we'll need the element of surprise. And I think I can guarantee a few surprises. But I'm still worried about Warrick. I'm not sure what, if anything, I can do against his magic."

"Have you not been studying the Grimoire of Honorious with Brian?" Shannon asked.

"I have," said Brewster, "but this magic stuff is not exactly something you can pick up overnight. And apparently, if you try to rush it and overreach yourself, it can be very dangerous. The other night I tried a simple fire spell before I was really ready and I burned one of the big tapestries in the great hall by accident. Brian gave me quite a stern lecture."

"Do the best you can, Doc," Shannon said. " 'Tis all any man can do. You have already done more than enough. 'Tis past time for the rest of us to do our part."

"What do you think Warrick's been doing all this time?" asked Brewster.

"Well, Warrick is not the only one with spies," said Harlan. "We've sent the Awful Urchin Gang as spies to Pittsburgh. However, they report that no one has seen Warrick recently. He has not left his Alabaster Tower, and there is no way of telling what he may be up to in there."

"Up to no good, that much is for certain," Mac said with a

grimace. "Still, there is no point in worrying about things we cannot control. He may be preparing spells to aid his army, but we shall have a few tricks up our sleeves, as well."

"I hope so," Brewster said as he watched Mick and his apprentices working on the armor plating for the tank. "I surely hope so."

By now, you're probably wondering what became of Warrick since he vanished in Brewster's time machine. Has he been transported to some limbo, doomed to remain forever trapped between dimensions and thereby written out of the story? Well, in a word, no. Much as I would have liked to have done something like that, I'm afraid it would have been anticlimactic. That wouldn't have satisfied you, would it? No, some of you would have thrown the book across the room and sworn never to buy anything I wrote again, others would have written me angry letters, calling me to task for being sloppy and taking the easy way out; and a few of you, I'm sure, would have come up to me at one of the conventions I attend and read me the riot act, telling me how you would have handled the situation better if you'd been in my place.

Well, never fear, your faithful narrator has not fallen down on the job. I may not have started this book off as smoothly as I'd have liked and I may have lost control a few times here and there, and I may have whined and bitched a bit about how frustrating life can be when you're a writer, but hey, that's just the sort of thing that brings us closer together, right?

No, huh? Well, okay, maybe not. But haven't I always told you to trust your narrator? Haven't I gotten us all this far without any major mishaps? All right, the occasional expository lump and authorial intrusion notwithstanding, we've made it to this point, haven't we? I mean, we're about three quarters of the way through the story, the big war is coming up, the subplots with Colin and Pamela have come together, we've found out that Queen Sandy is more than just another pretty face . . . well, that counts for something, doesn't it?

Okay, okay, so you want to know what happened to Warrick. The fact is, he really had me by the short and curlies. I can't tell you how many hours I spent sitting at my trusty Apple Mac, staring at the screen and trying to come up with some way to do him in that wouldn't completely screw up the story. I'd go to bed at night and lie awake for hours, wishing to God that I could get some sleep, but all I could think about was Warrick. Believe me, lying there at four-thirty in the morning, tossing and turning and staring at the ceiling, wondering why I ever decided to do this for a living, I knew exactly how Dr. Victor Frankenstein must have felt. I had created a monster and I couldn't figure out a way to get rid of him.

The worst thing about it was that I had laid the ground rules for my own dilemma. I had made Warrick a mighty wizard with no effective limitations to his powers—or his ambition—and I had given him the ability to stymie all my efforts to control him. Now, this might sound a little silly to some of you, but the fact is, a writer has to *believe* in his characters. It says so in all those books on writing you see in the stores. I believed in Warrick, and so his magic worked on me. And when he came up with a spell to prevent me from writing him out of the story, there was simply nothing I could do about it. I knew it was only a matter of time before he devised a spell that would allow him to take over the book completely. And what's more, he knew it, too. But there was one thing he *didn't* know.

Having cast a spell to prevent himself from being written out of the story, he thought he had me beaten. He knew I couldn't kill him off and he thought that by wearing me down and forcing me to show him the secret of the time machine, he could cross the boundaries between the dimensions of reality and nonreality and confront me where I lived. Well, no thanks. I've got enough problems with reality as it is. So guess where he wound up?

Pamela inserted her EnGulfCo Security ID into the machine to open the steel doors, then pulled her Jaguar E-type into the parking garage. It was late and everyone had long since gone home. She parked the car in her reserved space by the elevators and they got out. She gave Hightower a quick once over.

"Button up your raincoat," she told him. "No self-respecting scientist would wear anything like that frantic sport jacket of yours."

"Well, we can't all shop in Savile Row," said Colin, wryly.

"In your case, Skid Row is more like it," Pamela replied.

"Cute," said Colin.

"Now remember, if we're challenged, let me do all the talking," Pamela said.

"What if someone asks me something?" asked Megan.

"Don't answer," Colin said. "Just roll your eyes and look impatient. Let Pamela handle everything."

They got into the elevator and Pamela pressed the button for the top floor, just beneath the penthouse. As the doors slid shut and the elevator started to ascend, a voice came over a concealed speaker.

"Good evening, Dr. Fairburn. Working late again tonight?"

"No rest for the weary," Pamela replied with a smile. "Is that you, Jerry? How's everything tonight? Keeping it all safe for queen and country?"

The guard on duty at the station chuckled. "All locked up tight. Who is that with you, Doc?"

"Dr. Simmonds and Dr. Radinski."

"They're not on staff here, are they?"

"No, but they're consulting with me on a special research project up at the lab."

"I see." There was a slight pause. "I'm sorry, Dr. Fairburn, but I don't seem to have a clearance registered for them."

"Really? Are you sure?"

"I'm afraid so. I've double-checked."

"Well, that can't be right," said Pamela. "Dr. Davies told me earlier this afternoon that he'd taken care of it personally."

"I'm sorry, Dr. Fairburn, but there's no record of that on the computer."

"Oh, bloody hell," said Pamela in an irate tone. "He told

me he was going to take care of it himself. He must have given it to that new secretary of his, Miss Legs and Busoms." Pamela grimaced. "That woman is a bloody disaster. This is the third time she's dropped the ball on something relating to this project. It's simply insufferable."

"Well, I'm sorry, but I'm afraid I'll have to ask you to check in at the station," the security guard said. "We can give Dr. Davies a call at home and sort this thing out."

"Yes, I suppose—oh, Christ," said Pamela. "We can't reach Dr. Davies at home tonight. He told me he was leaving early for a weekend of fishing in the country." She turned to Colin and Megan. "I'm really sorry, this is all terribly embarrassing."

Colin merely nodded for the benefit of the hidden video camera while Megan shook her head and tapped her foot impatiently.

"Look, Jerry, we're on a very tight schedule here. Dr. Simmonds and Dr. Radinski have a late flight to catch at Heathrow in about"— she glanced at her watch,—"three and a half hours. That's barely enough time for us to go over . . . well, I can't really discuss it, you understand. I was fortunate to catch them at the Defense Ministry this afternoon and they've both got to be in Washington by tomorrow morning. If we miss this opportunity, it could set the project back by months and Dr. Davies will have an embolism."

"Well . . . I shouldn't really be doing this, you understand," said Jerry, "but seeing as it's you, Dr. Fairburn, I guess it'll be all right this time."

"You're a lifesaver, Jerry, thank you. But I want you to be sure to mention in your log that we had a problem with this."

"Uhm . . . if it's all the same with you, Dr. Fairburn, I'd really rather not, because then my supervisors will want to know why I skipped procedure. That, uh, could make things rather sticky."

"Right, of course," said Pamela. "Well, I certainly wouldn't want to cause you any problems, particularly since you're being such a dear about this. I'll just speak to Dr. Davies privately. That new secretary of his has simply got to go, but there's no reason to involve you. We'll just keep this between ourselves.'

"I appreciate that, Dr. Fairburn," said Jerry. "Well, have a good night then. I'll see you on the way out."

"Thank you, Jerry." She turned to Colin and Megan. "I apologize for this."

Colin simply shrugged. They rode the rest of the way up in silence, then stepped out on the top floor. Hightower noted the security cameras outside the elevator and in the hallway, and the security station, now unmanned, by the elevator leading to the penthouse.

"That was very well done," he said in a low voice.

"Relax, the corridors aren't wired for sound. But we're not out of the woods yet," said Pamela. "Getting in is only half the problem. Smuggling Marvin's notes out is going to be the trick."

"You think your friend Jerry's going to insist on searching us?" asked Colin.

"It's standard procedure for everyone working in a restricted area," said Pamela, indicating the unmanned security station with a nod. "During the day, there's always a guard stationed there, and there are checkpoints at every floor with restricted access. Not much goes on here at night, so they just use a skeleton crew. With all the surveillance equipment they have installed, they can monitor the whole building from the central station just off the lobby. Jerry's a good man, but he's already bent the rules by allowing you up without a registered clearance, merely on my say so. If I tried to get us out without checking in with him, I'd be pushing my luck."

"What if we're in a big rush to make our so-called flight to Washington?" asked Colin.

"It could be worth a try," said Pamela as she pressed her palm against the scanner panel of the elevator to the penthouse, "but Jerry's not a fool. EnGulfCo doesn't hire run-of-the-mill security personnel. They're all either former police officers or executive protection specialists. And some are former military. They're all very well paid. I told Jerry we have a limited amount of time, but he'll become suspicious if I press the issue. I know what the procedures are. And going through security on the way out wouldn't take more than a few minutes, anyway, so he'll want to know why I'm avoiding it."

"Okay," said Colin, "just how complete is the security check on the way out?"

"All personal baggage such as purses and briefcases are examined, and there's a body search," said Pamela.

"Are there any female security personnel on duty at this time?" asked Colin.

"No, I don't think so," Pamela replied. "Why?"

"I've got a miniature spy camera in my coat pocket," Colin said. "We could simply photograph what we need, and then conceal the camera. I can think of a good place to hide it. On a woman, that is."

Pamela stared at him. "Surely, you don't mean . . . "

"Well, I'm trying to be somewhat delicate about this," Hightower replied. "We could have Megan do it, but I think you'd be a safer bet. I doubt your friend Jerry would get that personal with you."

The elevator arrived and they stepped inside. Pamela simply stared at him, and her look conveyed exactly what she thought of his suggestion. Colin merely shrugged.

They got out at the penthouse and Pamela placed her palm against the scanner, then punched in the special entrance code. The laboratory doors opened automatically and they went inside. Almost immediately, Pamela halted in her tracks and caught her breath.

"What is it?" Colin asked.

Sitting in the center of the lab was the duplicate time machine she had constructed from Brewster's plans, an exact copy in every detail save that it was nonfunctional without the Buckminsterfullerine inside the torus that encircled it. And beside it was an absolutely identical machine.

"It's a second time machine!" she said. "It's Marvin's! It has to be!" She rushed into the lab, glancing all around her. "Marvin? Marvin, darling, where are you?"

She came to an abrupt halt as a man stepped out from behind the machine. He looked perhaps in his late thirties or early forties, but his shoulder-length hair was snow-white. He wore white robes, a loose-fitting white tunic, white breeches, and white velvet boots.

"And who might you be?" he asked in a demanding tone.

Pamela stared at him, shocked speechless for a moment.

Megan gasped. "Warrick the White!" she said, cowering behind Hightower.

Warrick glanced at her and smiled. "I remember you," he said. "You were one of my experimental subjects, were you not?"

"What are you doing here?" demanded Pamela. "Where's Marvin? What have you done with him?"

Warrick turned toward her and raised his eyebrows. "I do not know who this Marvin may be, but who are you?"

"My name is Dr. Pamela Fairburn," she replied tensely, "and you are in a restricted area. If you don't tell me where Marvin is and what you've done with him, I'm going to call security and have you taken into custody!"

"That sounds rather threatening," said Warrick, unperturbed.

"Oh, I can do a lot more than threaten," Pamela replied, heading for the phone.

"Watch out!" cried Megan. "He is a fearsome sorcerer!"

"I don't care what the hell he is," said Pamela. She put her hand on the phone. "Are you going to answer my question or do we do this the hard way?"

"Pamela, wait," said Colin. "The last thing we want right now is security guards up here. Let's try to sort this out on our own first." He approached Warrick. "So, you're Warrick, eh?"

"Aye," said Warrick, looking Hightower up and down with a critical gaze. "And who are you?"

"The name's Hightower. Colin Hightower. I'm a reporter. And I've heard a great deal about you, sir." He held out his hand. Warrick glanced down, but refused to take it.

"Have you? And just what have you heard, and from whom?"

"I've spoken with some of the people you've been sending here, from wherever it is you came from," Hightower said. "The Alabaster Tower, is it? In Pittsburgh? In a land of twenty-seven kingdoms? You mind telling me why?"

"Perhaps not," said Warrick. "But first, I have a few questions of my own that I want answered. I have only just arrived here and I would like to know exactly where I am. What is this place?"

"Fair enough. It's Dr. Marvin Brewster's research laboratory in the headquarters building of EnGulfCo International, in London, England," Hightower replied, and then added, "in the twentieth century."

"Brewster?" Warrick said, his eyes narrowing. "Brewster Doc?"

"Dr. Brewster, that's right," said Colin.

"Where is he?" Pamela demanded. "Is he all right? Have you seen him?"

"Oh, I would like very much to see him," Warrick replied, "but I have some other matters to attend to first. Where is the Narrator?"

"Who?" asked Pamela with a frown.

"The Narrator," repeated Warrick. "The voice in the ether. The demigod who governs this ethereal plane."

"I have no idea what you're talking about," said Pamela. "But you are illegally in possession of highly classified equipment, and you have gained unauthorized entry into a restricted area. That's enough right there to put you in prison for a very long time, so I strongly suggest that you cooperate or else suffer the consequences."

Megan made a soft whimpering sound behind Colin and shut her eyes.

"For a wench, you are exceedingly arrogant," said Warrick. "I take it you are in some position of authority here. Well, thus far, I have been tolerant, but there is a limit to my patience. I wish to see the Narrator at once. You will send word to him that Warrick Morgannan has arrived and demands an immediate audience."

"Now just hold on a minute, friend," said Colin, stepping between them. "I don't think you fully understand your situation. You're way out of line here. Now why don't we just—"

Warrick raised his hand in a sorcerous gesture and quickly mumbled a spell under his breath. Absolutely nothing happened.

"I beg your pardon?" Colin said. "I didn't catch that."

Warrick frowned, raised his hand once more, and gestured toward Colin dramatically, repeating the spell with no more result than the first time. (God, I love this . . .)

"Now see here, old chap," said Colin irritably, "I don't like people waving their hands in my face, and I didn't particularly care for the tone of that remark, whatever it was."

Warrick raised both hands high above his head, shouted out the spell at the top of his lungs, and swept his arms down at Colin, fingers splayed, inches from his face.

"Right, that does it," Colin said, and he cracked Warrick across the jaw with a right hook. The wizard crumpled to the floor, unconscious.

"That was constructive," said Pamela, wryly. "Now what?"

"You struck him down!" said Megan with astonishment. "You struck down Warrick the White, the mightiest sorcerer in all the twenty-seven kingdoms!"

"I don't care who the bloody hell he is," said Colin, gazing down at Warrick's prostrate form. "No one takes that kind of tone with me."

Pamela headed for the time machine in which Warrick had arrived.

"What are you doing?" Colin asked.

"Checking the temporal chronometer settings," Pamela replied as she got in. "I should be able to reset and return to his departure point."

"Now wait a moment," Colin said uncertainly. "Surely, you're not thinking of taking off in that thing!"

"Marvin is still back there," Pamela said as she started up

the engines. "And he'll be trapped permanently unless I go back for him."

"I'm going, too!" said Megan, rushing toward the machine. "I want to go home!"

"All right, get in," said Pamela. "I won't know my way around and I'm going to need some help in finding Marvin."

"Hold it!" Colin shouted over the noise of the engines. "You can't just leave! What about him? And what am I supposed to do?"

"He's not going anywhere," Pamela shouted back, over the rapidly rising whine of the engines. "Security will take care of him. Tell them what's happened."

"Tell them *what*?" Colin shouted. "That you've gone back in time to get your boyfriend? They'll throw me in the loony bin and leave me there to keep my mouth shut! Besides, if you think I'm missing out on this, you're crazy! It'll be the story of the century! Move over! I'm coming with you!"

"There's no room!"

"Megan can sit on my lap!"

"All right, I'm not going to argue. I'll need all the help I can get. Get in!"

Hightower got into the machine and readjusted the safety straps so that he could slip them over both himself and Megan as she sat on his lap, leaning back against him. "This isn't going to hurt or anything, is it?" he asked.

"I haven't the faintest idea," Pamela replied. "I've never done this before."

"Oh, Lord. Are you sure you know what you're doing?"

"All I need to do is throw this switch here when that indicator moves into the red."

"And then?"

"And then hold on to your hat!"

"Oh, Jesus . . ."

She threw the switch.

NINE

Well, your faithful narrator feels more in control now. Warrick has finally been neutralized. As we all know, magic doesn't work in modern London, for if it did, England would still have an empire and the royal family would probably be having a lot less trouble. Fortunately, Warrick did not suspect his powers would be useless in our world, otherwise your faithful narrator would be in a considerable pickle. As it is, Warrick is now trapped in London, at EnGulfCo headquarters, with no way of getting back home. And that means he can't interfere with this story anymore, to my immense relief.

In a short while, Jerry the security guard will realize that more than four hours have gone by since Pamela told him her consulting colleagues had to catch a flight from Heathrow Airport and he'll call upstairs to see if everything's all right. Warrick will not pick up the phone, because although he'll certainly have regained consciousness by then, he has no idea what a telephone is and he'll be baffled by the mysterious ringing noise. When Jerry gets no answer, he'll call in the alarm and discover that Dr. Davies, the head of EnGulfCo R and D, hadn't left for a fishing weekend in the country after all. Dr. Davies will immediately rush to the lab, where the reprogrammed palm scanner will admit him and a detachment of security and they'll find Warrick, take him into custody, and subject him to a long and strenuous interrogation.

Now, I realize that by telling you all this, I'm violating one of the cardinal rules of writing. Ask any of my students, and they'll say I always teach them that a good writer should *show*, not tell. However, I also teach them that good writers should avoid authorial intrusion, and I've already blown that all to hell and gone. But you see, this is the sort of thing that happens when you decide to push the limits of the envelope, as they say in *The Right Stuff*. The author of that book, Tom Wolfe, did it when he invented the New Journalism in *The Kandy-Kolored Tangerine Flake Streamline Baby* and Hunter Thompson did it when he invented Gonzo Journalism in *The Kentucky Derby Is Decadent and Depraved*. (Actually, he didn't really "invent" Gonzo Journalism, it was more like a freak accident, but that's another story and we've already gotten ridiculously sidetracked.)

The point is, I wanted to experiment with "Fantastic Metafiction," because I learned in grad school that this is what you do when you want college professors to take you seriously. You write something really weird and come up with a multisyllabic label for it—like "Literary Deconstructionism"—and then you become the acknowledged expert in that field, because nobody but you can understand what the hell you're doing. So, to explain it, you write articles for *The English Journal* and you give talks at academic conferences and then you write grant proposals to get money to conduct intensive research in this new field you've just invented. This is called "getting tenure."

Anyway, I'm getting sidetracked yet again. The point I'm trying to make is . . . what the hell *was* the point I was trying to make? Oh, yeah, right. I was trying to invent this new literary form and it just sort of got away from me. But . . . that's okay. That's part of it. That's the very nature of "Fantastic Metafiction." It's what was *supposed* to happen. Yeah . . . that's it, that's the ticket . . .

I could have chosen to write the scene where Warrick gets captured and interrogated, and actually show it happening, because I'd dearly love to see old Warrick squirm after all the trouble he has caused me, but the fact is it wouldn't really advance the main plot of the story and we'd only wind up getting bogged down in nonessential details (which is what I'm doing right now, come to think of it, but hey, that's how "Fantastic Metafiction" works. It's a technique known as . . . uh . . . "Narrative Transcendentalism." Yeah, right, that's it. I'll explain it more fully in the essay I'm planning to write for *The English Journal*). However, if we have a chance, we will drop in on Warrick once again, because it's not good storytelling to leave subplots unresolved.

Speaking of which, some of you may be wondering whatever became of all the people Warrick had teleported to our world with Brewster's time machine. Well, we don't really have the time to get into all the individual case histories, otherwise this book would be a Robert Jordan novel, so we'll simply look at a representative sampling.

Those of you who have been with us from the beginning will recall the dotty old wizard known as Blackrune 4, to whom the brigands sold the time machine after they discovered it in the Redwood Forest. Why does he have the number 4 after his name, you ask? Well, if you'd read the first installment of this metafictional adventure (*The Reluctant Sorcerer*, Warner Books), you'd already know that, but for those of you who haven't, it was because the Sorcerers and Adepts Guild registers all mage names, and there were already three other wizards named Blackrune, 1 through 3, respectively, registered with the guild. It was Blackrune 4 who had first stumbled on a magic spell to activate the time machine by tapping into its temporal field. He was teleported to Los Angeles, where his magic wouldn't work and he wound up becoming part of the homeless population. He met a lot of other homeless people who found him absolutely fascinating and made him into a sort of street guru, which resulted in his being featured in a PBS documentary about the homeless. A Hollywood producer saw the program and it gave him an idea for a sitcom called *Street Smarts*. Blackrune was found and hired as a consultant for the show, which starred George Carlin in his second series television venture, and it became an instant ratings hit. Blackrune 4 changed his name to George R.R. Blackrune, renegotiated his contract, and is now one of the show's executive producers, with a house in Sherman Oaks, a regular table at Spago's, and a Mercedes Benz convertible in his garage.

Blackrune's young apprentice, who delivered the time machine to Warrick and became his first test subject, wound up in New York, where he lived on the streets for a while until he took up with a nineteen-year-old performance artist who introduced him to all her friends in the East Village arts community. He adopted the name Johnny Snot, got a gig as a lead singer with a heavy metal band called STD, and their last CD, *Another Time, Another Place*, just went triple platinum.

Remember the Pittsburgh hooker who was teleported on stage in the middle of an Allman Brothers concert in Georgia? Well, after becoming hysterical on stage behind a mike, tearing her hair and wailing about going back home, she was given a five-minute standing ovation and hailed as a great white blues artist. She got a recording contract with Atlantic Records, got a great write-up in *Rolling Stone* after the debut of her first album, Shriek, then disappeared after giving birth to a beautiful blond baby boy. Rumor had it the father was Gregg Allman. Well, she and her son are now living in Arkansas, where she's happily married to a prosperous real estate broker who is currently under federal indictment for tax fraud.

One of Warrick's test subjects was teleported to Japan, where the urban density of Tokyo coupled with the sight of people unlike any race he'd ever seen and speaking a language he couldn't understand put his nervous system into overload. He ran hysterically through the streets, convinced he'd been transported to a world of demons, until he was finally apprehended by the Tokyo police. When questioned by an officer who spoke English, he fearfully told his story, which resulted in his being sent to a hospital for psychiatric observation, where he remained for about ten months. Once convinced no one would harm him, he stopped being violent and was allowed to mix with the other patients and watch television. This proved to be an immensely educational experience for him. He learned Japanese, discovered a great deal about our world, and was eventually released. However, having been a criminal in his own world, he naturally gravitated to what he knew best, and is now working as an enforcer for the Yakuza.

A great many of Warrick's test subjects wound up in various institutions, where some of them remain, perfectly content. However, most were eventually released. Television had made an immense difference in their lives and they have all more or less acclimated to their new environment. Many of them took correspondence courses and got their GEDs, and are now working in productive jobs in their communities. Some turned to crime, as they had in Pittsburgh, but most took advantage of the opportunities in their new world and started to build productive lives for themselves, working at such diverse occupations as short order cooks, highway construction workers, sanitation engineers, topless dancers, and postal service employees. One is now a deputy sheriff in Pima County, Arizona. Another is a popular veejay on MTV. Several became used-car salesmen and one, a former member of The Swindlers Guild, became a televangelist and is now running for Congress from the state of Louisiana. However, most of them, with the exception of Warrick's first few test subjects, had at least one thing in common—they were still under the spell of compulsion Warrick placed on them, directing them to return to him in his Alabaster Tower and tell of what they'd seen.

In many cases, drugs helped dull the uncontrollable compulsion. Given enough thorazine, even Godzilla would mellow out. The rest of them, however, were still driven by a relentless urge to reach the Alabaster Tower and tell Warrick what they'd seen. Unfortunately, there was really nothing they could do about it, save toss and turn all night and redirect the compulsion into such activities as overeating, gambling, alcoholism, sex addiction, and watching soap operas. Many of them wound up buying sets of Lego blocks and constructing large plastic white towers in their apartment living rooms, rather like Richard Dreyfus building a mountain out of mud in *Close Encounters of the Third Kind*. They were immensely frustrated, knowing there was no way they could get back home until one day something very strange happened to all of them simultaneously.

For no apparent reason they suddenly all felt compelled to

go to London. (Oh, by the way, did I mention that the EnGulfCo Corporate headquarters building was faced with white ferroconcrete slabs and known as "The White Tower?")

It was almost sunrise when Queen Sandy started heading back toward the castle. It had been a long and busy night. After leaving The Stealers Tavern, she had hurried to another end of town, not far from the market district, and a small stone coffeehouse and bakery known as The Smorgasbard. It was a place where one could partake of coffee and herbal infusions and a wide assortment of fresh baked bread and pastries while listening to bards regale the patrons all night long with their songs in exchange for gratuities dropped into their hats or instrument cases. The Smorgasbard was open until the wee hours of the morning, and was a popular gathering place for artists, bards, and craftsmen, as well as the occasional aristocrat. They even allowed filkers to perform. Their slogan was, "All the bards that you can stand."

On entering, Sandy pulled her hood closer around her face and headed straight for the door to the back room. She knocked three times, paused, then twice, then paused again, then once. A small panel set into the door at about eye level was slid aside and someone asked, "Who knocks?"

"One who seeks," Sandy replied, giving the password.

"Enter," said the voice, and the window slid shut. A moment later, the bolt was drawn and the door opened.

Sandy walked into the dimly lit back room, illuminated only by a few candles placed on a long table. There were no windows, and the walls were thick, ensuring privacy. The men and women seated around the table immediately got to their feet as she entered and pulled back her hood.

"Your Highness," said one of them, bowing politely and sweeping his hat from his head. He was middle-aged, with long, wavy brown hair, a luxuriant beard, and a wide, ruddy face. Beneath his dark cloak he wore a brown leather doublet, a lace-trimmed shirt, brown breeches, and high black boots. He also wore an extremely well-crafted sword.

"Good evening, Lord Aubrey," Sandy said, nodding to the other members of the Underground. "Please, let us dispense with formalities. Be seated, my friends. What news?"

"None that is good, I fear," Lord Aubrey replied, resuming his seat as Sandy took her place beside him. "The army is marching for Brigantium tomorrow. They have formed their own kingdom, separate from Darn, and apparently with King Durwin's support. His Majesty has received assurances of solidarity from all the other rulers—save King Durwin, who has sent no reply—but only three, King Vidor, King Alan, and King Rodney, have chosen to support his war with troops. Our forces have been augmented by six regiments of foot and three regiments of horse. It makes for a formidable army, the largest ever assembled in the twenty-seven kingdoms. Brigantium will never stand a chance."

Sandy sighed heavily. "I am the queen, and yet you know more about my husband's plans than I do," she said. "He never confides in me anymore."

"Your husband, madame, is a fool," one of the other men seated at the table said.

"Whatever he may be, Lord Edward, he is still your king, and I will demand you speak of him with respect," Sandy replied firmly.

Lord Edward merely inclined his head in response. Clearly, while Sandy commanded respect within the room, her husband, the king, did not.

"Let us be honest with one another, Your Highness," said Luke the Luthier, director of The Craftsman's Guild. "We all have our own reasons for being here. The aristocrats among us have lent their efforts to our cause because they see Warrick as a threat and they realize, with no disrespect intended to His Majesty, that the king simply lacks the capabilty to stand up to him. We commoners are here because with each passing day, our freedoms are eroded further and the people suffer more."

"You think I do not care about the people, Luke?" asked Sandy.

"No, Your Highness, clearly you do, and if you were on

the throne in place of your husband, I have no doubt the welfare of the people would be your first concern. But the fact remains that while your husband sits upon the throne of Pitt, Warrick and Sheriff Waylon rule in all but name. We had all hoped to avoid a violent revolution, but it may be the only answer."

"You speak treason, Luke," Sandy said.

"My lady, may I remind you that you are committing treason yourself by the mere fact of your presence here," the soft-spoken luthier replied.

Sandy compressed her lips into a tight grimace. "Well, I will have you know that I have just come from a meeting with two of the prime movers behind this revolution, and what I have learned may change your mind."

"You met with them *yourself?*" Lord Aubrey said with astonishment.

"I have met with them on several occasions," Sandy replied. "But you may relax, Lord Aubrey. They do not suspect who I really am."

"Still, the danger to you—"

"Is not as great as you may think," Sandy said, cutting him off. "However, 'tis not the point. The point is that The Stealers Guild foments this revolution merely to advance their own criminal purposes. If it succeeds, then they shall benefit from the removal of Sheriff Waylon and the period of disorder that is bound to follow until proper rule can be restored. And if it fails, then they shall take advantage of the fighting to line their pockets unmolested, for they have taken care to see that others will take the blame when it is ended. They have lit the fire, and now it has gathered its own momentum. Those who are vocal as the leaders of this revolution are but the unknowing pawns of The Stealers Guild. The support they now receive from them will quickly fade the moment anything goes wrong. And you may rest assured it will go wrong."

"With the army marching for Brigantium, what is to stop it?" one of the others asked. "They leave behind only the palace guard, augmented by some soldiers."

"And what do you suppose will happen when the army returns?" Lord Aubrey said. "The king may be deposed, and Sheriff Waylon and his deputies lynched by the mob, but Warrick will take care to keep himself protected, even if the mob does gather up the nerve to storm his tower, which I strongly doubt. Warrick will merely sit back and let it all happen, and when the army returns from Brigantium, they will seize power effortlessly and place Warrick on the throne. The crafty wizard has played his hand extremely well. He has convinced the king to send the army to put down this outlaw mage, whom Warrick fears as a rival to his power, and at the same time, the absence of the army tempts those who would plot against the king to action. With one move, Warrick seizes power and consolidates it."

There was silence in the room as they all saw the logic of Lord Aubrey's remarks.

"What are we to do, then?" someone asked.

"I can think of but only one solution, for the present," Sandy said. "We must abduct the king."

"*What?*" said Luke with disbelief.

"My husband does not wish to see the truth," said Sandy. "He must be made to see it. The revolution will doubtless come soon after the army marches on Brigantium. The palace will be their first objective. If they seize the king, his life is surely forfeit. But what if they cannot find the king? When the army returns and puts down the rebels, Warrick will not be able to assume the throne so long as the king lives. Then he will be seen as a usurper, and as such, will never gain support from any of the other kingdoms."

"True," Lord Aubrey said, nodding in agreement. "The other rulers would be fools to sanction such a blatant seizure of power. They would be forced to unite against him, if only to safeguard their own positions."

"A clever plan to save your husband, Highness," Luke said softly. "And once he is back upon the throne, what will have changed?"

Sandy gave him a hard look. "If you think I propose this plan merely to save my husband's life, then you have learned nothing about me since I joined you. He is my husband and my king, and I will do my duty by him. But I am also queen, and I have a duty to my people. My presence here is evidence of that. If I cannot prevent the revolution, then I shall do my utmost to prevent the people suffering from its results. If you can think of a better plan, then I am sure we are all eager to listen."

Luke looked down and remained silent.

"Fine then," Sandy said. "There is little time to waste. Now here is what I propose . . . "

"I think I'm going to be sick," said Hightower with a moan.

"Then let me up first," Megan said quickly, fumbling with the safety straps and jumping out of the machine.

"Where are we?" Pamela asked, looking around at the room in which they had materialized.

"Warrick's sanctorum, in the Alabaster Tower," Megan said. "We're home, in Pittsburgh!"

"Well, you're home, maybe," Pamela said as she got out of the machine and looked around. "But as a little girl named Dorothy once said, 'I have a feeling we're not in Kansas anymore.'"

The walls around them in the circular chamber were all constructed of large blocks of heavy, mortared, pale white stone. The floor was made of thick wood planks. The furnishings were well made, but crude by modern standards, fastened together with wooden pegs instead of nails. The windows in the thick walls were arched and shuttered. Everywhere Pamela looked, there were piles of ancient, leather-bound vellum books and rolled-up scrolls, just stacked wherever there was room. The tables and shelves were covered with ceramic jars and glass beakers containing dried herbs and powders and other unidentifiable objects, some of which looked like specimens from a pathology lab. There was a large carved desk that held a human skull, turned brown with age, with a hole in the top to hold a candle. Pamela examined some items spread out on what appeared to be an altar. There were candles of several colors, a large silver chalice, several cauldrons of varying sizes, amulets holding precious stones, ceramic bowls, ritual knives and crystals, oils and unguents and jars of powdered incense along with a mortar and a pestle.

"This looks like a set for a bloody horror film," said Pamela.

"If you think it looks strange in here, take a look outside," said Hightower, standing by a window.

Pamela came up beside him. What she saw made her gasp. The tower was built upon a hill, and spreading out below them was a medieval city, with several main avenues paved with cobblestones and twisting, narrow side streets and back alleys. The buildings were all constructed of wood and mortared stone, and the people moving through the streets were dressed in tunics and loose breeches, with thick leather belts and woolen cloaks. Several horse-drawn wagons rolled through the streets, containing wooden barrels and hay and produce from outlying farms. Nearby and to their left, rising high above the surrounding buildings, was a stone castle, complete with moat and drawbridge, walls and battlements and crenellated towers. It was shortly after sunrise. The city was slowly coming awake.

"If I wasn't seeing this with my own eyes, I'd never believe it," said Hightower. "It works, Pamela! We've actually gone back through time! We're in London in the Middle Ages!"

Pamela scanned the horizon. She frowned and shook her head. "No, I don't think so," she said. "The Thames should be over there," she said, pointing. "Where is it? And look at those mountains in the distance. We're not in London. We're somewhere else entirely."

"You're right," said Hightower. "But where?"

Pamela shook her head. "I don't know," she said. "But Marvin's here, somewhere. He's got to be."

"Are you sure this is the same place he went back to?" Colin asked.

"That man, Warrick, came from here," Pamela replied.

"This is his home, apparently. And he had Marvin's time machine. The question is, how did he get his hands on it?"

"Look," said Colin hesitantly, "I don't want to rain on your parade, but I think you should consider the possibility that something may have happened to him."

"I know," said Pamela. "I've already thought of that, believe me. It's been over a year since Marvin disappeared. But I can't give up until I know for sure."

"I understand," said Colin. "But now that we're here—wherever 'here' is—we need to make a plan." He glanced back at the time machine. "That thing's our only way back home. How do we know it's safe to leave it here while we go out looking for Brewster?"

"No one ever comes to Warrick's sanctorum," Megan said. "The people are afraid of this place. No one who's ever entered this tower has ever been seen again."

"Yes, and now we know why," said Pamela. She leaned out the window and looked to the left and right. "This tower doesn't appear connected to any other structure. But at the same time, except for the castle over there, it's the tallest building in the area. It seems hard to believe that just one person would be living here. Megan, what are we liable to find if we go out that door?"

"Warrick has his minions," Megan said. "They reside here in the tower, on the lower floors. Warrick's private living quarters are on the upper levels, but I have never seen them. I think no one has."

"Minions?" Colin said. "What do you mean?"

"Men-at-arms and servants," said Megan. "They dress in Warrick's colors, a white surplice with a light blue band across it."

"You mean soldiers?" Pamela said. She glanced at Colin uneasily. "That could present a problem. How do we get past them?"

"Ever play poker?" asked Hightower.

"You mean bluff?" said Pamela, uncertainly. "We don't even know what we're doing."

"Leave it to me," said Colin. "I'm an old hand at this sort

of thing. Look, Warrick's stuck back in our own time, right? Without that machine, there's no way he can get back here. So, instead of trying to sneak around, which always makes people suspicious, we put on a bold front instead and confront things head on. Warrick is some sort of royal sorcerer, right, Megan?"

"Aye, he is royal wizard to the King of Pitt," said Megan.

"That means he undoubtedly has some pull around here," Colin said. "So, since he's not here to contradict us, we'll simply claim he sent us here to take care of things while he's off in—what did he call it?—The ethereal plane?"

"Yes, I think that's what he said," Pamela replied. "But are you sure this is the smart thing to do?"

"It's our best chance," said Colin. "We're completely on our own here, and what we need more than anything right now is information. And these are primitive people, aren't they? It shouldn't be too difficult to pull the wool over their eyes."

Pamela took a deep breath and exhaled heavily. "I hope you're right. But it's going to be very risky."

"Risky?" Colin said, raising his eyebrows. "Are you joking? We've just traveled back in time, for God's sake, and we don't even know for certain where we are. Just how much more risky can things get?"

"I think from here on in, the risk is only going to escalate," said Pamela wryly. "But your suggestion's worth a try. We're simply going to have to make things up as we go along."

"Right," said Colin. "Okay, Megan, I want you to go out there and find whoever's in charge around here and tell him . . . hmm, let's see . . . just tell him Warrick wants him to report here at once. We'll just improvise from there. Go on, now. And be firm. Act as if you're carrying out Warrick's personal instructions."

"Very well," she said, and turned to go.

"Megan, wait," said Pamela.

She turned around.

Pamela moistened her lips nervously. "You . . . you will come back, won't you?"

Megan looked startled, and then she looked a little hurt. "Colin helped me get out of that awful place they kept me in," she said, "and you helped me get back home. Did you really think I would be so selfish and ungrateful as to leave you in the lurch?"

"I . . . I'm sorry, Megan," Pamela replied. "It's just that . . . well, I must confess, I'm more than a little bit afraid."

"Warrick is no longer here," said Megan, "so there is far less reason to be afraid. And now that I have seen him and returned to his tower, the compulsion he had placed upon me is gone. I will return to help you. I promise."

She turned and went out the door.

"Don't worry, she'll be back," said Colin. "She may seem a bit erratic, but she's a good girl."

"Well, in that case, I hope you're a good poker player," Pamela replied. She took out a pack of cigarettes and her lighter, and stared at them ruefully for a moment. "I'd quit smoking, you know. I started again when Marvin disappeared. I suppose I'll be giving it up again. I don't imagine I'll be able to buy any cigarettes here."

"Hold on a moment," said Colin. "Don't light up yet."

"What? Why not?"

"I've got an idea. Give me your lighter."

Puzzled, she handed it over.

"Let me have one of those cigarettes."

She shook one out and handed it to him.

"Take one and hold it between your thumb and middle finger, like this," he said, demonstrating, holding it so that his palm was cupped around it. She followed his example. "When Megan comes back, just follow my lead. I may not know my history all that well, but tobacco was a New World crop, wasn't it? It was never seen in Europe until old Sir Walter Raleigh started shipping it back home. So chances are these people have never seen cigarettes."

Pamela smiled as understanding dawned. "Very clever," she said.

"You just need to start thinking like a con man," Colin replied. "Anything we can do to play on these people's superstitions is only going to strengthen our position. You still have that pistol, don't you?"

"Yes, it's in my purse."

"Good. How many bullets do you have?"

"A full magazine, less one round," she replied. "And I always carry a spare, so that makes a total of thirteen."

"Well, we'll have to be very sparing of them," Colin said. "We don't know how long we're liable to be here. What else have you got in that purse?"

"My compact, a lipstick, keys, wallet, checkbook and change purse, some . . . some feminine things, a packet of facial tissues, an electronic organizer, a penlight, two ballpoints, a pocket tape recorder, a small canister of Mace, a rape whistle . . . can't be too careful, you know. Oh, and a small pocket knife, one of those Swiss Army things. Marvin gave it to me for a present."

"Regular Girl Scout, aren't you?" Colin said with a grin. "Let me see that tape recorder."

She took it out and handed it to him.

"Right," said Colin. "Now let's see if we can't prepare a small demonstration of our 'supernatural powers,' shall we?"

A short while later, there was a knock at the door.

Colin quickly lit their cigarettes. "Enter," he said imperiously.

The door opened and Megan came in with the captain of Warrick's personal guard.

"I have brought the minion you summoned, my lord," said Megan with a deep curtsy.

The captain of the guard stared at them uncertainly, taking in their strange clothes, and then his eyes grew wide as he saw both of them exhale smoke through their nostrils.

"Kneel, mortal, and show proper respect for the astral familiars of your master," said Colin, "or I shall burn you with my touch!" And with that, he snapped the cigarette lighter.

At the sight of the flame apparently emanating from Hightower's fingers, the captain dropped immediately to his knees and lowered his head. "Forgive me, my lord!" he said. "Do not burn me, I beg you! I . . . I did not know! The wench did not explain—"

"Silence!" Colin said.

The captain bit off his words and remained on his knees, his head lowered.

"Look at me," Colin commanded.

The captain swallowed hard and looked up, fearfully.

Colin put his hand into his jacket pocket and pushed the play button on the recorder. *"Shall I kill him now, Master? Shall I tear him limb from limb and feast upon his flesh?"*

The playback was his own voice doing a rather poor Peter Lorre impression, but it served its purpose admirably. The captain gasped and his eyes bulged. He turned white as a ghost and started shaking.

"Nay, Unseen One," Colin said theatrically. "There will yet be time for you to feast on human flesh. We have need of this one."

"I . . . I beg you . . . do not harm me, Lord!" the captain stammered, gazing wildly around him for the source of the disembodied voice.

Colin hit the playback once again. *"This one seems a poor servant for our purpose. Perhaps we should feast on him and find another."*

"Please, Unseen One! Stay your hand!" the captain cried. "I shall do whatever you ask! Give me but a chance to prove myself!"

Colin raised his hand to his chin, as if in thought, and took a deep drag on the cigarette he had cupped in his palm. He exhaled a long stream of smoke through his nostrils. "What is your name, worthless one?"

"I am Ivor, captain of the royal wizard's guard, my lord."

"Well, Captain Ivor, I bring a message from your master, Warrick," Colin said. "He has departed for the ethereal plane and sent us here to see to matters until his return. You and all here are to give us your unquestioning obedience, or suffer the fangs of the Unseen One. Do you understand?"

"Aye, my Lord, I shall do whatever you command!"

"Good," said Colin. He turned to Pamela. "Perhaps he will do."

"That remains to be seen," said Pamela, exhaling smoke.

"I have always served Lord Warrick faithfully! I shall prove myself worthy, Mistress," Ivor said. "I swear!"

"We shall see," said Colin. "Rise, Captain Ivor."

Ivor rose trembling to his feet, but kept his head lowered.

"What do you know of one called . . . Brewster?" Colin asked.

"The outlaw mage?" said Ivor. "I only know what people say, my lord. That he is a mighty wizard who works wonders and sets himself above all others. And I know he is my master's enemy. This very day, the army marches for Brigantium, to wage war upon his forces."

Pamela suppressed a gasp.

"Brigantium, you say?" said Colin quickly, before Pamela's alarm could be noticed by the soldier. "And where might that be? Remember, we are strangers to this world."

"Aye, of course, my lord. Brigantium lies to the west, near the foot of the Purple Mountains, about a week's journey hence by horse," the captain replied.

Pamela frowned, but Colin shook his head, forestalling any comment from her.

"And they march today, you say?" asked Colin.

"Doubtless, they have already departed, my lord," Ivor replied. "It is a mighty army King Billy has assembled, and victory is assured."

"I see," said Colin. "And the king is leading them?"

"Oh, no, My Lord," said Ivor. "King Billy lead an expedition into war? It is all he can do to find his way around the palace. The commander of the royal army, Lord Kelvin, leads the force, together with commanders sent with regiments from other kingdoms, and the mercenaries, who are led by one of their own number, a freebooter known as Black Jack."

"It sounds like quite an army," Colin said.

"It is, indeed, my lord. The largest ever assembled in the twenty-seven kingdoms. But Brigantium presents a threat that must be eliminated. The outlaw mage, Brewster Doc, is said to be a very mighty wizard, and a dangerous one."

"Listen to me, Ivor," Colin said. "Warrick has left strict instructions with us that this sorcerer, Brewster, is not to be harmed. He wants him alive."

"But . . ." Ivor looked worried. "But Lord Kelvin has sworn that he would return with the outlaw mage's head upon a pike!"

"That would make Warrick very angry," Colin replied as Pamela paled. "The wizard Brewster must not be harmed, under any circumstances."

"I fear that is not in my power to change, my lord," said Ivor, with a nervous swallow. "Only the king can issue such commands."

"I see," said Colin, trying to decide what to say next.

"Shall I summon the king to you, my lord?" asked Ivor.

Colin raised his eyebrows. "Summon the king? Is Warrick in the habit of doing that?"

"Lord Warrick sends word that he requests an audience," Ivor replied. "It is always made as a request, for the sake of appearances, but the king always comes whenever Lord Warrick sends for him."

"Well, then by all means send for him," said Colin. "But do not tell him who it is that summons him. Let him think it comes from Warrick. We would not wish to frighten him unduly."

"I understand, my lord. But . . . your pardon, my lord, I would not know who it is that summons His Majesty, in any case. How should I address your honored presences?"

"Our true names would sear your tongue should they ever pass your lips," said Colin, improvising. "However, you may address us as Lord Charles and Lady Diana. Those names will do as well as any others."

"Aye, my lord Charles," said Ivor. "I shall do as you command. Do I have your leave to send word to the king?"

"You do," said Colin. Then, as Ivor rose and started to back out of the room, he said, "Oh, and, Ivor . . . one more thing."

"Aye, my lord?"

"We could do with something to eat."

Ivor's eyes grew very wide and he swallowed hard. "Who . . . whom shall I fetch for your dinner, my lord?"

"Well, we shall try to refrain from consuming human flesh for the present," Colin replied. "In its place, some roasted animal flesh from your kitchens will suffice. Along with some vegetables, some bread, and some wine, perhaps?"

"It shall be done, my lord," said Ivor.

"Good. You may go."

Ivor backed, bowing, out of the room and Megan closed the door behind him, with a giggle.

"Charles and Diana?" Pamela said, raising her eyebrows.

"First thing that came to mind," said Colin, with a shrug. "Anyway, what difference does it make? That was a pretty good performance, if I do say so myself. I think we're off to a good start."

"A good start?" said Pamela. "Are you kidding? There's an army on the way to kill Marvin! What in the world has he gotten himself into? And what's all this about him being a sorcerer?"

"Makes sense, really, if you think about it," Colin said. "We just convinced old Ivor we were a couple of demons. Brewster probably did much the same sort of thing. And seeing as how he's a lot smarter than I am, I'm sure he did a much better job of it, all told. But it seems he's run afoul of the local power structure."

"That's putting it mildly," Pamela replied. "What are we going to do?"

"Well, the most important thing is not to panic. Act like you're completely in control. Attitude is everything when you're trying to con people. We're making pretty good progress. We've got Ivor terrified of us, we've got a rough idea of where Brewster is, we've snapped our fingers and the king is about to come running, and dinner's on the way. Not too shabby, really, considering we've barely been here half an hour."

"You're actually *enjoying* all this, aren't you?" Pamela said.

Hightower grinned. "It is a bit of a kick, isn't it?"

"This isn't a game, Colin. One mistake and we could easily wind up dead. I don't relish the idea of being burned at the stake."

"Oh, they don't burn people anymore," said Megan.

"Well, that's a relief," said Pamela.

"They draw and quarter them, hang them, or chop their heads off."

"I'm so glad you shared that," Pamela replied wryly. She glanced at Colin. "What are you going to tell the king?"

"I'm not quite sure yet," he replied. "It all depends on what sort of chap he is. Warrick apparently has the king under his thumb. Ivor's opinion of him certainly did not seem very high. If it proves accurate, then this whole thing may be a lot easier than we thought."

"Just don't get overconfident," said Pamela. "We're on a lucky streak so far. But lucky streaks run out."

"Believe me, I'm well aware of that," said Colin. "I've been on a streak of bad luck that's lasted damn near ten years, but I have a feeling all that's about to change. When I get back with this story, I'll be sitting on top of the world. I'll wind up editor of the bloody *New York Times*. Or maybe even *USA Today*."

"Let's worry about getting back in one piece first," said Pamela. "With Marvin. Somehow, we've got to get to this place Brigantium and find him before the army gets there."

"Well, now that we know where he is, we could simply take the time machine," said Colin. "If he's become some sort of famous wizard or whatever in Brigantium, he shouldn't be too difficult to find once we get there."

"There's just one problem," Pamela said. "I don't know how to get us there."

"What do you mean?"

"Exactly what I said. How do I program the destination? I can't just type in, 'Brigantium, at the foot of the mountains to the west.' I need specific coordinates. Aside from which, I'm not exactly certain how it works."

"What are you talking about?" said Colin. "You got us here."

"The *machine* got us here. I simply used the auto-return function of the program. If I alter the settings now, I'm not convinced I can reprogram the exact coordinates to get us back. I didn't design this system. Marvin did."

"But you're a cybernetics engineer," said Colin, with a frown.

"Yes, but Marvin's got his own way of doing things when it comes to computers. His mind works in a very strange way. The basic commands are easy, but the programming functions are like nothing I've ever seen."

"But you've read his notes. You've duplicated his machine."

"I've duplicated the hardware, but it's not functional," Pamela replied. "I know Marvin better than anybody else, and I've still got migraines trying to decipher his notes. He's totally nonlinear. Part of it was on the paper, and part of it was in his head. And I have no idea how to duplicate the software. Given enough time, I might be able to figure it all out, but even then there's no guarantee I'd get it right."

"Well, now wait a minute," Colin said. "What is it you're saying? You mean . . . you don't know how to get us *back*?"

"Oh, I can get us back, all right," she said, "so long as we don't alter the programmed settings."

"But . . . you can check them, can't you? I mean, can't you just bring them up on the screen and copy them down or something?"

"It's not that simple. If I changed them and then didn't reenter them exactly the right way, there's no telling what could happen. At best, it simply wouldn't work. At worst, we could wind up in outer space or something."

"Well, that's just bloody marvelous, isn't it?" said Colin. "Why didn't you tell me this before?"

"Look, I didn't twist your arm to come along, you know."

"Right. And where would you be now if I hadn't?"

"I must admit you've got a point there."

Colin exhaled heavily. "Well, we'll simply have to make sure no one mucks about with that thing and spins the dials on the combination. I don't imagine that will be too difficult. If nobody comes in here but Warrick's servants, then it's not too likely anyone would mess about with his things, his being the royal wizard and all. I suppose we could put the fear of God into old Ivor and have him and some of his soldiers guard it with their lives while we're gone, but the smart thing to do would be for us to stay right here."

"And what about Marvin?"

Colin shrugged. "Let the army bring him to us. We'll simply tell the king that Warrick wants him to send a message to his general that Brewster is to be taken alive and unharmed, and brought back here."

"And what if something happens to him during the fighting?" asked Pamela. "What if the message doesn't get through? We can't just sit here and do nothing. I'm not going to take that chance."

Colin sighed. "I was afraid you'd say that. Well, then I guess there's nothing else to do but set off for Brigantium and try to get there before the army does. We should be able to manage that. An army on the march doesn't move very quickly. I suppose we'll have to use horses, won't we?"

"I doubt they've got any helicopters," Pamela replied. "Can you ride?"

"I was on a pony once, when I was ten years old," said Colin. "Since then, my only relationship with horses has been betting on them."

"Then we'll have to see if we can get some sort of carriage," Pamela said.

"And an armed escort," Colin added. "I don't think traveling unprotected would be wise. We're not going for a ride through Hyde Park. We only have thirteen bullets, a can of

Mace, and a rape whistle. That's not exactly a formidable arsenal."

Pamela nodded. "No, it's not. I wish we'd had time to prepare for this trip."

"Bit late now. But leave it up to old Colin. I'll just record a couple of messages for His Majesty from our friend, the Unseen One. And you might get that rape whistle of yours out. A blast or two on it at the appropriate time could make for a nice effect."

Pamela shook her head. "The Unseen One, astral familiars, feasting on human flesh . . . where do you come up with this stuff?"

"Have you forgotten whom I work for?"

"Oh. Right."

"Relax. I'll get us through this. I've been in tight spots before. Trust me."

Pamela grimaced. "Whenever a man says, 'Trust me,' I grab a firm hold of my purse and cross my legs."

"Well, in this case, I don't happen to have an interest in either of those two commodities," said Colin. "Although I would keep a firm grip on that purse if I were you. It's about all we've got, aside from our wits."

"Perhaps we'd better look around and see if there's anything else here we can use," said Pamela.

"Take care," said Megan. "Warrick may have his possessions spell-warded. Wizards often do that."

"Spell-warded?" Pamela asked with a frown. "What's that?"

"Protected by magic," Megan replied. "If you touch any of his things, something terrible could happen."

"Don't be ridiculous, my dear," said Colin. "There's no such thing as magic."

"Well, then how do you suppose Warrick learned to use your chariot?"

"You mean the time machine?" said Colin. "He probably saw Brewster using it and copied what he did. Or else he simply experimented and threw a switch and—"

"He did no such thing," insisted Megan. "He never even

touched it. He stood ten feet away or more and spoke a spell and gestured."

"That's impossible," said Pamela.

"I swear 'tis true. He is a mighty sorcerer, I tell you, and all these"—she indicated the books and scrolls stacked everywhere,—"are his arcane spells and enchantments."

"Nonsense," Colin said. He put down the tape recorder he was holding and reached out to one of the stacks, picking up a leather-bound tome. "It's merely a lot of primitive superstition. See? I've touched this and absolutely nothing's happened." He glanced at the cover of the book. "The Grimoire of Honorious, eh? Sounds like something you'd buy in one of those New Age shops." He opened it.

There was a loud pop and a puff of smoke, followed by a metallic clang as Colin disappeared and a chamberpot fell to the floor where he stood.

"*Ow! Jesus bloody Christ!*" the chamberpot cried out in Colin's voice.

Pamela stared, wide-eyed with disbelief. "Oh, my God!"

"I told you," Megan said. "Now look what you've gone and done."

There was a pounding at the door.

Pamela looked toward the door, fearfully.

"My lord! 'Tis Ivor!"

"Now what do we do?" asked Megan.

Pamela took several deep breaths, trying to compose herself. "You'd better open it."

Megan opened the door and Ivor came rushing in, bending low as he dropped to one knee. "My lord, I rushed here as soon as I—" He looked around. "Where is my lord Charles?"

"Right here," said the chamberpot.

Ivor stared.

"Lord Charles has decided to change form," said Pamela quickly. "What news do you bring?"

"Terrible news, My Lady," Ivor said. "The king has been abducted!"

"*What?*"

"It occurred shortly before dawn, my lady," Ivor said. "Rebels had gained admission through a secret passageway unknown to the palace guard. It led to the queen's chamber. They overpowered the guards in the corridor and made off with the king and queen! The alarm has been given, and the palace guard is combing the city, searching for them. Sheriff Waylon has taken command in the king's absence and he requests an audience with my lord Warrick."

"Did you tell him Warrick wasn't here?"

"Nay, my lady, I did but do your bidding not to announce your presence. But what should I do? What should I tell the sheriff?"

Pamela thought fast. "Tell him nothing. The king and queen are none of our concern. We must make certain that the wizard Brewster is taken alive for Warrick, for those were his commands. Assemble an armed escort at once with provisions to take us to Brigantium. We will need swift horses." She glanced down at the chamberpot and swallowed hard, still unable to believe what had just happened. "Lord Charles will travel with me in his present form. But we must move quickly. Go!"

"Aye, my lady, as you command," said Ivor.

The moment he left the room, Pamela leaned against a table for support.

"That was quick thinking," said the chamberpot. "But what in the bloody hell happened to me?"

"I don't think you really want to know," said Pamela.

"Give me a hand," said the chamberpot. "I can't seem to get up."

"A hand?" said Pamela, shaking her head in dismay.

"Yes, give me your hand."

"All right, if you say so," Pamela replied. She reached down and picked him up.

"What . . . ?" said Colin. "How did you . . . ?"

"Prepare yourself for a shock," said Pamela. She carried him over to a small, ornate mirror mounted on the wall. "*This* is what happened to you," she said, holding him up to the mirror.

"*Holy shit!* It can't be! It's impossible! It's . . . it's some kind of trick!"

" 'Tis a spell of transformation," said the mirror. "You opened the Grimoire of Honorious, didn't you?"

Pamela stepped back from the mirror, startled.

"I'm having a bad dream," said the chamberpot.

Pamela slowly approached the mirror.

" 'Tis all right, I won't bite," the mirror said. "I am the Enchanted Mirror of Truth. How may I serve you?"

"I don't believe it," Pamela said. And then, involuntarily, she giggled. "Mirror, mirror on the wall, who's the fairest of them all?"

"Well, 'tis all relative, isn't it?" the mirror said. "Beauty is in the eye of the beholder. And there's much more to being beautiful than just a great body and a pretty face. There's a person's inner beauty to consider. Like, is she nice? Does she have a good personality? A sense of humor? A kind and understanding nature? I must admit, you score pretty well on those points. About an eight and half, I'd say."

"This can't be happening," said Pamela. "It's a two-way mirror. Who's there? Who's on the other side?"

"No one. Unless, of course, you mean the question in a metaphyscial sense, in which case, the answer would be rather lengthy and complex. The answer depends on which truth you seek, for as I told you, milady, I am the Enchanted Mirror of Truth."

Pamela shook her head. "Enchanted? But . . . that isn't possible. There's no such thing as magic!"

"Excuse me," said the chamberpot wryly, "you want to run that by me again?"

"This has to be some kind of hallucination," Pamela said. "Magic doesn't exist!"

"It does not exist in your world," said the mirror, "but it does in this one."

"In . . . this one?" Pamela said weakly. "What do you mean?"

"I think perhaps you'd better sit down," the mirror replied. "This could take a while."

TEN

Well, it looks as if things are coming to a head. Pamela has crossed the dimensional boundaries and is now in the same world as Brewster; Warrick is safely stuck in modern-day London, where he can no longer cause any trouble; Megan has found her way back home; and after years of sticking his nose into other people's business, Hightower has finally discovered that curiosity sometimes kills the cat . . . or in this case, turns it into a talking potty. It only goes to show that just when you think you've got things under control, life has a way of pulling the rug out from under you. The important thing is that I've finally got this story back on track. You see, I told you, always trust your narrator.

What? How did Colin happen to pick up a copy of the Grimoire of Honorious when Teddy stole it from Warrick and brought it to Brewster in the Bag of Holding? He had a spare copy, all right? Well, he had a spare crystal ball, didn't he? You mean to tell me you don't have duplicates among your favorite books? (Picky, picky, picky . . .)

The point is, Warrick had, indeed, spell-warded all his valuable possessions, and unlike Teddy, who knew the wards and canceled them before he stole the Bag of Holding, Hightower set off the magical ward the moment he opened the book. Now the same fate that had befallen Prince Brian has befallen him, and since opening the grimoire would only set off the spell again, Pamela can't help him by looking up the spell to change him back. Brewster could, of course, but neither Colin nor Pamela know that, yet. And Pamela's having enough problems just trying to deal with what the magic mirror told her.

Fortunately, the magic mirror *wasn't* spellwarded, because Warrick had not considered it a particularly useful possession. (Hah, thought you caught me on that one, didn't you?)

He had grown impatient with its equivocating, politically correct replies to all his queries, and so he had simply hung it on the wall and left it there, using it only on occasion to comb his hair or apply some magical disappearing salve to an outbreak of pimples. As a result, the mirror had grown terminally bored, and was only too happy to have someone finally ask it questions once again.

After a hearty, room-service dinner of roast venison and veggies provided by Warrick's staff, Pamela had Captain Ivor prepare some horses and saddlebags loaded with provisions. Then, together with an escort of half a dozen men-at-arms in Warrick's colors, she had set out for Brigantium, with Colin the Champerpot slung across her saddle and the magic mirror wrapped and safely packed away inside her bedroll. It was at least a week's ride to Brigand's Roost, and since she no longer had to worry about Colin being unable to ride, there was no need of a coach. Speed was of the essence if they were to beat the royal army, so they set off on horseback first thing after breakfast.

Meanwhile, King Billy was having a rather rude awakening. Over the recent months, Queen Sandy had taken to spending a great deal of time by herself, and they rarely slept together in the royal bedroom anymore. It seemed that everything he did made the queen angry and irritable. She was always complaining that he deferred too much to Warrick, and that his brother, Sheriff Waylon, was exceeding his authority and making himself more and more unpopular with the citizens of Pittsburgh. She complained that he was making the people pay too much taxes, that he didn't care about their welfare, and that, in general, he was a pretty piss-poor king.

All this only made Billy more stubborn and truculent, and he had taken to spending more and more time making grandiose plans for troop movements and strategies for the upcoming war. He would spend hours maneuvering his toy soldiers around on the sand table, updating his plans daily, and forwarding them to Lord Kelvin, the commander of the

royal army, who—being a man who knew his business—
promptly crumpled them up and threw them all away.

Now, with the royal army on the march against the upstart
new Kingdom of Brigantium, and Lord Kelvin promising
that with such a mighty force, a speedy victory was assured,
Billy was looking forward to basking in the glory of their
return. He wouldn't have anything to do with their victory,
of course, but it was *his* army and the credit would reflect on
him. He would have Lord Kelvin decorated, and there would
be a great parade—Billy simply loved parades—and the
people would be happy. The army would come back with
their spoils of war, Lord Kelvin would present Warrick with
the head of the outlaw wizard on a pike, and all this talk of
revolution would disappear. There was nothing like a war to
bring about national unity and lift people's spirits.

All in all, thought Billy, things were going very well.
Maybe Warrick would even be grateful enough to devise a
spell that would make the queen respectful and compliant.
She was a beautiful, seductive woman, with a body that
made his mouth water, but lately, she had been denying it to
him because she was upset with him and that made him feel
extremely frustrated. He was the king, after all. What was
the use in being king if you couldn't even command your
own wife? He would simply have to make sure that Warrick
did something about that. After all, hadn't he always done
everything that Warrick asked? Would it be too much to
expect him to return just this one small favor?

Thinking of Warrick made Billy realize that it had been a
while since he'd seen or heard from him. Word had it that
Warrick was cloistered in his Alabaster Tower, doubtless
conjuring spells to ensure the army's victory over the outlaw
mage. Well, now was not the time to interrupt him. Billy had
learned the hard way that sending for Warrick was coun-
terproductive. Warrick would always send the courier back
with the message, "What does the king want?" And then
Billy would have to explain to the courier what he wanted
and send him back to Warrick, and Warrick would invariably
reply that he was too busy to come right then, but he would

be happy to see to whatever His Majesty wished at the earliest opportunity. After a while of this, even the couriers had started smirking. Billy finally resolved that if he wanted anything of Warrick, it was best to simply go and see him himself. Well, there would be plenty of time for that after the war was over. In the meantime, Billy kept revising his battle plans, just to make sure, and sending updates to Lord Kelvin right up until the last minute.

The night before the army was due to depart, Billy had stayed up very late, maneuvering his toy soldiers and making detailed notes. He wanted to make absolutedly certain that Lord Kelvin had the benefit of the finest battle plan he could devise, because then he could take the credit for it when the army returned victorious. He was so intent upon his task that he never heard the scuffling in the hall when Sandy came back through her secret passageway with Lord Aubrey and some members of the Underground and overpowered the royal guards stationed in the corridor. The first inkling Billy had that anything was wrong was when the doors to his bedchamber burst open and a bunch of cloaked and hooded figures descended upon him. Before he could even cry out, a gag was stuffed into his mouth and his arms were tied behind him. Then a sack was placed over his head and he was frog-marched out into the corridor.

They spun him around several times and he quickly lost all sense of direction, so he had no idea that he was marched straight back to the queen's chambers and through her secret passageway. Eventually, he knew he was outside because he felt the breeze and the cobblestones beneath his feet, but almost at once he was hustled into a coach and forced down on the floor. He had no idea how long the jarring ride was, but before long he was rudely lifted up and carried out. He was marched a short distance down a street and then inside somewhere, and after a few more minutes he was pushed down into a chair and tied to it. The sack was not removed from his head, so he had no idea where he was, or who his captors were. And he was very much afraid. Terrified, in fact.

"Who ... who are you?" he demanded. "How dare you? What is the meaning of this? What do you want of me?"

"Please accept our humblest apologies, Your Majesty," a voice said, "and rest assured that we intend no harm to you. We truly regret the necessity for this, and we apologize for the inconvenience, but 'tis all for your own good."

"For my own *good*?" said King Billy with disbelief.

"Aye, Sire," the unknown voice replied. " 'Twas necessary to spirit you out of the palace and someplace safe, where your enemies could not reach you."

"My enemies?" said Billy. "Are you seriously trying to suggest that you are my friends? When I am bound and gagged and abducted from my own bedchamber, then held this way, with my hands tied and a sack over my head, like some common criminal?"

"The sack will shortly be removed, sire, and the bonds as well. I regret the temporary inconvenience, but I fear that 'twas necessary to preserve our anonymity. We are the Underground, you see, people dedicated to the cause of freedom and improving conditions within the kingdom."

"You are the rebels," Billy said, as his stomach contracted with fear.

"No, Sire, we are not. A number of us might even be known to you as members of the aristocracy, or perhaps even your own palace guard. Our members come from every walk of life, and we have one thing in common—to work against injustice and help those who have been oppressed. But we are not the revolution. Our methods are nonviolent, yet we are still branded as criminals under your regime. And ironic as it may seem, we have abducted you to save your life. We have learned that once the army had departed for Brigantium, the revolution would begin, and the first target of the rebels would surely be the royal palace. Your palace guard would never be sufficient to repel the force. You would have been seized and executed. 'Twas our intention to prevent that."

"And the queen?" asked Billy. "What of her?"

Lord Aubrey glanced at the queen, who stood beside him

as he spoke to her husband. King Billy, of course, was oblivious to her presence.

"The queen is not far from here," Lord Aubrey replied truthfully. He disguised his voice, to keep the king from recognizing it. "You may rest assured that we will keep her safe."

"I demand to see her," said King Billy.

"In due time, sire," Lord Aubrey replied. "For the present, you shall not be kept together. 'Tis purely a safety precaution, you understand."

"I do not understand. Why?"

"The revolution will certainly succeed," Lord Aubrey said, "at least in the short term. They shall seize control of the government, and one of their first priorities, on finding you and the queen gone, will be to search for you. Should anything go wrong, we cannot afford losing you both, so you will be kept separate."

"I see," King Billy replied. "If I should be found and executed, then the queen succeeds me. And if she should die, then I will still be left alive. Your reasoning makes sense. And when the royal army returns, they shall put down the revolution and proper rule shall be restored."

"Precisely," said Lord Aubrey. "But there is more to it than that, Your Majesty. You have enemies within your regime, as well. If anything were to happen to you and the queen, the blame would doubtless fall upon the leaders of the revolution, but the advantage would fall to your royal wizard, because then, since you are childless, there would be nothing to prevent him from claiming the throne."

"Warrick? Assume the thone? Don't be absurd!" said King Billy. "Warrick is a sorcerer. He cares only for his books and potions. Of what use would earthly power be to him?"

"Warrick is the Grand Director of the Sorcerers Guild, Your Majesty," Lord Aubrey said. "As such, he has already proven himself adept at politics. The recent edicts, which have so incensed the populace and were instituted in your name, were all written by the sheriff, at Warrick's behest. It is also a well known fact throughout the kingdom that whatever favor Warrick asks of you, you grant. And is not our army at this very moment marching off to war against Brigantium for no other reason than because Warrick sees this so-called 'outlaw mage' as a threat to his own power?"

" 'Tis not true," King Billy protested. "Brigantium is a threat to the entire economy of our kingdom. They steal our trade through unfair competition, they cause our currency to be devalued, and they steal our citizens by luring them away with the promise of riches gained at our expense."

"And who was it that told you this?" Lord Aubrey asked.

"Why, 'twas . . ."

"Warrick, was it not? The people who have left our kingdom for Brigantium fled from our repressive laws, which you empowered the royal sheriff to enact. And your brother, the sheriff, does whatever Warrick tells him. As for these economic grievances you cite against Brigantium, was there ever even an attempt to send a delegation there to negotiate our differences peacefully?"

"Well . . . no, but . . ."

"Is that not normally the first step when kingdoms have differences between them?"

"Well, perhaps, but in this case, Warrick felt that . . ."

"*Warrick* felt? I thought you said that Warrick did not concern himself with such earthly things, that he cared only for his books and potions. Yet here we see that he advises you on foreign policy. Or perhaps he dictates that policy?"

"Now you are sounding like the queen," said Billy. "She never liked him."

"Perhaps, sire, because Her Highness realized, as you did not, that Warrick was never your friend."

King Billy remained silent.

"Doubtless, sire, you do not reply because of your physical discomfort," said Lord Aubrey. "In a moment we shall see to that. A room has been prepared for you. The accommodations are paltry compared with those of your palace, but we have endeavored to make them as comfortable as possible. There is no window, I am sorry to say, and the walls are thick, but we shall provide you with an adequate supply of candles and as good a bed as we could find. You will be well fed, with the best we have to offer, and if there is anything we can provide to make your stay more comfortable, we shall endeavor to do so. Meanwhile, perhaps you can use the time to contemplate these things we have discussed, and consider the lives that will be lost in the coming revolution and the war against Brigantium, and the deaths that will occur when the army returns and finds it must put down a coup, all of which could easily have been avoided if you had listened less to Warrick and more to the people of your kingdom. And now, Your Majesty, I must say good night. My companions will conduct you to your room, where your bonds will be removed. I have other pressing matters to which I must attend."

The king was led away and Lord Aubrey turned to the queen. "Well," he said, "now we are guilty of an offense that could put our heads upon the block."

"You spoke well," said the queen. "Strangely enough, he seemed to listen to you, whereas he never listened to me."

"Had he done that, Your Highness, none of us would be here now."

"My lord," said one of the men, entering the room, "it seems that we have caught a spy."

"A spy!" Lord Aubrey said.

"He was following the queen," the man said.

"Then . . . he must know everything," said Aubrey. He sighed and shook his head. "Bring him in."

A moment later two men entered, holding a frightened Ferret Phil between them.

"I have seen this man before," said Sandy. "He was at The Stealers Tavern. Gentlemanly Johnny and La Donna must have had me followed from my meeting with them there."

"And you came directly to our meeting," said Lord Aubrey, "from which we left for the palace. If he has been following you all this time, then he could not have had a chance to report what he has learned."

The look of alarm that briefly registered in Ferret Phil's eyes told Aubrey he was right.

"Well, we can spare neither the time nor the effort to hold him," Aubrey said. "And there is always a chance he may escape. Besides, he knows too much and he has seen us."

"We agreed to use no violence," said Queen Sandy.

"Aye," Aubrey replied, "but given what's at stake, what other choice do we have?"

"There is one," said Sandy. She glanced at the men holding Phil and said, "Leave us."

They released Phil and left the room, shutting the door behind them and leaving Sandy and Aubrey alone with him. Sandy approached Ferret Phil, gazing deep into his eyes, and made a languid pass with her hand before his face. His eyelids closed and his body relaxed. In a slow, chanting voice, Sandy spoke a spell.

> "Of what you've seen and what you've heard,
> you shall utter not one word.
> From the moment we first met,
> everything you shall forget.
> All events of this past night,
> now will vanish from your sight.
> Tomorrow morning, when you wake,
> this night's memories you'll forsake.
> All of these commands you'll keep,
> now descend to dreamless sleep."

The moment she stopped speaking, Ferret Phil collapsed to the floor and immediately started snoring.

"Well, smite me," said Aubrey, staring at the queen with astonishment. "You're a witch!"

She turned to him and nodded. "Now there are no secrets left between us, Lord Aubrey."

He gave her a slight bow. "And unless you wish to cast a like spell upon me, Your Highness, I shall take this one to my grave."

She smiled and said, "I know your word to be more binding than any spell I could devise, Lord Aubrey."

"You honor me, my queen."

"And you me, Aubrey, with your friendship. Now, let us have this man taken to another part of town and find him a room where he may sleep in comfort. There is yet much for us to do."

"I am at your command," Lord Aubrey said.

"Then fetch us two fast horses and some provisions," said Sandy. "You and I must leave at once and try to beat the army to Brigantium."

"Brigantium!" said Aubrey. "But, Your Highness, do you realize what you're proposing? Quite aside from the risks of such a journey, if they realize who you are—"

"I intend to tell them who I am," said Sandy.

"And the moment that you do, they shall seize us both and take us prisoner."

"That is precisely what I intend for them to do," Sandy replied. "And then when Lord Kelvin arrives with his army, they can hold me hostage against his attack."

Aubrey shook his head with admiration. "With no disrespect intended to His Majesty, he does not deserve such a queen." He clapped his hand to his sword and bowed deeply. "It shall be my privilege to escort you to Brigantium, Your Highness."

Ah, adventure! Ah, romance! Ah, the courtly graces and the noble gestures! Don't you wish you knew people like that? Don't you wish we could still walk around in cloaks and boots and breeches, with leather doublets and flowing white dueling shirts and swords strapped around our waists? Of course, if we did, given the way things are today, there would be people out there lobbying for sword control, and we'd need a National Sword Association and bumper stickers that would read, "Swords don't kill people, knights kill people," and there would be a five-day waiting period and background check before you could buy a rapier. We'd have drive-by lungings and people would be afraid of children carrying broadswords to school. "Milady" would be regarded as a sexist term and feminists would go absolutely berserk if any woman called a man "Milord." Ralph Nader would probably get quarter horses banned because they are too small and unsafe in a collision and someone would figure out a way to put seat belts and air bags on our saddles. That's why people join the SCA and read fantasy novels, because the real world sucks.

Anyway, where were we? Oh, right, we were in the process of pulling together the various elements of what we laughingly refer to as "the plot" of this story. Don't worry, we'll get there, I promise. Remember, always trust your narrator.

And speaking of promises, I know I said we'd check back in with Warrick and see how he was getting on in modern London. Heh, heh, heh. Not too well, it seems. When last we left the royal wizard, he was making the unpleasant discovery that magic didn't work in our world and getting pasted in the jaw by Colin Hightower. Well, since then, as predicted, he regained consciousness and was discovered in Brewster's lab by Dr. Davies, the EnGulfCo executive vice-president of R and D, and a detachment of security. They handcuffed him and took him into custody and subjected him to a rigorous interrogation, which resulted in Dr. Davies placing a call to the EnGulfCo CEO.

Of course, it was illegal for them to detain him like that without calling the police, but since Warrick didn't know enough to demand to see a lawyer—or barrister, as they call them in England—they just went ahead and did it anyway. Even if he had demanded to see an attorney, they probably would have disregarded him in any case, because they were not about to go public with any of this stuff. There was just too much at stake. And we all know what happens when an individual tries to take on a huge multinational corporation. Can you say, "Bambi meets Godzilla"?

For twenty-four hours, Warrick was kept in a holding room in the security wing at EnGulfCo corporate headquarters. He was questioned by Dr. Davies, then hooked up to a polygraph machine and questioned once again, and finally he was brought to the opulent private office of the EnGulfCo CEO.

"Leave us," he said to the security guards as they sat Warrick in a comfortable leather and brass-studded chair opposite the massive mahogany desk. The security guards left, leaving Warrick alone with the CEO and Dr. Davies.

"Well, Mr. Warrick, is it? You've posed us quite a pretty problem." The CEO glanced down at the report lying on his desk. "No doubt, you are wondering just what it is that's happened to you, and where you are. At the moment, you are in the office of the chairman of the board of EnGulfCo International. That's me. I am a very busy man. A very wealthy and powerful man, as I imagine you were where you came from, wherever that may be. I've read the report of your questioning, you see, and you have the look of some-one accustomed to authority. Well, I am in authority here. I have only to say the word "Jump," and heads of state ask, 'How high?' Would you care for some wine?"

"Thank you, I would," said Warrick.

The CEO merely nodded to Dr. Davies, who went over to the sideboard and poured them both some sherry.

"You had come into possession of something that belonged to us," said the CEO.

"The time machine," said Warrick.

"Precisely. You understand what it is?"

"A device for traveling through the ethereal planes," said Warrick.

The CEO smiled. "I suppose that could be one way of putting it," he said. "The man who built it, Dr. Marvin Brewster, whom you apparently know as 'Brewster Doc,' works for me."

"I see," said Warrick. "He is your court wizard."

The CEO smiled again and took a sip of sherry. "In a manner of speaking. The woman you saw up in the lab was Dr. Pamela Fairburn. She is engaged to Dr. Brewster and is, uh, something of a wizard in her own right. At my direction, she had attempted to duplicate the machine that Dr. Brewster built, but unfortunately, it does not work. We lack some of the key components, and it seems the notes Dr. Brewster left behind were not entirely complete. What that means is the only working model of Dr. Brewster's time machine is the one in which you had arrived here, and which Dr. Fairburn apparently took back to wherever it is you came from, along with those two other individuals, one of whom it seems you know. The other one, the man who struck you, has since been identified. He is a rather unscrupulous reporter with a distinctly unsavory reputation."

"I am not surprised," said Warrick wryly.

"You appear to be a good judge of character," said the CEO. "We may be able to help each other."

"I was about to suggest the same thing," Warrick replied with a smile.

"Excellent," said the CEO. "It is obvious that Dr. Fairburn went back to get Dr. Brewster. If she fails to return, then there is probably nothing we can do but keep working on the machine she duplicated and try to find a way to make it function. The odds of that, however, seem slim and none. If she succeeds, however, then a world of possibilities will open up to us. She has proven to be an extremely resource-ful woman, and I have great confidence in her. Let us hope that she succeeds."

"And if she does?" asked Warrick.

"Then you and I will have a great deal to discuss," replied the CEO. "The situation could be of great profit to us both, if we were to work together."

"Perhaps," said Warrick, "but first, there is something that I want."

The CEO raised his eyebrows. "Really? And what would that be?"

"I am seeking someone who calls himself 'the Narrator.' It was for that purpose that I came."

Oh-oh. No, you don't.

At that moment, the door to the CEO's office opened and the head of security came rushing in.

"I thought I said that we were not to be disturbed," the CEO said, frowning.

"Yes, sir, but I think you'd better have a look at this," the head of security said, moving to the window and opening the blinds. The CEO got up and looked. Outside, there was a crowd of people jamming the sidewalk and spilling out into the street, blocking traffic. Police were trying to break them up, apparently without success. More police cars were arriving as they watched, along with several vans.

"What's going on down there?" the CEO asked. "Who are those people?"

"They started arriving about half an hour ago," the security man said. "It seems like some sort of protest demonstration. Their numbers have swelled dramatically in the last ten or fifteen minutes and a bunch of them have broken through into the lobby. We can't contain the situation and we've been forced to call in the police. And now we've reporters down there, too, along with several TV crews."

"What do they want?" asked the CEO.

The head of security glanced at Warrick. "They want him."

The CEO turned to Warrick with a frown. "What do you know about this?"

"They must be my test subjects," Warrick said.

"Test subjects?" The CEO suddenly remembered the report and what Warrick had revealed during his questioning. "But how could they have known you were here?"

"Before transporting them in the time machine, I had placed each of them under a spell of compulsion to find a way back to me and report where they had been and what they had seen," Warrick explained. He shrugged. "My spells are not effective here, but it seems the effects of the spells I cast in my own world linger on in this one. They must have been drawn to me by my arrival here."

"Wonderful. And we've got the media down there," the CEO said. "Can you imagine what will happen if any of those people talk to them?"

"Never fear, they will not speak with anyone about this before they have spoken with me first and fulfilled the conditions of the spell," said Warrick.

"And then what?"

"Then they will no longer feel the effects of the compulsion."

"I see." The CEO turned to the head of security. "Let them in," he said.

"Sir?"

"You heard me. Let those people in. But the media stays out. And if they want to know what's going on, just tell them 'No comment.'" He turned back to Warrick. "Well, since this is your doing, I guess you'd better speak with them."

"*All* of them?" said Warrick.

"All of them," said the CEO.

"But it could take days for them to tell me all that's happened to them since they have arrived here," Warrick protested.

"I imagine it will probably take several weeks, at least," the CEO replied. "It makes no difference to me. I want this situation brought under control. Besides, it isn't as if you have anything better to do for the present. Afterward, I'm sure I can come up with something useful for a man of your peculiar talents, but meanwhile, I want you to take care of this. You can use one of the offices downstairs." He turned back to the security man. "I want the names of all those people, and their addresses and telephone and social security numbers. I want us to be able to find each and every one of them again if we have to. Find accommodations for them and put them all on the payroll until Warrick's finished with them. Make sure they sign the standard contract and that they read and understand the security clause. Got it?"

"Yes, sir."

"It would appear as if I have unintentionally caused you a great deal of inconvenience," said Warrick. "Such was not my intention. I apologize."

"Oh, you'll make it worth my while, Warrick, one way or another," said the CEO. "As of now, you work for me."

Well, the plot thickens. Brewster and the others, whom we shall join in the next chapter, are frantically working to prepare for the upcoming invasion. Harlan's spies have reported that King Billy's army is on the move, and things are indeed hectic right now at the keep. The fortifications are almost complete, and the assembly lines are running at full tilt. Mac is busily trying to whip the newly recruited Army of Brigantium into shape with the assistance of the mercenaries he has hired; Rachel Drum, bearing Dwarfkabob, the enchanted Sword of the Shaman, has flown with Rory to the convocation of the elves to seek their help; and Harlan, having freshly returned from his mission to King Durwin, who has decided to sit this whole thing out and see what happens, has departed for a meeting with the dwarves to see if he can negotiate an alliance with them against Lord Kelvin's army. All in all, things have been pretty busy in the newly formed Kingdom of Brigantium.

Meanwhile, Pamela and Megan are on their way to Brigand's Roost, escorted by six of Warrick's men-at-arms, while the rest of Warrick's guard remain behind with Captain Ivor, who is convinced that Warrick has sent the two demons to aid in the invasion. It has not occurred to him to wonder why two powerful demons from the ethereal plane would need an armed escort to travel to Brigantium, or why they would travel on horseback rather than fly or teleport themselves, or even why one of them would choose to assume the rather unusual form of a chamberpot. Ivor had long since learned not to question magical goings-on.

Time after time, he and his men had dragged prisoners from the royal dungeons into Warrick's sanctorum and none of them ever came out again. So far as Ivor was concerned, what Warrick or any of his conjured demons chose to do was their business. He simply followed instructions, taking up watch on the time machine, which he was careful not to approach too closely. There were, to be sure, easier gigs to be had in Pittsburgh for skilled men-at-arms, but Warrick's minions were paid very well, even better than the palace guard, and they had generous benefits, such as free health care, a uniform and weapons allowance, free room and board and even a retirement plan. If that meant putting up with the occasional supernatural manifestation, Ivor figured it was worth it.

And finally, Queen Sandy and Lord Aubrey are also galloping at full speed toward the town of Brigand's Roost in a desperate effort to stop the war before it gets started. Sandy did her best to reason with The Stealers Guild, but clearly they would have been unable to stop the revolution even if they wanted to, and the most Sandy could hope for was a minimal loss of life among her subjects. To be sure, the palace guard would be overrun, but she doubted they would put up much of a resistance once they realized how greatly the odds would be against them. Unlike Warrick's minions, they were poorly paid and had no benefits. Chances were they would simply cut and run, or even throw in with the forces of the revolution, and the palace would fall without much of a struggle.

Sheriff Waylon and his deputies would be the ones who would be most hard-pressed. The people had no reason to despise the palace guard, but they had plenty of reasons to hate Sheriff Waylon and his men, who had comported themselves like thugs. Waylon would be the first to feel the mob's wrath, especially once they discovered that the king had gone into hiding. Unless Waylon was able to escape, he was probably going to have his neck stretched, and Sandy couldn't think of a more deserving candidate for such a fate. What worried her was Warrick.

She had no idea what the Grand Director of the Sorcerers Guild was liable to do when the revolution started. She had no way of knowing that he would be sitting in a London office, drinking pots and pots of coffee while he conducted interminable interviews with his test subjects, who would regale him with long tales of what they had experienced and learned since he had transported them to our world.

Okay, have we left anybody out? No, I don't think so. I think that just about covers it as this story approaches its dramatic climax. It's time we checked back in with Brewster, who is feeling very ambivalent about this whole thing. He had never thought, when he first arrived in Brigand's Roost, that his efforts to improve the lives of the town's residents would lead to such a crisis. He felt responsible, and he was determined to do everything he could to help them. To that end, he has been driving himself mercilessly, working around the clock to prepare for the coming battle. And if you think this story's been pretty weird so far, just wait 'til you see what happens next.

ELEVEN

Brewster was exhausted. For the past several weeks, he had averaged at best three or four hours sleep each night, and the last few days he had gone almost completely without sleep, just grabbing a quick nap here and there whenever he could. Mick had the weapons crews working in shifts around the clock and last minute construction was being completed on the fortifications. The keep had taken on the appearance of a factory. All work on the palace had been abandoned, and it stood unfinished as they concentrated on the walls and gun emplacements. The grounds of the keep had become a crowded tent city as people from Brigand's Roost and the settlement just outside the walls moved in for protection from Lord Kelvin's army, which was fast approaching. Advance scouts had already been sighted.

The land beyond the settlement had already been cleared in preparation for new construction. Now, it would become an open field of fire. Bloody Bob's work crews had cut down small trees to make large stakes, sharpening them at the ends, crisscrossing and bracing them and setting them into the ground at angles in staggered lines, to impede the advance of troops in large formations across the open ground. Frenetic activity was taking place everywhere. Whenever Brewster wasn't checking on the work in progress, he was huddled in the great hall of the keep with Mac and Shannon, going over crudely drawn maps of the surrounding area in an effort to come up with defensive strategies.

"It looks as if they will avoid the town on their approach," said Mac, as they stood around the table, looking down at the map he'd drawn. He pointed to it with a dagger. "The watch reports the army here at present. Their advance scouts have crossed the river and are now swinging around to the west, this way. That indicates they will be taking a circuitous approach."

"Why not simply continue down the road and through the town?" asked Brewster.

"Because the road to Brigand's Roost is narrow," Mac replied, "with thick woods all around. The troops would be stretched out along it for a good distance, which would afford too many possibilities for ambush from cover. Lord Kelvin is too good a general for that. He will circle round the forest, through the meadows here, and approach us from the west, down the road from Franktown. 'Tis a wider road, and it skirts the forest, following the river before bending around past the keep here, and going on toward Brigand's Roost." He outlined the course with the tip of his dagger as he spoke.

"That will still take them through part of the forest," Shannon said.

"True," Mac replied, "but for a much shorter distance. 'Tis the logical approach. Lord Kelvin knows that if we come out to meet him in force, we'd have to meet him on ground of his own choosing, here in this rolling meadow"—he pointed with the dagger—"where he will doubtless dispose his troops upon the rise. Otherwise, he will expect us to attack when he moves his troops down the road and through the forest, toward the keep. If I were him, I would send one column down the road, and wide flanking columns of skirmishers through the forest on either side. That way, if the main column was attacked, he could bring his skirmishers in and trap the attacking force, then advance upon the keep, saving the town for last. 'Twould make a good incentive for his troops to have the town to plunder once the keep had fallen."

"The keep isn't going to fall," said Shannon firmly.

"If it does," Mac replied, "then there will be nothing standing between Lord Kelvin's forces and the town."

"What do you propose to do?" asked Brewster.

"Well, we are vastly outnumbered, and our force is poorly trained," said Mac. "Lord Kelvin would have the decided advantage if we met in open combat on a field where he could maneuver. There has been no word from Rachel?"

Brewster shook his head. "No, and we have heard nothing from the dwarves, either. So, unless something happens very soon, we cannot count on any help from either the elves or the dwarves. We may have to do this on our own."

"Then our best bet is to make our stand right here," said Mac. "I will position the main body of our force here in the woods, to the east of us, between the keep and Brigand's Roost, so that they may strike Kelvin on his flank as he comes at the keep and then fight a defensive action and retreat back toward the town as necessary. The remainder of our force will man the walls. What progress are you making with your special weapons?"

"They're just about ready," Brewster said. "We've only got two of the big guns finished, but there hasn't been much time for field testing. We'll just have to hope they work, that's all."

"You look tired, Doc," said Shannon. "You have done all you could. You need to get some rest."

"Yes, I'm about dead on my feet," Brewster replied, running his hand through his hair. "I feel as if I could sleep for a week. I just wish there was some way we could avoid all this. I feel as if it's all my fault."

"There is no sense in blaming yourself, Doc," Mac said. " 'Tis not you who is responsible for this. We are the ones being attacked."

"Yes, but it's all because of me," Brewster replied sadly. "If I hadn't come here in the first place, none of this would have happened."

"But think of all the wonderful things that have happened because you did come," Shannon said. "You have changed many lives for the better, Doc, ours included. If you were to leave, there is no one who would not be deeply sorry to see you go. And no one holds you to blame for this war."

"Aye, 'tis Warrick who is behind it all," said Mac. "And he remains the unknown factor in this conflict. We know what Kelvin will do. As to Warrick's plans, we can only guess. Get some sleep, Doc. There is nothing more that you can do for the present. Fear not, 'twill all turn out for the best."

"I sincerely hope so," Brewster said. "I don't know how I'm going to get any sleep, thinking about all the people who are going to die soon, but I suppose I'll have to try."

They watched him go off toward the stairs, moving slowly and slump-shouldered, like a man bearing the weight of the entire world. Shannon turned to Mac and said, "What do you really think of our chances?"

"Well, it depends on how well Doc's weapons work," said Mac. "Lord Kelvin will not expect anything like Doc's guns. They just may turn the tide. But without them . . ." He shook his head. "Have you noticed that Thorny has disappeared?"

Shannon frowned. "Doc's pet bush? No, I had not."

Mac nodded. " 'Tis been over a week now. There is an old saying among sailors about rats leaving a ship before it departs upon its voyage. They say it means the ship is doomed, and the creatures know somehow."

Shannon gave him a sharp glance. "Say nothing like that around Doc," she cautioned him. "He has enough worries. I have never seen him like this. He looks drawn and haggard. Despite all we say, he still blames himself for this."

"Aye, I know," said Mac grimly. "He only wanted to change things for the better, but change never comes easily."

"Mac," said Shannon, "however things turn out, I just wanted you to know that if I should—"

He placed a finger lightly up against her lips. "Hush now," he said. "Let us not speak of such things. Remember the lessons of my father. Admit neither the possibility of victory nor defeat. Address the task at hand. Live in the moment. Now come, let us see if those mercenaries I've appointed to instruct our troops have killed anybody yet."

Shannon grinned. "They have been driving them hard," she said.

"As they should be," Mac replied, rolling up the map.

"Do you think we can really count on them?" asked Shannon. "I mean, they are mercenaries, after all. And they know the odds against us."

"They know," said Mac. "As they know the benefits that they can reap after this is over. We have hired the best, my love. And their worth shall go up considerably when they can claim they've turned back the mightest army ever assembled in the twenty-seven kingdoms."

"You really think that we can do it?" she asked.

"Trust in your sword," said Mac. "And trust in Doc. He has never let us down before."

"And what of Warrick?"

"We shall deal with Warrick when the time comes," Mac replied. "We cannot anticipate what he will do, so there is no point to worrying about it."

"Mac . . . I must confess, I am a little afraid."

"Only a little?" He grinned. "Shannon, my love, I'm scared out of my wits."

"You?"

"Aye, is that so surprising?"

"I never thought you could be afraid of anything," she said.

"Well, fortunately, it does not happen very often," he replied. "But when it does, I simply accept it. As my father used to say, why waste time fighting fear when there are other things to fight?"

"Your father was a wonderful teacher," Shannon said wistfully, recalling the man who had taught her all she knew.

"Aye, as I intend to be. But first, there is the minor matter of an army to dispose of." He offered her his arm. "Shall we, Your Highness?"

She took his arm and smiled. "We shall, my general."

Queen Sandy and Lord Aubrey reached the river with Lord Kelvin's army perhaps several hours behind them. They lost valuable time in circling through the forest, around the troops, and when they reached the crossing, the ferry was on the opposite shore. Aubrey rang the bell to summon the ferryman, and after a few moments, they could see the ferry raft moving out slowly from the far bank, along the guide ropes that kept it from drifting away with the current.

Seeing the ferry's slow progress toward them, Sandy shook her head with impatience. "Why must it take so long?"

"Patience, my queen," said Aubrey. "The delay will work for us, in the long run. We will gain significant time here. There is but the one ferry, and even if Lord Kelvin constructs additional rafts, which he will undoubtedly do, 'twill take days for the entire army to cross."

" 'Twill take even longer if we cut loose the raft once we reach the other shore," said Sandy.

Aubrey grinned. "Funny you should mention that," he said. "I was just thinking that very same thing." And then the grin slipped from his face as he glanced back sharply toward the road. "Horses," he said, "coming fast."

"Could it be the army already?"

Aubrey shook his head. "No, they are still several hours behind us. But it could be an advance party of scouts. We had best get out of sight, and quickly."

They rode their horses to a stand of trees, behind some shrubbery, dismounted, and covered the mouths of their mounts with their hands to prevent them from whickering and giving their hiding place away. Moments later, a group of riders came into view.

"Warrick's men!" said Aubrey, softly as he recognized their colors.

"Are they after us?" asked Sandy.

Aubrey shook his head. "I do not know. 'Tis possible. Warrick may have divined our plan somehow."

"What shall we do?"

"Keep still and wait," said Aubrey. "I do not think they saw us."

"But what of the ferryman?" asked Sandy.

"Perhaps he'll think 'twas they who summoned him," said Aubrey.

They watched as the riders reined in at the riverbank, by the crossing. The ferry was not quite halfway across the river.

"There are two women with them," Sandy whispered. "Do you recognize them?"

Aubrey frowned and shook his head.

"The ferry comes, milady," said one of the men at arms.

"Good," said Pamela. "How much farther?"

"Once across the river, 'tis but a few hours ride to Brigand's Roost," the man replied.

"So we should be there by nightfall," Pamela said. "How far behind us is the army?"

"Perhaps three, four hours march, at most, milady. We could have made much better time had we not gone around them. I confess, my lady, I still fail to see the necessity for that. Would it not have been more prudent for us to join Lord Kelvin and—"

"It is not for you to question my decisions," Pamela replied curtly.

"Aye, your pardon, milady. Yet, once we cross the river, we shall be in enemy territory, and we are wearing Warrick's colors, which are well known throughout the land. If we were to ride into an ambush—"

"You say the road on the opposite shore leads straight to Brigand's Roost?" asked Pamela, interrupting him.

"Aye, milady."

"Then you need not cross with us. We shall proceed alone from here."

"If that is what you wish, milady," said the man-at-arms, with obvious relief. "Have we your leave to go then?"

"We need some coin with which to pay the ferryman," said Megan.

The man removed his purse from his belt and tossed it to her. "With my compliments, milady," he said.

"Thank you. You may go," said Pamela.

"Good fortune to you, milady," said the man-at-arms. He signaled to the others and they wheeled their horses round and rode away.

"Most strange," said Aubrey, watching from their hiding place. "I have never known Warrick's minions to take orders from anyone but Warrick, much less a woman. I wonder who they are."

"Well, there is one way to find out," said Sandy, mounting up.

"Your Highness, wait!" said Aubrey, but she was already riding out toward the two women. He hurriedly mounted and rode after her.

Pamela turned quickly at the sound of their approach, her hand going into her purse for her pistol. "Stop right there!" she said. "What do you want?"

"I might well ask you the same thing," Sandy replied, unaccustomed to being challenged in such a tone, but reining in a short distance away as Aubrey rode up beside her. "You ride with Warrick's men-at-arms, and you give them orders, yet you are unknown to me. And you are dressed most strangely. Who are you?"

"Who wants to know?" asked Pamela, her hands grasping the butt of the pistol in her purse.

Sandy pulled back the hood of her cloak. "You do not know me?"

"No," said Pamela cautiously. "Why should I?"

" 'Strewth!" said Megan. " 'Tis the queen!"

Lord Aubrey unsheathed his sword. Pamela quickly drew her pistol, aimed, and fired. The bullet struck the guard of Aubrey's sword and he dropped it with a yell.

It would have been very dramatic as a threatening gesture if it had simply ended there, but as anyone familiar with both firearms and horses can attest, if you plan on firing a gun from the back of an unfamiliar horse, you'd best bring along a parachute. Horses and loud, sudden noises don't really mix too well, unless the horse is used to such things and trained not to react. These horses had never heard the sound of gunfire before, and while a Walther .38 semiautomatic does not sound anywhere near as loud as a .44 Magnum going off, it does have a very sharp report, enough to make all four horses in this case start plunging around in consternation.

Lord Aubrey's horse reared up and almost threw him, but he managed to hang on, struggling to keep the animal from bolting. Megan's horse whinnied in alarm and plunged into the trees, where an overhanging branch swept her out of the saddle and the horse took off, galloping back down the road the way they came. Pamela's horse started bucking like a rodeo bronc, and though Pamela was an expert rider, Larry Mahon she wasn't. She tried to ride it out, but was unable to remain in the saddle for more than a few seconds. She went over the side and rolled down the bank into the river as the horse took off. Sandy managed to stay in the saddle, but only because the moment her horse reacted to the shot by neighing and veering off sideways, she clamped tight with her knees and reached out to grab the animal's mane, speaking a spell to calm it down. All in all, it was a rather ludicrous scene, fully worthy of *F Troop*.

Aubrey finally got his horse back under control, twisted the reins around his fist, dismounted, and snatched up his sword. Megan was still groggy from being struck by the tree branch. She lay on her back in the underbrush, moaning and clutching her head. Pamela managed to grab on to some reeds growing by the riverbank and slowly pulled herself out of the water, streaming wet and gasping for breath. Sandy dismounted and walked over to where Pamela had dropped her purse and her gun. She bent to pick up the pistol, examining it curiously. She turned it and looked down into the bore.

"Don't!" Pamela said quickly. She held out her hand in a warning gesture. "Don't move! Don't even breathe!"

Sandy glanced at her with a puzzled frown.

Pamela approached her, cautiously, water streaming from her hair and clothes. "Be careful!" she said. "Please, point that thing away from you, and to the ground."

Sandy did as she was told.

"The safety was off and a round was chambered," Pamela said. "You could have been killed."

"Safety? Round?" said Sandy. She glanced at the pistol and shook her head in confusion. "I do not understand."

"No, you wouldn't, would you?" Pamela said. She retrieved her purse. "It's a weapon. It, uh . . . shoots very small projectiles with a great deal of force and speed. And it's very lethal."

"If you try to harm her, then you shall have to kill me first," said Aubrey, stepping between them with his sword. Pamela backed away.

"Take it easy, Mister," she said. "I wasn't trying to hurt anyone."

"Wait, Aubrey," Sandy said, placing a hand on his shoulder. "Stand aside."

"But, Your Highness . . ."

"You drew your blade. She was merely trying to defend herself. Go see to her companion."

"As you wish, my queen," Aubrey said, glancing at Pamela uncertainly before leading his horse over to where Megan lay, groaning.

"I have never seen nor heard of such a weapon," Sandy said, carefully holding it out to Pamela in her open palm. "It seems so small to be so fearsome. I have never seen such magic."

"It's not exactly magic," Pamela replied, taking the gun back and clicking on the safety.

"Are you not a sorceress?"

"No, not really. Just a stranger in a strange land." She grimaced. "A really strange land."

"Who are you, then? And why do you ride with Warrick's men at arms?"

"It's a long story," Pamela said, "and I really don't have the time to get into it right now." She glanced toward the ferry, which had almost reached the bank. "I've got to get to Brigand's Roost before the army does."

"As do I," said Sandy.

"Oh, my God!" said Pamela suddenly, glancing around with alarm. *"Colin!"*

"And who is Colin?" Sandy asked with a frown.

"Somebody who really should have stayed home," said Pamela with a sigh of resignation. "He's probably halfway back to Pittsburgh by now. And I can't spare the time to go after him."

"Hallo!" shouted the ferryman, having heard the noise and seen all the commotion. "What goes on?"

" 'Tis all right!" Sandy shouted. "All is well! We need to get across!"

"We?" said Pamela.

"We have the only horses," Sandy replied. "Without us, you will have a long walk ahead of you to Brigand's Roost."

"Wait a minute," Pamela said. "If you're the queen, and your army's marching to war against Brigantium, then what are you doing trying to get there first?"

"I am trying to prevent the very war of which you speak," said Sandy. " 'Twas all Warrick's doing, and not mine. And 'twas the poor judgment of the king, my husband, to lend his sanction to this venture. If you are in Warrick's service, then you shall have to try and stop me. Yet you are not with Warrick, are you?"

"No, I'm not. It looks as if we both want the same thing," Pamela replied. "As for Warrick, you don't have to worry about him. Where he is now, there's nothing he can do. But how did you intend to stop the war all by yourself?"

"By offering myself as hostage to the wizard Brewster Doc," said Sandy. "Lord Kelvin will not attack if he knows they hold me prisoner. He will be forced to negotiate, and thus many lives may be spared."

"Girl, we need to talk," said Pamela. She glanced toward the ferry pulling up to the bank, then looked to see Aubrey approaching, leading his horse with Megan sitting astride it groggily. "You'd better brace yourself," said Pamela. "You're going to find this real hard to believe."

Sandy glanced at the pistol as Pamela put it back into her purse. "Somehow, I doubt that," she replied. "Come, let us go. I am most curious to hear your tale."

Okay, now we're cooking. The big climax is approaching, Warrick's finally out of my hair, all the different plot elements are coming together, and the stage is set for the grand finale. Lord Kelvin's army is coming up hard on Pamela and Sandy's heels, but they still have to cross the river, which will give them plenty of time to reach Brigand's Roost and find out that Brewster's at the keep. There will be a touching reunion between Pamela and Brewster, Sandy will find out that Brewster wasn't at all what she had thought, and when Lord Kelvin finally gets his army into position, he'll discover that the queen is being held hostage in the keep and he won't dare to attack.

Flags of truce will be sent out and they will commence negotiations, with Harlan arriving in the nick of time to handle the talks on Brewster's end. He'll inform Lord Kelvin that an alliance has been agreed to with the dwarves and they are on their way in force with their deadly little crossbows and their nasty little warhammers—boy, let me tell you, nothing hurts as much as being kneecapped by a dwarf—and at the last minute, Rachel will arrive on Rory's back to bring the news that the elves are on their way, as well. Lord Kelvin, realizing that the odds have shifted, will be compelled to agree to a truce while riders are sent back to King Billy with the terms, and . . . wait a minute. What the hell is so dramatic about that?

Brewster won't get to use any of his neat new weapons, and the dwarves won't have anything to do but stand around and rap, and we haven't even *seen* the elves yet, except for Rachel, and she still hasn't had a chance to use the magic sword which we made such a big deal about, and Rory won't get to breathe fire on anybody, and Mac and Shannon and the brigands won't get a chance to show what they can do, and Mick will have gone to all that trouble with his work crews to make all those weapons which never get used and that wouldn't be much of a climax at all, would it?

Of course, on the other hand, using Queen Sandy and her hostage ploy to force negotiations with Lord Kelvin would avoid a violent ending, and then we could have a nice romantic scene with Pamela and Brewster, where the focus would be on how she braved the dangers of the unknown, all for love, and went back through time and across dimensions to get her man and rescue him.

Queen Sandy would have saved the day, and once her subjects learned about the treaty she had negotiated with Brigantium, which included economic benefits and trade agreements that would lower taxes and provide thousands of new jobs, the revolution would fizzle out and she'd be hailed as an enlightened ruler. Sheriff Waylon and his corrupt deputies would all be thrown into prison; King Billy would finally come to his senses and realize the error of his ways and rule with Sandy in a comonarchy, or else abdicate in her favor and simply be her consort (that would please the feminists among the readership) and we could even have Teddy appointed Royal Mascot and Thorny made the state tree or something. (The environmentalists would like that.) Actually, that would be the perfect, politically correct ending to the story.

Nah . . . that sucks.

I know why you people buy these books. You want action. You want adventure. You want ferocious dragons and valiant elves and courageous dwarves and swashbuckling heroes and heroines and all that hack-and-slash, role gaming, Tolkien kind of stuff. Whoever heard of politically correct fantasy? Hell, you can't even teach Snow White and the Seven Dwarves anymore, because it shows a woman in a subservient role to little men. They're saying that the Brothers Grimm are much too violent and could traumatize small children; Hansel and Gretel depicts cannibalism and cruelty to senior citizens; Little Red Riding Hood and The Three Little Pigs shows cruelty to animals; Sleeping Beauty promotes sexual molestation, because the prince kisses her while she's suffering from diminished capacity; Peter Pan has Native Americans functioning in racially stereotyped roles and promotes a negative image of the physically challenged in Captain Hook; and Cinderella depicts class envy and has disturbing overtones of foot fetishism. I tell you, enough's enough. Somebody's got to draw the line and take a stand.

Never fear. Remember, always trust your narrator. And your faithful narrator still has an ace up his sleeve. In this case, it happens to be a character we've met before, in the second novel of this trilogy (*The Inadequate Adept*, Warner Books). Remember Black Jack, the freebooter who captured Shannon and would have taken her in for bounty if not for Brewster's dramatic rescue at the end of the last book? You may recall we mentioned that he's now leading the mercenaries with Lord Kelvin's army. (Yes, I know he's been off-stage for the length of this entire book, but that's what really minor supporting characters are for. You introduce them briefly in the beginning or somewhere near the middle and in the end, it turns out they have a key role to play in the resolution of the plot. Well, they do it all the time on *Murder, She Wrote*.)

Anyway, it so happens that Black Jack was riding out ahead of the main body of the army with the mercenaries under his command when what should come galloping down the road toward them at breakneck speed but Pamela's horse, with Colin the Chamberpot tied to the saddle and screaming at the top of his lungs.

Now, the sight of a riderless horse coming straight at you and apparently screaming "Help!" is enough to give most anybody pause, unless your name happens to be Wilbur Post and you're used to talking horses. Some of the mercenaries freaked and started shouting, "Sorcery!" and "Witchcraft!" However, Black Jack was made of sterner stuff and he rode out and stopped the runaway horse, at which point he discovered it wasn't the horse that was screaming after all, but the chamberpot tied to its saddle. We'll take it from there . . .

"What in blazes are you supposed to be?" Black Jack said, cutting the chamberpot loose and holding it up before him.

"Ohhh, thank God!" said Colin with a groan of pain. "I never want to see another bloody horse as long as I live!"

Black Jack took out his dagger and smacked the chamberpot with its hilt. "I asked you a question, pot!"

"*Ow*! Jesus! Take it easy, for Christ's sake!"

"I will ask you one more time, before I crush you beneath my horse's hooves. Who and what are you?"

"All right, all right! Just hold your bloody horses! No pun intended. My name is Colin Hightower, and I'm a reporter."

"A reporter of what?"

"Of news, what do you think?"

"You are a paid informant?"

"No, I'm not a . . . oh, never mind. You wouldn't understand."

"What are you? Are you human?"

"Of course, I'm bloody human! I'm under a spell or something!"

"How came you to this state?"

"I was standing in Warrick's place and I picked up a book and opened it, and the next thing I knew, *poof*! I was a bloody bedpan."

"I see," said Black Jack. "And how came you here? Whose horse is this?"

"It's . . . excuse me, but do you mind telling me exactly who you are?"

"Ohhhhh, someone get me out of here!" came a voice from the bedroll tied to the back of the saddle.

"What's this?" asked Black Jack with a frown. "More enchantment? Here, hold this." He tossed Colin to one of his men, who bobbled the chamberpot a moment before getting a firm grip on it.

"Watch it!" Colin said.

The man stared at the chamberpot wide-eyed, holding it well away from him while Black Jack cut loose the bedroll with his dagger and unwrapped it, revealing the magic mirror.

"Many thanks, kind stranger," said the mirror. "I thought I was about to be jarred loose from my frame!"

"And what are you supposed to be?" asked Black Jack, holding up the mirror and staring into it at his own reflection.

"I am the Enchanted Mirror of Truth. Ask me any question, and the truth shall be revealed."

"Indeed?" said Black Jack. He frowned, thinking of a way

to test this claim. "All right, then. What was my father's name?"

"Ah, well, it depends, you see," the mirror replied. "The truth is always relative. There is the truth you know, or think you know, and then there is the truth as 'twas told to you, which is the truth the teller knew, or thought she knew, and then there is the objective truth, which often has subtle shades of meaning—"

"What in thunder are you babbling about?" demanded Black Jack. "I asked you a simple question!"

"No question is ever truly simple," the mirror said. "You believe your father was called Jack the Red, a legendary freebooter with whom your mother fell in love while he was passing through your town on the way to the War of the Three Kingdoms. But in fact, while there really was a Jack the Red, and he was a legendary freebooter, your mother never even met him. She simply told you that story so you would have a strong male role model to think of as your father. Your mother always believed your real father was a man named Walt the Tinker, an itinerant peddler who sold pots and pans, dry goods, and herbal suppositories. He also did odd jobs and small repairs. Your mother was almost certain that he was your father, for it could have been any one of about a dozen men or more and he seemed the most likely candidate. But in truth, 'twas your Uncle Fred."

"My Uncle Fred!" said Black Jack with astonishment. "But . . . you mean my mother's *brother*?"

"Well, half brother," said the mirror. "They had different fathers, although your grandfather never knew that. You see, your grandmother—"

"Enough!" said Black Jack, scowling. "Was the pot telling the truth?"

"Colin? Well, reporters are supposed to tell the truth, though of course, accuracy in reporting is always subject to a certain amount of inherent bias on the part of the reporter. In Colin's case, telling the truth was never really one of his strong suits, but in this particular instance, his reporting of the facts can be considered essentially reliable."

"I am getting a headache just listening to all of this!" Black Jack replied. "Whose horse is this?"

"Yours," said the mirror.

"Not the one I'm sitting on, you benighted piece of glass! The runaway one bearing you and the pot!"

"Ah, well, you didn't really specify which horse you meant. The one you're asking about belongs to Warrick the White. 'Tis part of the stable used for his men at arms."

"I meant who was *riding* it?"

"Well, you did not ask me who was riding it, did you? You asked to whom it belonged. If you wish a correct reply, you need to ask the correct question. The horse under discussion was being ridden by Dr. Pamela Fairburn, who was on her way to Brigand's Roost in search of her intended, Dr. Marvin Brewster."

"You mean the sorcerer, Brewster Doc?"

"He is also known by that appellation, although in truth his real name is—"

"Was she traveling alone?"

"She was traveling in company with a wench named Megan and a squad of Warrick's men-at-arms, but Warrick's men had left her at the river crossing, where she met two others."

"Aye, those men passed us but a short while ago. They seemed in a great hurry. Who are the two others that she met?"

"Lord Aubrey of Ravenhurst and Her Highness, Queen Sandy of Pitt."

"The queen!" said Black Jack. "Impossible! What would the queen be doing on this road?"

"She is en route to Brigantium, to offer herself as hostage to the wizard Brewster, so that Lord Kelvin will be unable to attack and will be forced to negotiate, instead, thereby averting the war."

"Blabberglass!" said Colin.

"Quiet, you!" said Black Jack. He scowled. "If there is to be no war, then there will be no spoils. We shall not be able to pillage the town."

"Indeed, 'twould be bad form to despoil a town after a truce had been agreed upon," the mirror reflected.

"Shut up. I'm thinking." Black Jack frowned, considering the situation. "All right, I have it. We shall tell Lord Kelvin that this tale of the queen held hostage is merely a ploy of the sorcerer, Brewster Doc, meant to prevent our attack. 'Tis not really the queen, but only an apparition. The real queen is safe in her palace, back in Pittsburgh. And you, mirror, will confirm this."

"Excuse me, but I am the Enchanted Mirror of Truth. And that is not the truth, you see. I cannot tell a lie."

"Then I will smash you into a thousand pieces."

"Well, actually, now that I think of it, the queen's heart is with her people back in Pitt, and since home is where the heart is, then I suppose an argument could be made that she really is at home, in a sort of metaphysical sense."

"I rather thought you'd see it my way," said Black Jack, with an evil grin.

"Captain, what should I do with this?" asked the burly mercenary to whom Jack had thrown the pot.

"I have no use for that baggage," Black Jack replied. "Keep it, if you wish, or else throw it away."

"Now wait a minute . . ." Colin said.

"I never had a chamberpot that talked before," the mercenary said. "And 'twould be more convenient than squatting in the bushes."

"No!" Colin said. "You wouldn't!"

"Aye, I think I'll keep it," said the mercenary, tying Colin to his saddle. "I could always sell it later."

"Let's move on," said Black Jack. "Send word back to Lord Kelvin about the wizard's ruse with the queen, and tell him I have Warrick's enchanted mirror to confirm it. I want to be across the river within the hour. I want to see what sort of preparations these Brigantians have made."

As the riders galloped off, Colin jounced helplessly against the saddle of the mercenary, clanking painfully against his scabbard.

"Oh, no, not again!" he wailed. "If I ever get out of this, I swear to God I'll quit this bloody job and become a CPA!"

And as Colin Hightower contemplated the unpleasant prospect of being used as a field latrine, the mercenaries moved on toward the river, with the main body of Lord Kelvin's army just behind them.

TWELVE

Sandy and Aubrey's horses had traveled a long way, and for the last few miles, they had carried two people each, so they needed rest. The group dismounted several miles past the river crossing, so the horses could be walked a bit to cool them down. As they walked, Pamela told Sandy and Aubrey the story of how she had arrived in their world and where she had come from. Aubrey and Sandy listened with fascination, and when she was done, they peppered her with questions, which Pamela tried to answer as best she could.

"So your intended, Marvin Brewster, is not really a sorcerer, after all?" asked Aubrey.

"I suppose it depends on what you mean when you say sorcery," Pamela replied. She took out her pistol. "In my world, this is not considered an example of sorcery. It's an example of technology. Given the proper knowledge and skills, and the proper tools and materials, anyone could make one of these."

"But one could say the same of sorcery," said Sandy. "Given the proper knowledge and skills, and the proper tools and materials, anyone could cast spells. The trick is in acquiring those things."

"Exactly," Pamela replied. "No reputable scientist in my world takes magic seriously, and yet, a lot of what science has produced would have been regarded as sorcery in days gone by. Who knows, maybe the laws of physics are different somehow in this dimension. Warrick was unable to work his magic in my world. So perhaps, here, given the proper knowledge and skills, even Marvin or I could learn to do it."

" 'Tis possible," said Sandy. "I had been taught the Craft from the time I was a child. Had Aubrey been given the benefit of the same instruction, he too could have been a witch."

"It just all seems so amazing," Pamela said, in an awed

tone. "For years, there have been theories of parallel universes existing in other dimensions, and now we have proof. When I think of what this could mean for our respective worlds . . ."

"Indeed," said Sandy. "We have much to learn about one another. I would be most curious to see your world. Carriages that move without benefit of horses to pull them, flying machines, boxes that transmit sounds and images through the ether, devices that allow one to speak with people many miles away . . . It sounds like a truly wondrous place. We must seem so simple to you by comparison."

"In a way," said Pamela, "but at the same time, I can think of countless people in my world who would give anything to live as you do here, in pristine, natural surroundings, without all the stress and noise of our modern society. There are many people in my world who long for the simpler times of the past. I think I could easily make my home here. And I'm not all that sure there are many things about my world that I would miss. Toilet paper, maybe. And hot showers."

"Toilet paper?" Aubrey said with a frown.

"Hot showers?" asked Sandy. "You mean the rain is hot in your world?"

Pamela shook her head. "I'll explain all that some other time," she said. "Right now, I'm more concerned about—"

"Horses!" Aubrey said, turning suddenly and looking back the way they had come. "And they're coming up behind us."

"It couldn't be the army," Pamela replied. "They couldn't have crossed so soon, could they?"

"I do not see how," said Aubrey, "but whoever they are, we will never outrace them mounted two up, on tired horses. We had best take shelter and let them pass."

They led their horses into the trees and underbrush by the side of the road. Moments later a large party of about forty mounted men galloped into view.

"Mercenaries!" Aubrey said in a low voice. "They must have crossed right behind us. I recognize the one in front, a murderous rogue named Black Jack."

The riders reined in almost parallel to them as Black Jack

raised his hand to indicate a halt. He glanced down at the road, looking for tracks, then scanned the trail ahead of them. Then he looked off to the side of the road and smiled.

"You may as well come out, Your Highness!" he shouted. "I know you're there. You cannot escape. Come out, or must I send my men to beat the bushes for you? If they find you, they will be none too gentle, I assure you."

Sandy sighed with resignation. "To have come so close and failed!" she said miserably.

"We haven't failed yet," said Pamela. She reached into her purse and palmed her rape whistle, then took out her Walther. "Come on," she said. "When all else fails, take the bull by the horns and spit in his eye!"

They stepped out of hiding.

"Ah, there you are, Your Highness," said Black Jack with a grin. "And Lord Aubrey, the great friend to the common people. A bit far afield, are you not? Have you lost your way?"

"If you lay one hand on the queen, you rogue, you shall answer to me!" Lord Aubrey said, placing a hand on his sword.

"I tremble," Black Jack replied. His gaze fell on Pamela and his eyes widened appreciatively. "And you must be the Lady Pamela, the outlaw wizard's woman. I must say, he has exquisite taste. But you waste your beauty on a sorcerer, my lady. They are not known for indulging in the pleasures of the flesh. Whereas I would indulge with you at every opportunity." He grinned.

"In your dreams, you arrogant ass," said Pamela. "I am more than merely a sorcerer's lady. I am a sorceress myself. And if you do not turn around and ride back the way you came, you will find out just what sort of pleasures I indulge in."

"Indeed? Pity your manners do not match your looks. I will have to teach you how to address a man with more respect."

"I would do as she says, Jack," said Aubrey. "You have

already overstepped your bounds. I am surprised she has not already struck you down."

Black Jack smiled. "You expect me to fall for such an obvious bluff? You disappoint me, my Lord Aubrey. I thought you gave me credit for having more intelligence than that." He turned to Pamela. "Very well, then . . . sorceress, if that is truly what you are. Go ahead and strike me down."

"If I call upon the power of the thunder," Pamela said, "you and all your men shall die."

Black Jack made an airy gesture. "Call away."

Pamela raised her rape whistle, took a deep breath and blew a shrill and piercing blast. The horses of the mercenaries all started plunging about and rearing. Several of them bucked their riders off. Black Jack's horse shied, but he got it back under control after a moment and shouted out an order to his men. "Hold your ground, you fools! Are you frightened of a child's penny whistle?"

"Well, so much for that idea," Pamela muttered.

Black Jack brought his horse around to face her. "Is that feeble trick the best that you can do?"

"I have only called upon the power of the thunder," Pamela replied. "And now it grows within me. If you force me to unleash it, you will all be doomed."

"Enough of this nonsense!" Black Jack replied irritably. He drew his dagger and flipped it around expertly, holding it by the point. "Now then, Sorceress, I shall call your bluff. You have until the count of three to strike me down with this so-called power of thunder. For when I say three, I shall lodge this dagger in your heart. One! . . . Two! . . ."

Pamela flipped off the safety on her pistol, brought it up quickly, aimed and fired.

"Three," she said.

The knife fell from his hand as Black Jack tumbled from the saddle, a bullet right between his eyes. The horses of the mercenaries, already skittish, reacted violently to the gunshot and started neighing and rearing about wildly, plunging off the side of the road as the men shouted out in fear and confusion. And then there came a new sound . . . the sound of frenzied, bloodcurdling screams from some of the mercenaries whose horses had bolted into the trees.

"What the hell?" said Pamela, staring in the direction of the sounds.

"Flee!" one of the mercenaries shouted. "Flee, or she shall kill us all!"

But in that moment, a hail of arrows erupted from the forest all around them, every shaft finding a target as the mercenaries tumbled from their saddles one after the other.

"Get down!" Aubrey cried, pulling both the queen and Pamela to the ground with him.

Within seconds, all the mercenaries lay dead and their horses either took off, bolting into the trees or back down the road, or else reared and pawed the ground where they stood, neighing and eyes rolling in confusion.

Pamela looked up. She saw bodies sprawled all over the road. And a moment later several slim figures, all dressed in black, stepped out of the woods. They had long, spiky black hair, sharp features, pointed ears, and piercing eyes. They wore studded black armbands and chokers and they carried longbows, with quivers on their backs and swords buckled round their waists. More joined them, and still more, until they were completely surrounded.

"Elves!" said Aubrey. "We are lost."

"Elves?" said Pamela.

And then a large shadow passed over them and a fearsome roar reverberated through the sky. Pamela looked up and her jaw dropped. "Oh, my God!" she said.

"A dragon!" Sandy said.

Rory banked and came gliding in for a landing in the middle of the road. Rachel jumped off his back and came toward them, the Sword of the Shaman buckled round her waist. " 'Tis all right!" she said. "Have no fear! We shall not harm you!"

"Who are you?" Sandy asked.

"I am Rachel Drum, the warlord of the elven tribes. And this is my friend, Rory."

"How do you do?" said the dragon.

"Oh, my God! It talks!" said Pamela.

"Actually, it would be more correct to say, 'It speaks,' " said Rory. He glanced down at Black Jack's body. "I've seen this one before," he said. "A most unsavory individual. He looks much better with a bullet hole between his eyes. What did you use, if you don't mind my asking?"

Numbly, Pamela held up the pistol, her hand trembling slightly as she showed it to the dragon.

"Ah, a Walther PPK," said Rory. "The gun made famous by Agent 007, James Bond, of Her Majesty's Secret Service."

Pamela swallowed hard, blinked, and shook her head. "I don't believe this," she said weakly.

"Brewster Doc has a gun, too," said Rachel.

"Brewster?" Pamela said. "You know Marvin?"

"Marvin?" Rachel's eyes grew wide. "Is your name . . . Pamela?"

"Yes! How did you know?"

In response, Rachel came rushing up to her and gave her a big hug. "Oh, but this is wonderful!" she said. "Rory, do you know who this is?"

"I heard," said Rory. "But who are these other two?"

"I am Lord Aubrey of Ravenhurst," Aubrey said with a slight, nervous bow. "And this is Her Majesty, Queen Sandy of Pitt. And we are indebted to you all."

"The Queen of Pitt?" said Rachel, glancing at Sandy with astonishment.

"I came in search of the wizard, Brewster Doc," said Sandy, "to offer myself as hostage in an effort to forestall the war so that a negotiated peace might be achieved, instead."

"*Will somebody* get me off this bloody beast?"

They turned to see an elf holding one of the mercenaries' horses. Tied to the saddle was a chamberpot that rocked back and forth as it yelled.

"Get me the hell off this thing!"

"Colin!" Pamela said, rushing forward with relief.

"Another one?" said Rachel with a frown.

"What do you mean, another one?" asked Pamela, as she untied the chamberpot from the saddle.

"Prince Brian was afflicted with the selfsame spell, until Doc spoke the magic words to free him."

"What magic words?" asked Pamela turning around with the chamberpot in her hands.

"Abracadabra, change back," said Rachel.

With a loud pop, Colin reverted to his normal form and both he and Pamela tumbled to the ground.

"Jesus bloody Christ!" said Colin. He picked himself up unsteadily, his clothing and hair disheveled. He reached out and helped Pamela to her feet. He stared at Rachel. "You mean that was all it took?"

Rachel shrugged.

"Where is Marvin?" Pamela asked. "I've got to see him!"

"Hop on," said Rory. "I will take you to him."

"Oh, no," said Colin. "Being a chamberpot strapped to a horse was bad enough, but if you think I'm going riding on a bloody dragon, you're out of your bloomin' mind!"

Pamela grinned. "I wouldn't miss this for the world," she said.

"Pamela! You're not . . . I mean, you can't seriously—"

"Just watch me," Pamela said, climbing up onto Rory's back. Rachel got up behind her and held her hand out. "Come on, Your Majesty," she said. "Don't worry, 'tis quite safe, I assure you."

"Come, Aubrey," Sandy said. "You shall have a marvelous tale to tell your grandchildren!"

"If 'tis all the same to you, Your Highness," Aubrey said, "I think I would prefer to ride on horseback."

"I'd rather take a cab," said Colin wryly. "But if it's a choice between Rodan there and a horse, I think I'll take the horse."

There was a knock at Brewster's door up in the tower of the keep and he groaned as he sat up in bed. "Yes, I'm up, what is it?"

The door opened and Shannon came in. "You have a visitor," she said with a smile, and stood aside to let Pamela come in.

Brewster was out of bed like a shot. "Pamela? Good God! Is it really you?"

They rushed into each other's arms as Shannon closed the door behind her to give them some privacy. They kissed and held each other, squeezing tight, as if to reassure themselves of the other's reality.

"I can't believe you're here!" said Brewster.

"I can hardly believe it, either," she replied with a smile. "God, I could just *strangle* you! You've disappeared on me before, but this time, you've really surpassed yourself!"

"How on earth did you get here?"

"It's a long story. I tried to duplicate your machine, but I couldn't get it to work. As usual, your notes were incomplete, and we didn't have any more Buckminsterfullerine."

"So then, how . . . ?"

"Warrick."

Brewster's eyes grew wide. "Warrick? Do you mean to tell me *he* brought you back here?"

"No, he's still there," said Pamela.

"Where?"

"In your lab, at EnGulfCo. Colin knocked him out and we took the machine back, using the auto-return function."

"Colin? Who's Colin?"

"A reporter." She shook her head. "Darling, we've got about a year's worth of catching up to do, and we don't have the time to do it. There's an army on the way here even as we speak, and you're the one they're after."

"Yes, I know."

"Listen, I've got some of Warrick's guards keeping an eye on the time machine back at his tower," she said. "They think I'm a demon Warrick sent back from the ethereal plane to take care of things for him while he's gone. If we leave now, before the army gets here—"

"I can't," said Brewster.

She stood back away from him. "What do you mean, you can't?"

"Just that. I can't leave. I've got to stay here and help these people."

"Are you crazy?"

"Pamela, I got them into this war. This whole thing is my fault. I can't just leave. Besides, these people are my friends. They helped me. I don't know what I would've done without them."

Pamela gave him a level stare. "Yes, I saw one of those friends just now. She looked like something out of *Penthouse*."

"Oh, you mean Shannon."

"Yes, I mean Shannon. She seemed very comfortable walking into your bedroom."

"Shannon would be comfortable around King Kong," said Brewster.

"Exactly who is she?"

"Oh, she's the queen."

"Another queen?"

Brewster frowned. "What do you mean, another queen?"

"Well, I've got one, too. Queen Sandy of Pitt. She's downstairs."

"What?"

"As I said, it's a long story. I'll try to give you the abbreviated version, but first, since it looks as if we're going to be staying, do you think you could find me a change of clothes?"

"I'm sure some of Shannon's stuff will fit you."

Pamela grimaced. "I think you need your eyes examined. But I'm flattered that you think so. Ask her if she can lend me something not too tight to wear. Meanwhile, I'll bring you up to date while we go down to the stream, so I can wash some of this road dust off me."

"Wouldn't you rather take a shower?"

She stared at him. "You're kidding."

"Oh, no, we've got hot and cold running water, flush toilets, electricity, the works," said Brewster.

Pamela shook her head. "You know, somehow, I'm not surprised. No wonder they think you're a sorcerer."

"They think you're one, too."

Pamela grimaced wryly. "Well, right now, I wish I could make both of us disappear. Well, all right, where's the bathroom? We can try to catch each other up while I wash."

They stood up on the battlement of the tower, watching as Lord Kelvin's army approached from the west of the keep. "Jesus, look at them all," said Colin, who had recently arrived with Aubrey.

"I cannot understand how they could have crossed the river so quickly," Sandy said.

"Warrick gave Lord Kelvin a spell to freeze the river," said the magic mirror, which was being held by Aubrey. "They simply marched across."

"Nice trick," said Brewster. "I hope they haven't got too many others."

"I will show myself upon the battlement when they approach," said Sandy, "and you can send out a rider with a flag of truce to tell them I'm being held hostage here."

"Uh . . . I fear that shall not work," the mirror said.

Aubrey frowned. "What do you mean? Why not?"

"Black Jack made me tell him what your plan was, and he sent riders back to Lord Kelvin with a message that Doc had conjured an illusion of the queen, a sorcerous apparition, and that the real queen was safely back in Pittsburgh. So I don't think he'll go for it."

"I ought to toss you right over the side," said Aubrey to the mirror with a scowl.

"You'll get seven years bad luck . . ."

Brewster tensed as he watched the army forming up on the open ground beyond the settlement outside the walls of the keep. "Are the guns ready?"

Mick used signal flags to communicate with Pikestaff Pat, who was in charge of the gun crews on the walls. He waited for the return signal, then turned to Brewster and said, "Ready."

"I wish we didn't have to do this," Brewster said with a sigh. "Well, maybe we can scare them off. They've never seen cannon fire before. You're sure Pat knows to aim short for the first volley, right in front of them? *And* over the village?"

"Aye, I told him," Mick replied.

"All right. Give him the signal to fire."

Mick gave the signal and the two big guns mounted on the wall emplacements roared. There was a huge flash from each of the guns and smoke from the explosive wine propellant as pieces of iron and stone were hurled up into the air. Several of the brigands on the walls screamed.

"What the hell happened?" Pamela said.

"The barrels blew up!" said Mick. "That idiot, Pat, used too much propellant!"

"Do you think anyone's hurt?" asked Brewster.

"Well, 'twill be some burns and cuts and bruises, to be sure, but if there are any injuries more serious, they bloody well deserve it!" Mick replied. "Now we have no guns!"

"I don't know, it might've done the trick," said Pamela, watching the soldiers. "They surged back in alarm when the guns went off and now they're milling around and looking very disorganized."

"They will not remain that way for long," said Aubrey. "Kelvin is a good general, and afraid of nothing. He will rally them."

"Then we'd better press the advantage before he does," Brewster said. "Send out the tank."

"The *tank*?" said Pamela, staring at him with disbelief. "You're joking."

But Mick had already given the signal. As the gates in the walls slowly swung open, a ferocious roar and clatter erupted from the courtyard below. The doors to Mick's shop opened and the tank came rolling out, belching peregrine wine steam and sounding like a locomotive.

"You've *got* to be kidding!" Pamela said as she stared at the contraption that rolled and lurched toward the gates. It looked like a dilapidated, mobile Quonset hut with a stubby gun barrel protruding from the turret, and as it rolled forward, several squads of armored men carrying swords and shields fell in behind it as tank support troops.

"I don't believe it!" Colin said as he stared down at the tank rolling out through the gates. "Christ, I wish I had a camera!"

Some of the troops were rallying, but when they heard the tank lurching toward them, through the settlement beyond the walls, they froze with shock and turned with apprehension in the direction of the sound. When they saw the tank come clattering down the road and toward the open ground, they simply stared, slack-jawed.

"Okay, prepare the Wild Bunch," said Brewster.

Pamela glanced at him, puzzled. "The Wild Bunch?"

Mick gave the signal, and in response, a roaring, thunderous noise exploded from below in the courtyard. And from behind the work sheds by Mick's shop, a dozen incredibly crude-looking motorcycles powered by peregrine wine internal combustion engines wheeled out into the central courtyard. Bloody Bob was in the lead, attired in his "magic visor" helm and chain mail, and the other brigands fell in behind him, blipping their throttles. Long Bill and Froggy Bruce, Fifer Bob and Malicious Mike, Fuzzy Tom and Silent Fred, Winsome Wil and Lonesome John, and Mac's three apprentices, Hugh, Dugh and Lugh, all sat astride the bikes, looking like a bunch of Hells Angels at a Renaissance fair. Bloody Bob looked up toward the tower battlement, waiting for the signal.

"Who's driving the tank?" asked Rachel.

"Brian," Brewster said. He grinned, despite his tension. "He said after being trapped as a chamberpot for years, what's a few hours inside a stove? And Robie's manning the gun."

The tank was rolling across the open ground and toward Lord Kelvin's troops, belching smoke and sounding like a laundry dryer inching its way across a tile floor. Lord Kelvin was forming up his cavalry for a charge. About a hundred yards away from the troops, Brian opened fire.

"All right," said Brewster. "Mick, tell them to drop the hammer!"

Mick swept his signal flag down and the Wild Bunch roared out through the open gates, spreading out as they hurtled through the village toward the troops. The first shot from the tank struck the ground just in front of the cavalry and the already skittish horses went berserk, rearing up and throwing their riders, plunging and bucking all over the place as the men desperately tried to control them. And then the Wild Bunch came roaring up, pulling wheelies and sweeping diagonally across the front ranks of the disorganized troops and tossing grenades into their midst. The ranks were completely broken up as men scattered in all directions, yelling with panic.

"All right, Rachel, it's your turn," said Brewster.

Rachel stuck two fingers in her mouth and whistled loudly. From behind the tower, Rory rose up to the battlement, flapping his great, leathery wings. Rachel leaped astride his back as he took off from the parapet. As Rory swept down over the walls and toward the opposing army, Rachel drew her sword, holding it high above her head, and yelled out, *"Dwarfkabob!"*

Already panic-stricken by the tank and the grenades lobbed by the Wild Bunch, Lord Kelvin's troops just flat soiled their breeches when they got a load of the fire-breathing dragon. And then the elves came streaming out of the forest behind them, screaming out their war cry, "Dwarfkabob!"

"Doc!" yelled Mick. *"Look there!"*

Brewster looked in the direction Mick was pointing, and for a moment he wasn't sure he was seeing right. From the west, the same direction that Lord Kelvin's army came from, a forest was moving down the road.

"Do I see what I think I'm seeing?" Pamela asked with disbelief.

No, it wasn't a scene from *Macbeth*, it was, indeed, a moving forest, or more precisely a herd of peregrine bushes. (Actually, "herd" isn't quite the right word. You can have a herd of cattle, but I guess a bunch of bushes would be called a "hedge.")

"It's Thorny!" Brewster shouted. "He didn't desert me, after all!"

"They're cutting off Kelvin's retreat," said Aubrey.

Indeed, they were. Several platoons of soldiers had taken off en masse down the road to the west, running back the way they had come, but when they saw the gigantic hedge of adult peregrine bushes moving toward them, with thorns large enough to impale Dracula himself, they turned and ran the other way. And then, over the noise of the battle, a new sound came from the east, the sound of hundreds of deep voices rapping in unison:

> *"Heeyyy, Hooooo! Heeyyy, Hoooo!*
> *We're marching to Brigantium,*
> *So stand aside and let us pass!*
> *We're marching to Brigantium,*
> *We're gonna kick some Pittsburgh ass!"*

"It's the dwarves!" said Mick.

And as the dwarves came marching down the road, carrying their nasty little crossbows and their mean little warhammers, the Army of Brigantium appeared, with Mac leading the foot soldiers and Shannon leading the cavalry. Lord Kelvin's army suddenly found itself completely boxed in.

Okay, now I know what some of you are thinking. These guys are going to get cut to ribbons and Brewster's forces are going to win the day, because it would be a real letdown if they lost, but at the same time, it's downright cruel to make Queen Sandy watch her people being slaughtered. After all, she did everything in her power to avert this battle and at considerable risk to her own safety, she rode all the way to Brigantium to offer herself up as hostage in an effort to save lives. Now, it looks as if all her efforts were in vain and the Army of Pitt is doomed.

But then again, some of you are thinking, "Hey, this is the good part. This is where we get to see all the hacking and slashing that we read high fantasy for. We've not only got brave dwarves and valiant elves and a fire-breathing dragon, but we've got medieval bikers with grenades and a handsome prince driving a tank! This is going to be really good!"

Well, now, your faithful narrator has a problem. If I try to please the group that wants to spare Queen Sandy and have the entire Army of Pitt simply surrender en masse, thereby achieving a nice, nonviolent ending to the story, the hack-and-slash freaks will be disappointed. And if I try to please the hack-and-slash freaks by having all sorts of mayhem break out on the field of battle, then the first group will be upset. And it really doesn't seem as if I can please everybody, does it?

Well, never fear. Remember, always trust your narrator. So far, all I've had is a couple of big guns blow up, causing superficial injuries to the gun crews, and the tank has fired at the feet of the cavalry, causing all sorts of consternation. True, the Wild Bunch has thrown a bunch of grenades, but I didn't say what *kind* of grenades they were, did I? I mean, they could be fragmentation grenades, or they could be just smoke grenades, designed to frighten the troops. So far, we haven't really had any serious violence, have we?

Well, all right, Black Jack did get shot between the eyes, but he was a real bastard and he was sexually harassing Pamela, as well as threatening her life, so no one will argue that he had it coming. And the elves did kill a bunch of mercenaries, but hey, they were mercenaries, and nobody really likes mercenaries very much. Well, except maybe those guys who read *Soldier of Fortune*, but you can't have a war without offending *somebody*. So, in the best traditions of interactive fantasy, here's what we'll do. You get to pick your own ending. All you hack-and-slash freaks just skip the next paragraph.

Now, for all you people who don't want to see Queen Sandy's noble gesture be in vain, imagine the Army of Pitt going into an absolute panic at all the fireworks and being struck dumb with terror by the fire-breathing dragon, the tank, the Wild Bunch, the coffee-drinking beatnik vampire elves and the rapping Rastafarian grunge dwarves, Shannon charging in with the cavalry, Mac coming up behind her with the foot soldiers, and Thorny attacking with his hedge, whereupon Lord Kelvin realizes it's an utterly hopeless situation, and in an effort to forestall wholesale slaughter, he has his troops throw down their arms and surrender. After that, Lord Kelvin and his officers meet with Brewster and Harlan and Shannon to negotiate a treaty that will benefit both kingdoms and it all ends more or less peacefully, with a minimum of bloodshed. Okay, now skip the next paragraph.

Now, for all you hack-and-slash freaks, imagine this: Lord Kelvin manages to rally his panic-stricken troops and launches a desperate counterattack. The cavalry regroups to face Shannon's charge from down the road to Brigand's Roost and a wild melee breaks out as the two units collide at full gallop, with steel ringing against steel and men shouting and horses neighing and all that stuff. The rapping Rastafarian grunge dwarves join up with Mac's infantry and they wade into Kelvin's left flank, swords flashing and spears thrusting and dwarven warhammers shattering human kneecaps. The Wild Bunch wreck havoc with their fragmentation grenades and then Rory swoops down over the panicked troops with Rachel on his back and roasts entire battalions to a crisp. A number of Lord Kelvin's soldiers, mostly the low-paid mercenaries, break and run for it, only to get impaled on the deadly thorns of the peregrine hedge. The coffee-drinking beatnik vampire elves let loose with volley after volley of arrows from their longbows, then charge in and start munching on the surviving troops, just like in *Night of the Living Dead*. Now, when the body count rises high enough to satisfy your bloodthirsty appetites, imagine the remains of Lord Kelvin's army—assuming there are any—throwing down their arms and surrendering.

Okay, so much for the big, climactic battle scene. At the end, there was a bad moment when the dwarves and elves almost went for one another, because they never did like each other very much, but fortunately, in the nick of time, Thorny maneuvered his peregrine hedge between them and a nasty brawl was narrowly avoided. Arrangements were made to send Queen Sandy back to Pittsburgh with the survivors, with Harlan going along as a representative of Brigantium to arrange a final peace settlement and begin trade negotiations.

The revolution had taken place in Pittsburgh, meanwhile, and Sheriff Waylon and his deputies were all tarred and feathered and then thrown into prison awaiting execution, but Sandy would grant them clemency when she returned and sentence them to twenty years of community service, along with Gentlemanly Johnny and La Donna and the rest of The Stealers Guild. King Billy, upon being released by the Underground, would realize what a fool he'd been and what an incredible asset he had in his wife and from that moment on, they would rule together in a comonarchy, which basically meant that Sandy called the shots, and all the repressive edicts would be repealed and the citizens of Pitt would all rejoice.

All that remains now is the final, closing scene, where Brewster and Pamela, reunited once again, decide to remain in Brigantium and settle down. Harlan will make sure the time machine is dismantled, and since EnGulfCo doesn't have a working model, and only Pamela was capable of deciphering Brewster's notes, no one from our universe will ever again be able to journey to the land of the twenty-seven kingdoms, which means that old Warrick will—

Excuse me a minute, my phone is ringing.

"Hello?"

"Simon? This is Wayne Chang, from Warner Books."

"Oh, hi, Wayne. I was just finishing up the book. I was about to write the closing scenes and—"

"Good, that's what I was calling about. Look, Betsy wants to talk to you. Can you hold on a second? She's on another line."

"Sure. I'll hold."

"Simon? Betsy Mitchell."

"Hi, Betsy, what's up?"

"Look, I was just speaking with management and they want some changes in the book."

"Changes? What do mean, changes? I haven't even submitted it yet. I was just about to write the closing scenes and . . ."

"Never mind that. Just stop it where you are and send it in. We'll complete it in house."

"Huh? What are you talking about? You mean you just want me to cut it off right where it is, when it's almost done, and you're going to finish it?"

"Yes, that's right."

"Wait a minute, are you kidding me? That's the most ridiculous thing I ever heard! There's not a single writer I know who's ever gotten a request like this!"

"There isn't a single writer I know who's ever written a book like this, either. Besides, it's not a request. This comes straight from upstairs, from the new management at the parent company."

"What parent company?"

"EnGulfCo International. They've just concluded a leveraged buy-out of Warner Communications and they're taking direct control of the publishing branch. I just got off the phone with their vice-president of acquisitions—"

"No! Don't tell me!"

"—a Mr. Warrick Morgannan, and he specifically instructed me to have you stop work immediately and submit the manuscript as is."

"Oh, no! Forget it! There's no way! We've got a contract!"

"And in case you've forgotten, there's an acceptability clause in that contract that gives us the right to edit the book, which means we can make any changes deemed necessary in order to make it publishable. Look, Simon, I know how you must feel and I'm really sorry about this, but there's nothing I can do. My hands are tied. And I have to tell you that if you rock the boat on this, it's probably going to jeopardize our next contract."

"No, no, noooo . . . this *can't* be happening!"

"Listen, I know this stinks, but I'll try to make it up to you. I'm not really supposed to tell you this, but Mr.

Morgannan told me we're going to get the contract to do a series of novelizations based on a new British TV program about an intergalactic starship that's a bar. It's one of those high concept things, *Cheers* in outer space. And they want you to write it."

"Aaaaarrrrrrrrgghhhh!"

EPILOGUE

A Note from the Publisher

Literary satire has often been considered one of the most challenging of art forms, with a long and honorable tradition behind it. Some of the finest writers of our time have published satirical works, among them such diversely talented and influential authors as Robert Heinlein, Paddy Chayevsky, Gore Vidal, John Irving, and Hunter S. Thompson. Simon Hawke, while not even remotely in their league, has nevertheless been a popular and prolific author for close to twenty years, and Warner/Aspect has been proud to publish some of his most successful novels. It is, therefore, with deep regret that we must announce that Mr. Hawke, the author of this novel, has recently suffered a nervous breakdown and has been admitted to a private psychiatric facility for treatment.

Close friends and associates of Mr. Hawke have informed us that they have seen this coming for a long time now, as evidenced by his recent move to a secluded location in the Arizona desert and his erratic behavior on the relatively few occasions that he has recently been seen in public. For legal reasons, we will refrain from commenting on those occurrences, other than to say we understand the extreme stress that creative individuals are often subject to and that, as publishers, we try to sympathize and follow a policy of reasonable tolerance wherever and whenever possible. As such, we fully sympathize with Mr. Hawke, and with his friends and family, and hope for his eventual recovery. Warner/Aspect stands by its authors and we shall continue to consider Mr. Hawke a valuable talent, and hope to continue publishing his works, when and if he is able to start writing once again.

In the meantime, due to contractual obligations and production deadlines, we are publishing Mr. Hawke's current, unpolished manuscript as written, without any changes or revisions, in part to show the erratic and often fascinating inner workings of an undisciplined creative mind at work, with all its hebephrenic narrative asides and the uncontrolled flow of the novel's satirical devices, and in part to help defray the author's medical expenses.

In the process of experimenting with the new literary form he was creating, "Fantastic Metafiction," Mr. Hawke unfortunately laid the groundwork for his own mental breakdown, and while we commend his efforts to stretch the boundaries of literary convention, we feel that as regards the issue of liability in this matter, we must stress that Warner/Aspect does not in any way endorse, sanction, or recommend the practice of "Fantastic Metafiction," and we earnestly caution all our readers not to try this at home.

In closing, we would like to add that Mr. Hawke's family and friends have requested that we do not disclose the name of the private facility at which he is currently being treated, and they ask that in lieu of sympathy cards, letters, and donations, fans lend their support to struggling new authors by purchasing their books. Mr. Hawke's family and friends have also requested that we do not disclose *their* names, either. As the parent company of Warner Communications, we at EnGulfCo International join in extending all wishes of a speedy recovery to Mr. Hawke, so that the time may someday come when we may, once again, "trust the Narrator."

> Warrick Morgannan
> Executive Vice-President
> EnGulfCo International
> London, England

The executive secretary finished reading back the dictation and looked up at her boss. "Was that correct, sir?"

Warrick leaned back in his chair and lit up an expensive cigar. "Yes, I think that will do quite nicely. Go ahead and send it off."

"Sir?"

"Yes, Emily, what is it?"

"Sir, I've read the manuscript, and I was just wondering . . . well, you know he's named the villain of the story, the evil wizard, after you?"

"Yes, I believe Ms. Mitchell mentioned something about that."

"Well, sir, don't you think we should have that changed? Or at least make some sort of comment about it in the epilogue?"

Warrick smiled. "No, I don't really think that will be necessary. I think the readers will understand that Mr. Hawke was merely venting his spleen in frustration, a pointless little gesture of defiance against the new corporate management of his publishing company. Let it stand. Personally, I think it's rather amusing. After all, in a manner of speaking, the evil wizard does win in the end, doesn't he?" He winked at her.

Emily smiled. "Well, it's certainly the strangest book I've ever seen. And it was rather amusing, in places. It really is too bad about poor Mr. Hawke."

"Aye, 'tisn't it?" said Warrick with a smile.

"I beg your pardon, sir?"

Warrick shook his head. "Never mind, Emily. It was nothing. Nothing at all."

ABOUT THE AUTHOR

Simon Hawke became a full-time writer in 1978 and has sixty novels to his credit. He recieved a BA in Communications from Hofstra University and an MA in English from Western New Mexico University. He teaches writing through Pima College in Tucson, Arizona.

Hawke lives alone in a secluded Santa Fe-style home in the Sonoran desert about thirty-five miles west of Tucson, near Kitt Peak and the Tohono O'odham Indian Reservation. He is a motorcyclist, and his other interests include history, metaphysics, gardening, and collecting fantasy art.

Don't Myth, uh, *Miss* Out On These Hilarious High-Fantasy Adventures From Jody Lynn Nye!

HIGHER MYTHOLOGY
(0-446-36335-9, $4.99 U.S.) ($5.99 CAN.)

MYTHOLOGY 101
(0-445-21021-4, $4.95 U.S.) ($5.95 CAN.)

THE MAGIC TOUCH
(0-446-60210-8, $5.99 U.S.) ($6.99 CAN.)

"A great sense of humor."
—Piers Anthony

"A wonderfully whimsical new fantasy writer emerges in Jody Lynn Nye."
—Anne McCaffrey

Available wherever Warner Books are sold.

607-c